REMBRANDT'S WHORE

REMBRANDT'S WHORE

Sylvie Matton

Translated by Tamsin Black

CANONGATE

First published in North America in 2002
and first published in English in the UK by
Canongate Books Ltd,
14 High Street, Edinburgh EH1 1TE.
First published in French in 1997
by Plon, Paris

10 9 8 7 6 5 4 3 2 1

The publishers gratefully acknowledge general
subsidy from the Scottish Arts Council towards
the Canongate International series

British Library Cataloguing-in-Publication Data
A catalogue record for this book is available on
request from the British Library

ISBN 1 84195 273 7

Typeset by Palimpsest Book Production Limited,
Polmont, Stirlingshire

Printed and bound by
CPD, Ebbw Vale, Wales

www.canongate.net

... For some time, he had been living with Hendrickje, and this remarkable woman (setting aside those of Titus, only the portraits of Hendrickje seem somehow steeped in tenderness and the splendid old bear's gratitude) must have amply satisfied his need for both physical and emotional tenderness.

Jean Genet

1649

God has been good. He gave our ancestors the strength and courage to win the sea-locked lands of our fathers. I believe in God, the All-Powerful Father. The Protestants are the people of the Bible, the Dutch are the elect. God is good, but you have to obey Him. If you forget Him, He will unleash tempests against you, and the dykes will burst. He already has done. The angry water floods the land that men have lost through their sins. In this new flood, amid terror and screaming, the water drowns, it washes away. In the distance, a few steeples still rise out of the milky mud of the countryside.

The doors slammed and the word echoed. And again, and once too much. A whore, that's what I was, yours, Rembrandt's whore. Shaking and pinned to the ice-cold wall. Breathless, speechless. Panting. Whore, she said, and the word resounded up the stairs across the russet rays of the sun. Long after the echo, it reverberated in my head, so I was a whore now, yours for Geertje Dircx.

I've always known it, even in my sleep, even when dreaming of those revolting little white squirming worms. I'm asleep and I think that these creatures of God's are full of horrible little teeth at work. Living means working, everyone knows that, even the poor women in the Spinhuis.* When they're disobedient, they shut them in a cellar and open the pump. The water slowly rises. In a quarter of an hour the cellar will be full of water. If you don't want to drown, you have

* Women's prison

to pump. And fast. It's more tiring than work. More dangerous too.

It's you I'm talking to, and memories are still talking to me about
you. You're everywhere in me, in my life, in the air I breathe, in
the cherry tree in the garden, in my belly. It's you, my love, I'm
talking to. It's God I talk to when I pray. I always pray. Without
thinking, words grow in the tunnels of my head. I can't write or
read, but I can stop time. I capture the moment and remember
it later, even the screams, I can still hear them.

I've let go the brass door-knocker, I've stepped back on the bricks
of the Breestraat to get a better look at the house, bigger than
I've ever seen. She's opened the door. Legs apart, hands on hips,
round face flattened in the sun. Her eyes on mine. In the blink
of an eye, she's judged my strength, my smile, my pallor and the
bundle of dirty blue cloth at my feet, the poverty and courage of
my family, my honesty. She said 'Come in,' and the heavy door
closed behind me.

He was conceived of the Holy Ghost. He was born of the Virgin
Mary. He suffered under Pontius Pilate. He was crucified, words
one after the other, the prayer wells up in me.

My eyes get used to the shadows everywhere. You'd think
there were no walls in Rembrandt van Rijn's house, you can
hardly see them between the paintings, but I know there must
be walls behind the paintings to hang them on. There's that
smell I've never come across before; it smarts and brings tears
to my eyes.

    Geertje Dircx is staring at my muddy clogs, her glare tells my
feet not to come any further. On a white tile on the floor, against
the wall on the right, her finger shows me a pair of *mules**.
Naked on a table, two plaster children have fallen asleep. Beside

---

* Dutch leather slippers

them, beneath a painting with a pink sky (so pink I want to climb into the picture), a human skull with two eye holes, as dark as a rabbit's burrow. I hurry out of my clogs, put on the *mules* and tiptoe behind Geertje across the transparent floor.

I don't know how to write. Where I was born, the schoolmaster taught the boys the letters of the alphabet, even the butcher's two snotty-nosed sons, and by heart the Our Father and the Ten Commandments. Some days he asked them whether Eve ate an apple or a pear. I didn't go to the village school, though, girls didn't. But I always listened to the Bible tales of love and vengeance, which my mother used to tell every evening, and the great toothy mouth of the preacher on Sundays. I thank thee, O Father, Lord of Heaven and Earth, that thou hast hid these things from the wise and prudent, and hast revealed them unto babes.

I can't write or read, and I never will. I let my eyes rest on those who look at me, and I hear the thoughts their eyes hide. That's what I call reading. I hear, fear and lies especially. And in the distance, very far off, the lash of waves on the dykes, singing and moaning, beating and breaking.

I've left my childhood and family behind, I've not yet come of age* but, where I come from, money is scarce. Especially since the Treaty of Westphalia.†' As they wait for the next battle, soldiers with no families and war wounds in one or more parts of their bodies beg all along the canals through the small towns. They stretch out their hands, and they carry around the death of a part of them where the dismembered bones and spurting blood were burnt. In the street, I turn away: it's not the sight of them, it's the smell. When they stretch out their hands, the worms stir in their bodies.

---

* Boys came of age at 25, girls at 24.
† On 30 January 1648, the Treaty of Westphalia (or Münster) assured the United Provinces their independence from the Spanish.

Before I left Bradevoort where I was born, my mother cried and men talked.

'The city is a dangerous place, and Amsterdam is a big city': my sister's husband told me – he's never been there, and never said anything that someone else hasn't already thought before him. It's like swallowing food someone else has already chewed. For once, I said what I was thinking out loud, and anger shone in my sister Marina's eyes:

'Go, go to Amsterdam. Go and be a servant-girl in that house our mother has the address of. Go, since you've never liked our country people.'

Some people always say what they think, even when they've not been asked. I didn't reply, I don't like fighting. But I did want to leave. It's not really the countryside where we live, and our little town isn't a real town, it's a garrison town. In winter the soldiers take up quarters in houses where families take them in, and in spring, when the horses have had their feed and the garrisons pitch camp, many's the girl whose belly is swollen with child. I may be the child and sister of soldiers, but I shan't become a soldier's wife like my sister Marina.

Since the Treaty, she's been putting black henbane and belladonna in her husband's beer at breakfast, so his passions aren't aroused till later. And then I could pass right by him without him putting out his hand with that missing finger. Always trying to touch me up. The wound in his stomach has never really closed up, it's a great fire that rages inside him, that's what Marina says. I'd never look at an open wound that shows the little worms inside. I believe the fire from outside will never leave his innards. Men love war. The fire is the poison the Devil casts on the Earth.

I followed Geertje Dircx. I told myself the young servant-girl was following the older one. We repeated each other, two shimmering figures in the black-and-white-tiled floor that shone so brilliantly that it seemed I could see myself on the other side.

'You're to wash in front of the house every morning with three buckets of water. Use the little brush to scrub between the bricks, and also clean the planks over the drains on either side of the road.'

Rotting matter falls to the bottom of the canals, and the rats eat it. What they haven't cleaned flows out to sea, where it's washed and reduced to nothing. Father often used to say the United Provinces of Holland is the cleanest country in the world. It's got the least vermin and the least Plague, thanks to the canals and the rats.

She seemed to glide noiselessly towards us from a long way off, quick little steps across the shining tiles. Judith's arms clasped the month's great basket of washing with dried blood on the linen. Red in the face from the weight of it. She looked straight into my eyes until she passed me, right up to the last moment, and then she smiled, with that smile of hers that draws her whole face up towards her wide forehead. 'That's Judith,' said Geertje.

The corridors disappeared in the shadows and wound up the stairs into the bowels of the house and, the further they went, the more the suffocating odour I'd noticed in the hallway drew me on step by step; more fragrances, more stench. They sting, you have to breathe with your mouth open, and I could tell that there'd be even more revolting smells behind the closed door. I can hear voices and laughter from the other side, lots of soft voices, young, I think. I try hard not to breathe and I close my mouth. I know that smells from outside get into our bodies and wake up the worms asleep there. And when a smell from inside gets out and settles on the outside, that's when you vomit. Then you can smell the worms inside.

Geertje puts a finger on her lips and turns round. She's not whispering, her voice isn't pleasant, it's gruff and very deep, like a sigh. Walk slowly in the studios, the master's and the pupils', and above all never raise the dust so it settles on the fresh paint on the canvases. Don't let a pupil's hand feel and examine the shape of your body, even (and most especially) if he says it's so he can gauge the correct weight of your flesh. Geertje Dircx says this without laughing, not even a smile.

She opens the door, there's a sudden hush among those smells that catch in the throat, a silence so empty we can hear fresh laughter instantly build up. Shy, though. I can't see anyone. Five alcoves are hidden behind long curtains of raw linen; they look like they've been dug out of the great wall. From the way the material bellies out, moulding the shape of a body, I can make out each pupil at work, alone and hidden from the others. Smothered titters. My cheeks burn as I sense their eyes on me and I want to laugh too. Geertje claps her hands, I look down.

'She's come from Bradevoort near Winterswigle this morning. She's called Hendrickje Stoffels. She'll bring you herrings and beer in the afternoon. And from next month it's her you'll ask every morning to fetch the peat brick for your foot-warmer.'* She turns to me: 'If they are stiff with cold when they work, the young men don't crush their colours properly in the oils they haven't warmed up enough.'

Heads appear, smiling, blushing, half strangled by the linen curtains, some more serious, aloof, almost solemn; they're the pupils and apprentices who work in Rembrandt's studio, twenty years old just like me. City life's not going to be miserable, that's for sure; a giggle welled up inside me – freedom: with no father, no brothers, no brother-in-law; and boys of my own age who aren't simply dreaming of blood and war. I stood biting my bottom lip. Just raised my lashes at first, then, with a great effort, I raised my whole head.

That morning I had kissed my mother as though I would never see her again. Gently I placed a kiss on her eyelids, one after the other, so delicate they scarcely contained the pearls forming between her lashes. I wanted to warm her fingers and her weeping heart. I said my life was beginning; I said I'd take care

* A foot-warmer was made of a wooden or metal box pierced with holes, in which a peat brick slowly burned.

of her Bible which she had given me, and that whenever I turned its pages and remembered the words, moving my forefinger from top to bottom of the page, I would think of her. I would never forget that He sits at the right hand of God, the Father Almighty: from thence He will come to judge the quick and the dead. Those who have been good will be raised again for Life, those who have sinned will be raised for the Day of Judgment. I said, no, I wouldn't forget that man is the master of woman, that he honours her and that she bears him in sorrow. I said, yes, I knew what life before death was and that, after death, life for the chosen is eternal. And mine will be what God wills.

Then I climbed into the horse-drawn barge for the two-day, two-night canal journey from Bradevoort to Amsterdam between the banks of soaking grass. Hidden in the hood of her *huik*,* my mother was crying behind me; I fixed my gaze on the horizon without seeing anything.

Tiptoeing hurriedly from room to room, I followed Geertje Dircx. In front of the leaded windows blazing in the orange sun, his face in shadow, was Titus. A little ball of pink flesh, a greedy smile playing round his pointed teeth: spring-loaded, athirst for life. 'I'm seven,' he told me. I can't remember when I began to love him. The hurried figure of the dry-nurse, while he waits. While he looks at me trustingly. And I tell myself that I'd have gladly carried him in my arms too, when he was tiny. When his first teeth cut through his gums, I'd have been able to rub them with juniper oil. Make compresses of rye flour mixed with milk to put on his little red stinging buttocks, squeeze some drops of blood onto a hot-iron to stop nosebleeds. I'll know how to do it. When I grow up, when I'm a mother. I stop these inside-out dreams about a past that's gone. Titus is seven and I don't know why, but I can hear my jealous regret.

Geertje was scolding: 'Go to the kitchen, Titus, go and eat.'
But the pink child with his ruddy locks doesn't hear her. He

* A long Dutch cloak with a hood

doesn't go to the kitchen. Perhaps he's not hungry. His hose skate over the black-and-white tiles into the shaft of light. He wants to take a closer look at me. He slips his warm little hand into mine.

The bitter smells make my eyes smart. Or is it just what they're seeing, what they're seeing for the first time? Words fall from Geertje Dircx's mouth, and I ask no questions: the great hall at the front, the little room at the back, the antechamber next to the courtyard and the cabinet of curiosities. Every wall in every room is hidden behind paintings and objects. Weapons I've never seen before, but I know what they are because they're sharp and stuck with fur and feathers, weapons from distant places. Sailors from the East India Company must have brought them back. White heads and shoulders of men and women (in matt plaster or hard stone that glints in the light), brightly coloured clothes that no Dutch person would ever wear in any town in our country of toil. Paintings of Jesus, all telling of Christ's sorrowful goodness; others of fruit, silver jugs, landscapes and, on a table, a beaten-copper helmet that shines like gold.

Geertje Dircx turns to face me in front of the closed door to your studio, she's thought out every word: 'And now I'm going to introduce you to the Master. He works from morning to night, and nothing in the house must disturb him.'

In the shadows between the brushes and easels, Rembrandt slowly shuffles the room's smells. With an other-worldly expression. There's too much to breathe in and see, I don't dare, my eyes glide a little further over the floor in front of me. You said: 'I hope she'll be happy.' I told myself you liked me, and backed out of the room. I thought, maybe the stench dries with the painting, and one day you can get close to the paintings without choking on the smell. Titus was waiting for us by the door. Nothing must disturb him. That's what Geertje Dircx said, that was long before all the shouting.

Where I come from, everyone shouted except my mother. My father, my two brothers and my sister Marina's husband all hammering on the ground with their privates' and sergeants' boots flapping open over their thighs. They could blow bubbles in their great fat bodies that sweated beer froth day in, day out. See who could belch the loudest. Then they'd start shouting. And I'd hide, especially from Marina's husband with that maimed hand that had caught hold of my hair once already, while the other one, the one with five fingers, stopped my mouth so I couldn't scream.

The more they shouted, the more they drank and the more our mother faded away. As if she'd suddenly grown old and frail, suddenly transparent, our mother. And she used to cry, the tears falling slowly as though they'd never stop. I go to sit on her knee to wipe the long, shining streaks that divide her cheeks in two. Like when I was a little girl, making my bottom teeth chatter against the top ones as if I was feverish, she'd tell me the story of the war against the Spanish, a hundred years ago, and how the United Provinces of Holland became one country, our homeland beloved by God. Because you always have to learn how to defend yourself. So that those Spanish barbarians won't torture or cut the throats of the men and women in our towns ever again.

That first evening, Judith came down to the mezzanine to wish me good night and see if there was enough air and if I was warm enough in the corner of the pantry where I've got my bed, and if we would be friends. She talks very quietly. It's not that she's shy, but she doesn't want to disturb anyone; that's what she says, very quietly. Judith is a year younger than me. She's married. Her husband works in the dyers' mill. Every evening, he waits for her in front of the Breestraat door so she doesn't have to walk home alone beside the black canals to the new district of the Jordaan, where they rent the first floor of a house on the Bloemgracht.

I asked one question, just one that evening: the objects and paintings cluttering the walls in every room in the house – where were they before they were here? And why? Does Rembrandt make them, or are they by his pupils?

'He buys them. They're paintings and sculptures by other art-ists that he likes.' My face must have said I didn't understand.

Judith laughed: 'He comes back with his purchases, and he's happy. He needs to be surrounded by beautiful things, he has to see what he loves all the time. And then, all those pieces of material and those clothes and objects get used in his paintings. He lends them to his painter friends, too. At least once a month he goes to auctions. Used to a lot more, though, ten years ago with Saskia.'

I started to laugh as well. Without really knowing why.

My new bed is hidden in the wall like in Bradevoort, but it's longer. My feet fan out, I stretch myself to my full length, for the first time in my life I'm not going to sleep sitting up. I count the bones in my back; one after the other they sink into the pillow. I've put my *mules* upside down at the end of the bed so the Devil's witches don't impale me on their burning pokers. Upside down. But that night (my first in Rembrandt's house), I'm woken every hour by the night watchman's trumpet, telling the city of passing time. Between calls I stare into the darkness of my room, listening to time flowing through the great twelve-hour sandglass.

I turn over, still sighing. When you can't sleep, it's like pain, this feeling, but the middle finger of my right hand can cure it. Then sleep will take over. I lick the end of my finger; on the small hardening ball the saliva's almost cool. In the sweet softness between my thighs, in the moist place among the hairs and the warm secrets that not even my sister's husband has broached, my finger's already dry and rolls the bud that comes alive like an ember. Again I stick my tongue out for a bit more saliva; no one to see me or the drops that fall on my chin. Alone inside myself, so I can hear myself, I moan and sigh, finger moving quicker, quicker.

So I don't forget, my mother used to tell me how our country was born out of blood and tears: 'The Spanish mercilessly stab a 70-year-old man in the neck, then make him drink his own blood until it stops flowing. They flay men alive and stretch the skin over their regiment's drums.' Then my mother stops. She looks down, wanting to see if she's rocked me to sleep yet. But I give her a little smile to say 'go on'. She remembers what her mother told her, and she rocks me as her mother used to rock her. 'The Spanish stab men and rape women. They tear the women's clothes and chase them from the town, blood pouring from their wounds. Some scoundrel finishes them off, and they're soon rotting, abandoned in the street among bodies without arms or legs, their heads ripped off.'

She used to stop there, my mother did, praying silently that the dead would get their revenge. His hoar head bring thou down to the grave in blood.

I spread my thighs still further, my feet pushing against each other. My mouth's open on my own kiss, my wild hair hides me, lashes me, I turn my head this way and that. Finger, saliva, feverish bud. And behind the swelling secrets, I'm drowning in a new heat. From far off comes the rising wave, I feel it beneath the foam. I groan, I want to cry. Like a tide that goes out and out and never stops. I've stopped moving now, I'm scarcely breathing, legs and arms flung wide, mouth open in a kiss of my own invention. Then I open my eyes, sigh, wanting to laugh, I tell myself I'm going to sleep.

Gently my mother rocked me. I used to fall asleep in her lap, till I was woken by the clank of my father's and brothers' boots.

At the first pink glimmer in the sky over the port, the baker comes along dragging his cart noisily over the Breestraat bricks: 'Hot rye rolls, barley biscuits. Piping hot rolls!'

As soon as I'm up, I get dressed. I always shiver when I change my shift: the one I wear in daytime clings icily to my damp skin. I lace it up and, quick as I can, pull on my woollen stockings. Then round my waist my petticoat, and over it my linen dress, the one I wear for working every weekday. The other one, the one our mother sewed in the same material, I put by for church every seventh day. Tight bodice, collar and jacket. Then I wash my hands and face in the pewter basin. In the little mirror propped against the leaded window, I brush my long, dark red hair; the curls get tangled when I can't sleep. Put my hair up in a knot that my fingers recognise even in the dark, and quick, in go the three yellow brass pins.

I bring my face to the mirror to adjust the new cap that covers my ears and the back of my neck. Pretty, no. I look at my eyes, then just one, more closely. I tell myself I know for sure, but it's like a prayer. And every time I wonder if it's God I'm praying to or the Devil. The pupil expands, I go down that black tunnel, falling to the very bottom of it. I'll never grow old.

I look at myself one side, and then the other, in the mirror. When I smile, my teeth appear in a row between the two scratches at either side of my mouth; they're like little bones that will never go yellow with age. I screw up my eyes, put out my pointy tongue, pull a face for a moment, like the Devil. The skin stretches again, my forehead grows. I love myself, but I don't know who will love me. One thing's for sure: neither wind nor cold nor time will spoil this face, this skin that twenty years have formed. Time won't notice it, time will pass it by, there'll be a miracle. Slowly I leave my gaze, back to my life again.

I tie my big blue-striped apron behind me, and pull on the fawn-coloured sleeves from elbow to wrist. It's the start of a new day. I'll drink hot milk quickly from a pewter bowl, I'll eat a slice of hot bread from the hearth and cumin-flavoured cheese from Leiden. I've not drunk beer at breakfast for a year, not since I noticed, as I served my sister's husband, that beer doesn't wake you up, not even the best, not even brown ale from Rotterdam.

The summer leaves are falling from the tree, slowly drifting past the pink glass in the kitchen window. I open the door, watch them settle on the bricks in the courtyard; I'll sweep them up. On the topmost branches of the cherry tree a few stones still hang, a few cherries the birds have left behind. Black cherries; they're black. Where I was born no tree bore black cherries. They're the fruit of the Plague, eat them and you die. Unless, at least once in your life, you've sucked the teeth of a man who died from the Plague.

Black cherries – just to look at them is dangerous. Because the Plague never dies, it lurks in the earth, waiting for the wrath of God. I will say of the Lord, He is my refuge and my fortress: my God; in him will I trust. Quick, shut the door again, fear beating furiously beneath my breasts. Ask the Devil for forgiveness. Then God. They nail the doors and shutters up on the cries of the sick; the neighbours wait in the street, listening; one night, silence will stifle the prisoner. My fingers are crossing themselves. Surely he shall deliver thee from the snare of the fowler, and from the noisome pestilence.

I like work that's well done, I like going about my work. Geertje Dircx and Judith inspect the kitchen cupboards with me. The drawer where the salt and spices for meat are kept. The vegetable cupboard that's always cold because of the little courtyard next to it – that's where savoy cabbages are stored, and leeks and cheeses. Fresh herrings in jars of oil, and smoked meats hanging over the hearth. Great pewter pitchers for the good warm frothy beer the beer merchant comes and ladles into them every Monday and Thursday morning. And in the Spanish cupboard, the white porcelain service and the transparent glasses for when grand clients visit.

I peel and chop, then throw things into the great copper pot. When I told Geertje Dircx I had the recipe of my mother's *hutsepot*,* she said: 'I'll taste it first before the Master,' then she left the kitchen. Finely minced mutton and beef, cucumbers, seasoning, parsnips diced small and prunes, zest of orange to soak, and strong vinegar, then simmer it all in the stock flavoured with ginger. The best *hutsepot* is in autumn, when my mother serves it with chestnuts. And now into the fat copper pot go the last bits of shallot; I put a lid over the bubbles. Leave to cook for three hours. A meal for twenty people. About a dozen times in three hours, I'll lift the lid to take a look and sniff

* A typical national dish

the fine smell of the spicy stock cooking, then I'll go back upstairs.

That morning, I wanted to play with Titus. The cold gives him a chill, and he's not allowed to skate on the frozen canals in winter. His father prefers him to keep warm in front of the fire. You can understand why he's afraid for him, what with the first three dying when they were babies. It's like Saskia gave her life for this child, worn out by giving life to the one that wasn't going to die. He puffs out his cheeks, then blows into a ring greased with soap, from dawn till dusk he blows bubbles coloured by the light, Geertje even slipped on the colours the light made on the tiled floor. Titus heard her, he won't forget.

He plays cards and dice, like all the Dutch, but he doesn't know funny games like *cut-the-bird*. Before they turned soldier, my brothers often used to play. Blindfolded, with a sharp knife, you must cut a duck's neck as it hangs on a rope by its feet. You take turns and you mustn't cheat. I wanted to teach Titus to play *cat*. You shut the cat in a little barrel tied to a rope. Then take turns to hit the barrel with a wooden stick. When the barrel starts to split, the cat miaows so loudly, and then the game becomes really good fun. When the barrel breaks, out jumps the cat, trembling with fear, his tail all swollen, hairs on end like the bristles on a hedgehog. Then you stop hitting the barrel and hit the cat instead. The one who kills him wins. Titus didn't want to play; he wandered off and I heard him snuffling. He doesn't know – and I'll tell him – that there are a lot of barrels in a garrison town and too many cats everywhere. Rats, now, they clean canals of lice and Plague, whereas cats and dogs carry the contagion in their fur from house to house.

I've knocked on the door to the pupils' studio. 'Come in,' the voices echo, and there's laughter, but no one opens the door for me. I've put down the pitcher of beer and, without dropping the cheese and herrings off the great plate, I've pushed the door, propped it open with my foot, taken a step forward, and now I've encountered the smell. Two pupils run up and introduce themselves. Barent Fabritius picks up the heavy pitcher from the floor; he's older than me, he's handsome, with long hair and dark eyes. And Nicolaes Maes who goes around the alcoves serving out the herrings, cheese and bread onto plates for the other pupils and apprentices is very young, and laughs all the time. He chortles but doesn't seem to hear himself. His forehead and neck are covered with big red spots. I think we're going to be friends.

Geertje asks me to peel the potatoes. But, where I was born, deep in the heart of the United Provinces, far from the sea, far from the world, we didn't eat potatoes, and we didn't grow them either. There, we knew there was poison in them. I say this quietly, not everyone knows this, and I don't want to displease Geertje Dircx. In the silence, she looks deep into my eyes, then shrugs her shoulders. She says to Judith: 'You can peel them later on.' I am to join her in the bedrooms upstairs. She goes out of the kitchen, with Judith behind her.

I'm going to market with Geertje, so I can get to know the city a bit; she told me so, but I don't know which day we're going. All I know of the city is what Marina's husband used to tell me, what I've seen between the jetty and the Breestraat, and the noises that reach us in the house through the pink and orange diamonds of the leaded window panes; they're closer and harsher than in the country.

Two lines of ducks were following the barge's furrows in the canal water. In the countryside silenced by the rain, the ducks were quacking away. I sheltered under the barge awning. The man wore a big black hat, and drops of rain were bouncing off it. He only had one eye. The other was a burnt hole, and the skin had made folds and closed over it. His clothes hung about him like they'd been burnt, too. His long arms were circling wildly, and he was talking loudly. He spoke to everyone in the barge, to all those people he didn't know and who were going along the canal to Amsterdam, and I said to myself he must be mad, because you don't talk to all those people you don't know unless you're mad: '. . . in the taverns, they'll light pipes for you over the embers; they'll have drugs in them from the Indies mixed with bad tobacco that grows in our fields.'

A woman with painted lips round her yellowed teeth shouted that we'd seen the Spanish leave our Dutch land, and that we should have got rid of all the madmen, too, that even the ducks behind the barge were quacking in agreement, and that in our churches we already had to suffer the threats of swollen-faced preachers, and that enough was enough.

'God will soon wreak vengeance on so much money, on our Exchange and our insurance policies, just as he did ten years ago when he punished the tulip sellers and merchants selling empty nothings, putting their head in the noose one after the other . . .'

'Be quiet . . .' shrieked the woman and the ducks.

'Thousands of piles . . . You'll see, like the Temple of Solomon, built in seven years, the new Town Hall . . .'

He was talking to Heaven, the man in black. He was waving his fist at Heaven: '. . . Worse than the Flood in the Bible . . . everything will be washed away, and everything the merchants have soiled will be wiped out. The air will be filled with the screaming of infants, but it will be too late, they'll already be drowned . . .'

The barge struck the jetty hard. In front of the landing-stage was a man selling spices, his face grizzled by a foreign sun. He carried them in big fat sacks round his neck, like a huge necklace. A smell of old fish bones oozed from him, clung to him, floated before him and announced his coming. He'd caught and eaten and defecated so much fish he'd almost become half-fish himself. Probably grown scales under his clothes. In a singsong voice, he chants that he's brought back East India spices himself, that he's known the danger of storms and savages, because, he says, everything that's not Dutch is savage. He gives a black-toothed smile beneath the fan of feathers of the green bird sitting on his head. The green bird's big yellow beak echoes his last words and phrases. But suddenly, there's a peal of bells, repeating over and over their crisp joyous notes. The bell music continued, and the bird replied with raucous cries. Smiling again, the sailor revealed all the scales in his mouth. Then he moved away.

Barent Fabritius paid me a compliment. He said he'd never eaten a better *hutsepot*. Nicolaes took three helpings.

Amsterdam – the dangerous city; I watched, I listened, I breathed. The sun bounces off the canals; they smell of herrings, of whatever people throw into them, and of rats. Children's voices echo over the bricks of the street, their cries tumbling over each other; they're beating drums, blowing trumpets. Others come into the narrow street on stilts. They're happy, dirty, noisy. They're beautiful.

Where I was born, on the first blue day of autumn we used to fly kites. Mouths open, round eyes, children watch the colours dancing in the sky. But every mother remembers the sad story of Jacob Egh de Zaandam. Mouth open, round eyes, Jacob watches the colours being drawn in the sky. He is running, the kite dancing behind him. One of his father's bulls bellows and charges at the boy. Father and heavily pregnant mother fly towards the raging animal, crying out, calling to get his attention. Maddened, he impales the father on his horns and kills him, then hurls the mother skywards. Before she dies, she gives birth to a baby in mid-air; it only lives a few months. I shan't see any kites in Amsterdam. The three- and four-storey houses take up too much of the sky; pity. There aren't any bulls either. A galloping bull always carries the miasmas of the Plague in its hide. The country is more dangerous than the city.

Before leaving the barge, I asked the woman with the painted lips where the Breestraat was, and I was soon immersed in the strong scents of the canals. Harsh raucous sounds of shouting and laughter suddenly greet me from across a narrow street nearby; I change direction to have a look. Two roads further on, in a little square, a woman in a white shift stained with dirt and blood, buttons torn off, ripped collar, is shaking her head, her hands held fast in the wooden stocks. There's a board swinging round her neck, and on it, in red paint, are words I recognise but can't read; they're words of punishment used throughout our United Provinces to denounce an outlawed whore.

The whip's leather thongs score her shift with crosses. They're long slashes of blood, cutting into the bursting flesh, ripping through the cloth. Every lash from the torturer is echoed by a scream from the outlawed woman. A scream as long as a breath. Every outcry is answered by the hatred and mockery of the crowd that's come to watch.

From a distance, you'd say she's young, this woman. But closer to, you can see the years have touched her often and often. Smallpox has pitted her face; her teeth are black, or else they're missing; her bare shoulders are stained dark brown and crusted, telltale signs of years of the branding iron and the lash. I hear the words, I clasp my hands together. He took on Himself our curse to deliver us, and He was hung on the cross. The woman's rage (more than fear or pain) answers the insults that threaten to send her back to the Spinhuis. For with what judgment ye judge, ye shall be judged.

There's a leper's clapper coming; it always foretells resurrection. A ship's mast on the canal glides slowly past the jagged gabling of a house, rising up taller, higher than the roof. He went down to Hell, on the third day He rose from the dead. A horse's hoofs clatter on the bricks of the street, nearer and louder with every step. I hurl myself against a wall suddenly, or I fall, I don't know which, thrust aside by the galloping horse that pulls a little waggon with a roof and curtains, and gold everywhere. A huge horse, all gold. Behind the half-drawn curtain, like a vision, I've seen the man in black. He didn't want to kill me, his long nose shining like a knife above his pursed lips. The city's dangerous. No, he didn't want to kill me, the man in black, blinded by gold – he hadn't seen me.

* * *

I know that God is good and that He loves Holland. God has chosen us. The waters withdrew before us and You led us safe and sound to port, like the people of Israel to the Promised Land. But, if we drown ourselves in gold and sinfulness, You will pour out your anger on us, the great death will rise up from the Earth and the Flood will swallow us up.

When evening came and the last pupils had left for the city or were in bed in the windowless garret, Rembrandt's heavy tread would cross the vast rooms in the house. Judith and I, we'd raise our heads, we'd listen. There was no laughter now, and no talk; just murmur. The voice of Judith, who never wants to disturb anyone, was no more than a breath. Silence allows no forgetting. Only Geertje's *mules* clattered on the cold tiles. You could still hear her voice ordering about; only Geertje couldn't hear the sorrow welling up in the darkness.

In the kitchen, Judith whispers secrets. Seven years after Saskia's death, Rembrandt still couldn't bear her absence; the silence, emptied of her presence and laughter, had now become his. In your studio you lived in this silence, Saskia's silence, day after day you went on living with her. You talked to her and you survived. Under the big red velvet hat, you kissed her lips, the lips you'd painted on canvas. So there'd be no more dying, so there'd be no more dying ever again. Seven years after her death, Saskia was still alive. Alive before you.

I look at you tonight and I remember. I think your smile has changed. It says the pain's less. With one quick breath you blow out the candle, your arms round me.

I always used to look down when I went in to see you. Even when Geertje sent me to your studio in her place with the herrings and the beer. I'd knock gently, three little taps at the door. Come in, you said, and I'd go in. And I'd wait, holding the plate and pitcher, and behind your back I'd watch the picture emerge from your painting. I could see that great greasy crust on the palette of dark nameless colours, and bladders of paints and pots of oil that smelled of garlic, the hen's feather, and lavender. I'd learnt to breathe slowly with my mouth open, and my eyes no longer stung.

Barent Fabritius has given me his hand and brought me right into the pupils' studio, where the artist who crushes the paint watches the oils heat till they become clear; then he can break up the colours into them. Not too hot, make sure the hen's feather doesn't fry in the turpentine. Beside him, an apprentice is stirring the bones and skin of a rabbit till they melt in a *bain-marie* – the steam coming off it's disgusting. If they're mixed with powdered chalk they'll turn into skin glue.

Another three dabs at the painting and, as if regretfully, your brush left the canvas; you turned round. Your voice was deep, I answered, looking down. I couldn't look into your eyes that were gazing into mine, face to face, I didn't dare. Yes it was a nice day, yes I was happy here, I played with Titus, yes, as often as possible, as soon as my work in the house and Geertje Dircx allowed. I didn't say Titus didn't like my games. Whenever you talk about your son, your brow grows smooth, as if your whole face is smiling, not just your mouth. And from deep down in your throat, a low gentle laugh makes its way through your teeth. It's a sad laugh, Rembrandt van Rijn's laugh. I love laughing, but I don't know why, sometimes when I hear yours, I want to cry.

Your voice that day, your deep voice, is asking me not to go back downstairs, not to clean the kitchen, and no, not to ask Geertje Dircx for anything. For the first time, I look at your eyes gazing into mine. You have a vision for a new painting, you need a model, this very minute.

On the seventh day, I step beneath the great archway of the Oude Kerk.* It's by the grace of God we were saved, it's through faith. But it doesn't come from us, this salvation, it's a gift from God. I walk forward, my head up, not seeing the city and the circles of

---

* *Oude Kerk* means 'old church'.

men and women laughing and haggling around me. So as not to hear them, I fix my eyes on the man in black in the pulpit.

He's put down his brush and palette. He comes out from behind the canvas, his steps coming towards me. Approaching me, his hand grows, it smells of blue pigment and a mixture of oils of cloves and poppy seed. Then it tucks back a lock of my hair, stroking my ear as it passes. I look down at the floor; no, you won't see the drops of pink perspiration under my eyes and above my lip. You lean towards me. A great shadow, you close in on me.

The pewter caster is in the district. At each word he strikes a ladle against a misshapen holey dish someone's thrown out: 'pewter caster' . . . Pewter makes less noise than copper in the street but it rings louder in your chest. I hold the plates up to the light of the windows, I pick out those that time and knives have worn away till they're transparent, sometimes with holes in them. Titus's cup and three dishes. I wait by the door. The caster will work the metal and, in the evening, he'll bring back the same number of plates and dishes but they'll be thick again. Just have to pay for the pewter and his labour. Make sure, though, like my mother taught me, that the mix he's used isn't poorer or weaker than before. I'll rub the pewter with a knife and see how it shines.

I pose now for Rembrandt. For hours I stare out of an open window, gazing far beyond my thoughts into nothingness, or into the shadows of the kitchen; hours without moving, leaning on a broom handle, just changing my weight so the cramps pass from one leg to the other. Time stands still, my body grows cold. In his paintings, I'm born again.

I hear him sniffing the paint, the sharp smells of the oils cooking. His brush stirs the paste about on the palette, spreading and scratching the wood or the canvas. Then he comes over to me, one hand under my chin, wanting to see his model closer to. His eyes wander, reshaping my face, which changes colour. I'd like to leave my pose and close my arms round him, round you. And stifle the love that's drowning me on his breast, stifle the tears to come, all of myself. Don't know why it's so strong suddenly, this yearning for you.

In the distance, like a mighty fear, enough to make the Devil's teeth chatter, the lepers' clappers were emptying the streets. Those who ran furthest from the unclean dropped a few coins on the bricks. I will: be thou clean. And immediately his leprosy was cleansed. High up in his pulpit that Sunday, the man in black drawled on beneath the great vaulted roof of the church. The poor need the charity of the rich, but the rich need the poor so that their souls may be at peace. It's Printers' Monday, the great lepers' procession. I throw coins out of a window. The leper's clothes and eyes are torn, as if he's in mourning for himself. Love for our neighbour is like God's love for us. Yes, I love them but, to come face to face with an unclean person, no: no nose, no hands, and the flesh slowly being swallowed up, digested by the worms inside so small you can't see them – no, I don't want that.

You've bent down. You've kissed me. With closed eyes, we kissed each other. As if we'd been waiting for this moment, as if we'd known beforehand. For days. And she, suffocating, no air in her mouth, she saw. The first kiss.

You couldn't bring yourself to say 'leave'. You'd have liked it to be different, you're fond of Geertje Dircx, you become attached to people who are kind to you. You'd have liked her to understand and stay with you, with us, if she wanted. But can you imagine it? I don't know much about men, but I believe they want everything, they don't want to lose anything, but they don't want to harm anyone either. Even when the harm's already been done.

I let my thoughts wander beyond what I can see, out into nothingness. I tell myself what Rembrandt paints isn't me. I think, with his brush and paste of colours, it's more than my image he's painting, he's giving me life. You'll never see living people in a picture, breathing and walking about, the flat image of people speaking and weeping, of little lives in a pool of light, like ghosts that haven't yet died. In his paste of colours, I learn how never to die, I smile out at him.

His arms carry me, carry me away. I hear his sad laugh in my ear, I'm floating in the dark rooms of the house. I open my eyes. On his bed. My lips seek his and moan. Tremors; I stop breathing. No breath comes. My body's quartered beneath yours, my desire is a wound. Your lips and mine at last, feverishly, wildly joined together. I breathe in, breathe you in, and I cry out. As if there was a great emptiness, because suddenly the emptiness has gone. Instead, there's you, hard and tender, my love, more burning. Never again without you here beside me. I give thanks in my head, I also give thanks to my God, it's too sweet, too much, more. Walk with the Spirit and do not give yourself to the lusts of the flesh. More. And then I'll tell you later: never anyone before you and no pain, not even the man with the missing finger. I scratched a red mark on his cheek. For the flesh has desires that conflict with those of the Spirit, and the Spirit has desires that conflict with those of the flesh. Blood on the sheets, of course, I'll see it in the morning. You're withdrawing, no, slowly, no, you leave me trembling.

A moan, a long sigh like regret, and I stretch myself. A smile: you pull away to get a better look. Then with closed eyes, I greedily breathed in these new smells, salty and sweet, the smoke from the studio has seeped into your skin and into the sweat of bodies in love. Your lips, like petals, wander over me, your arms round me, your thigh against me. Your caress up and down my body. You slide up and down, firm and gentle. And when the moment came, you cut me in two, my love. My legs crossed round you. Night has begun. The first night.

I was still asleep when the piping-hot rye rolls and barley

biscuits were announced on the Breestraat next morning. The first morning. In your arms.

For seven years after the death of Saskia, Geertje Dircx organised and fed Titus. She'd carried him in her arms and washed him, she'd loved all his smells and never let him out of her sight after he'd learnt to crawl. She played with him, mixing his soap bubbles and throwing dice for his games of *passe-dix*. And even though she hadn't become your woman, except a few times, seeing another woman in your eye shattered her life. When she's not screaming, she's holding in her agony behind pursed lips and her mind is burning with it. I don't know how to confront her jealousy or anger, and I look down when I'm with her.

The preacher thunders from his pulpit. In the echoing church, conversations have died down, the spice merchants stop their Sunday sales for a moment. Women lean against the broad columns and stop feeding their infants, or else feed them only so they don't cry. Even the dogs stop rummaging under the paving in the open tombs. '. . . His name is Galileo . . .' The voice rings. The Italian doesn't believe it's the sun that turns any more: it's the Earth that moves around the sun. He's dared go against what Genesis says. Muttering. The Catholics have imprisoned him. Muttered approval. On his knees before the Inquisition, Galileo has confessed his mistake.

On your brushes, the hairs had dried, stiff and splayed. Grey dust hid the crusted paint on your palette, a great neglected wound. You missed Saskia. Terribly. The emptiness in the house had entered you. You'd kiss Titus, tell Geertje to care for him with all her might, and go out into the city. Judith often ran after you onto the Breestraat, she tells me in a whisper. She used to carry the lantern you forgot nearly every time. For the streets leading down to the port are dangerous, they aren't lit with the oil lamps that you get on the houses. Few people complain, because these little lights lick at the wood and often cause fires in the city. But, in the morning, there are corpses floating in the canals down near the port. Sometimes the night patrols accompany people walking in the streets without a light. They take them home, or else they arrest them and take them off to the jails at the city gates.

You'd walk on, avoiding the thieves and rats, and in the distance you'd see the lighted windows of a harbour tavern. Night uncoiled around you with its whores, fortune-tellers and knife-throwers, but this night-life no longer interested you. In the pipe-smoke you screwed up your eyes. Between two glasses of gin you'd answer yes, you'd smoke one with tobacco mixed with *cannabis sativa* from the East Indies. And you wouldn't remember getting home, but you'd be easier, you'd have drowned some of your sorrow, and your lips and skin would be swollen with beer and gin. On such nights, Geertje didn't go to bed. She'd wait up all night, listening to Titus's breathing in his little bed. You can't say now if your wanton hands found their desire, or if it was her hands that clutched you to her. You say it with a wicked grin and one eye half shut: without Geertje, you'd never have found your way to your room. Still less your bed. She'd slip beneath you. Your bed was beneath her where she had lain down.

On sad mornings, I tell myself this is no life for a humble servant-girl, sleeping in her master's bed. I ought to leave, I should. That's what I say, but I've nowhere to go, and I won't go back to Bradevoort, not ever, even though I sometimes miss my mother, my gentle mother, and the stories she loved to tell. I don't think I could bear the smell of soldiers' boots now. I give thanks, and I pray that I'll never feel the gaze of an unkind man on me ever again. As if I've just been born at twenty, here in Amsterdam, in the arms, the scents and the kindness of Rembrandt van Rijn. In his bedroom, a peat fire burns half the night, and there's a heavy green cloth round his four-poster bed to keep the heat in. I stretch out, I don't want to think any more, happy in his arms, I forget, I'm never cold.

So, to make myself afraid, I remember stories of servants sent

away and shut in the Spinhuis because they fell pregnant. Like
Janeke Wellhoeck, a servant at Master Bickingh's in the good
town of Edam. Everyone knows that Edam is a nice town, and
that it was niceness that tamed the siren who was captured there.
While her belly swelled, Janeke wouldn't let on who the father
was. As she was suckling the newborn child, she whispered the
name of Master Bickingh's eldest son. And Master Bickingh
immediately had her shut away with the child crying from
hunger, so that she'd confess she was lying, and especially
so that she wouldn't ask to be married. The story goes, she
didn't ask for anything. Call on Me on the day of your trouble.
I shall save you, you will glorify Me. In her prison she hanged
herself before the eyes of the baby she'd just winded. But Master
Bickingh demanded that the dead body be executed, hanged in
the square, as if his honour still wasn't cleansed, and to avenge
himself again on the poor young woman whose hungry child
now cried because it was orphaned. Hanging a dead woman.
The whole nice town of Edam came to see. History doesn't
reveal whether Master Bickingh's son was there, or if the baby
died of hunger or from too much crying.

With a movement of your hand, you take out the pins, and the
curls of my long hair frame my face. You murmur that you only
want my good and that I'm too young, twenty, while you, you're
forty-three. It's not the years, my love, that I see in your eyes,
on your brow and all around you – it's suffering I see. All your
deaths are there. It's all our deaths that make us old.

And you say you've got nothing to give me, that painting
demands all of you, and that you're more and more alone,
alone inside yourself and in your painting. That you don't want
Geertje Dircx to hurt me, that I must work less and take Titus
to the zoo.

We'll go tomorrow. It's been built near the harbour, with
little gardens and cages. Rembrandt will show us the King of
the Animals from distant lands which he has drawn. He's king
because he's not afraid of any other animal. He's a big cat with

long hair and big teeth. But here, amidst the smell of herring and the cries and clappers from the port of Amsterdam, his eyes fixed on an impossible escape behind the bars of his cage, he paces up and down roaring a prayer which never ends.

You pull a face and groan loudly. Threatening that your ancestors will get their revenge, you stretch your head back as far as you can, you search (deep in your lion's memory) for a roar, the sudden anger of the King of the Animals in his lonely solitude. Frightening. Above us, Geertje Dircx's *mules* cease to clatter over the floor for a moment, for just a moment before we start to laugh.

Rembrandt is working. He doesn't eat at midday. Everyone eats the midday meal in the kitchen, as much or as little as they want. But we eat dinner round the table in the great hall. These dinners are a miserable affair. Barent and Nicolaes rarely sit with us; they mostly eat at about five o'clock and aren't hungry in the evening, or else they're out visiting other apprentices and pupils in the city. Barent takes the barge to see his brother, Carel, sometimes, too. He used to be Rembrandt's pupil and he opened his own studio in Delft. Geertje sits with a closed face, not eating. I said, yes, I'll sit with the Master, but also with Judith who never disturbs anyone. The earthenware dish steams in the middle of the table rug. We bend our heads over our knives and plates, Rembrandt shuts his eyes. Bless us, Lord, bless this meal and come to the aid of those who have nothing to eat.

Fishermen have seen three whales half a day away by boat. I pray to God, and perhaps the Devil, too, for them not to be stranded in the port; everyone knows that a whale that comes to die on land is a portent. God will punish us for our sins.

I listen, still amazed that Rembrandt, instead of repeating his memories to himself, has chosen to tell them to me. Saskia no longer left her bed. He would watch her sleeping or he would talk to her. About the light on the canal and, yes, the baby woke up in the night, they do at four months old, she must rest and Geertje Dircx, the dry-nurse, was very devoted and, of course, she would soon get better, the good doctor Ephraim Bueno had said so several times, so why the sad smile?

He watched the shadows round Saskia's sleeping eyes, or he talked to her, and always he drew her. And with Saskia he forgot about the painting that had taken up nearly all his time, *The Company of Captain Frans Banning Cocq*,* so big that his pupils had to fix it with a rope tied to its frame in the courtyard where Rembrandt could stand back far enough to see the whole thing. Months of work. And Saskia was leaving him. She coughed and, through her fever and the cough that was destroying her, she watched Titus grow.

You told me about Saskia and the three children, dead after three short weeks of life: Rombertus followed by the two Cornelias. And you blinked your eyes to hold back the tears. I didn't know men could cry. Just from sorrow, without having first drunk brown ale from Rotterdam.

This time, I saw the golden chariot and horse before hearing its hoofs on the bricks. In the distance coming down the Herengracht. Coming towards me.

No mother will ever get used to seeing the life from her belly fade until it's a corpse. I think Saskia died of grief at seeing the three babies in their coffins, and of the fear that gripped her belly.

Among the swords and boots of the militia of Captain Frans Banning Cocq, your brush rekindled her, like a prayer she'd rise again before she coughed her last cough.

Doctor Ephraim Bueno comes to see Rembrandt because he's a friend, but also to treat his gums and his teeth, which are growing into his head the wrong way and keeping him awake at night. He said the woman who's doing Rembrandt good ought to see,

* *The Night Watch* is the unjustified title that the 18th century bestowed on this painting.

and that he'd take me to the room where the civil guard meet. Candle smoke has blackened the painting; he wipes it away with his finger. Behind the greasy powder, the sun that lit the painting ten years ago is slowly going out. Its rays will soon be the moon's. That's what Ephraim says as a joke.

I heard your grief; I heard you give a great roar, like a lion, abandoned and alone in himself, as you looked at the small blonde woman, a will-o'-the-wisp of living light that sets the painting ablaze. God raised Jesus Christ, He delivered Him from the torments of death because it wasn't possible for death to hold Him in its power. Among all those soldiers' boots, Saskia looks like those portraits you kiss in your studio, and yet she's no longer quite flesh and blood. There's a transparency about her that's not life, she's already a figment of your nostalgia.

They asked you: 'How did this girl-figure of light get into the painting from nowhere?' You raised her out of the depths of your grief, and she rose up from her deathbed, but they didn't recognise her.

That was seven years ago. God blessed the seventh day and made it holy. The end and the beginning. The seventh year, too.

Seated on the tiles against my chair before the flames in the hearth, Titus has laid his head in my lap. My feet have gone to sleep on the foot-warmer beneath my skirts. A warm sleepiness has settled over Titus and he is closing his eyes. I search through his hair, his fine russet curls. They're not worms, they're lice, but they squirm like worms. I catch them between finger and thumb, I squeeze them hard with my nails, like they're fleas, but they beat the thin air uselessly with their little legs. I drown the louse, plunging it in the pewter basin full of molasses at my feet, I hold it there a long time. I start again, my nails squeezing like a peg, gently I slip my thumb and index finger away from the infested scalp to the end of the hair; then I drown the nits in the basin. I start again. It's a story my mother told me. The story of a man eaten alive by his lice.

You don't know these stories that grow in the country, and I keep them to myself. Sometimes I tell myself that, if I don't let them out, they'll take root like nightmares. A nightmare you have again and again can come true. Eaten alive by his lice.

The drypoint gouges out the copper. The acid eats into the metal where the varnish has splintered. There's a grinding from the cylinder on the press and, on the damp paper, a first print appears beneath the inked plate. I'm learning to like the smells of ink and turpentine and don't need to screw up my nose; I even like the smell that curled the feather and blackened the garlic. I stay by the door, a plate of cheeses in my hands. Standing in the pink light from the leaded window, I watch your face in the shadow. You bend your head, call me lovingly to you, wanting me to see the big engraving. I'm not ashamed in front of the pupils, I'm touched, and I cross the studio, tiptoe across the cavernous studio. With your hand on my shoulder, I'm learning to see. 'Suffer the little children to come unto me . . .' Jesus cured the sick and they followed Him. To His left I recognise the young man with bowed head. 'Yes,' you say. 'Verily I say into you. That a rich man shall hardly enter into the Kingdom of Heaven.'

They didn't recognise Saskia. Blind, you call them, there are hundreds of them with their possessions and their certainties, as if they'll never die. And they're the ones that go to church on Sunday. The more you talk, the more I learn.

They come to see you. I open the door, my eyes fixed on my apron. You ask them in, and they swarm about you, showing off their fat bellies and their self-importance like, if it weren't for them, the sun would stop moving round the Earth. (You drink a glass of gin.) They pose for a few weeks in your studio, choking in the white ruffs they've squeezed their ruddy faces into. They're the ones with money, their parents' money and money from war and cannon-fire, whale blubber, spices and insurance policies. My possessions are my certainty, that's what their faces say, that's what their portraits will say. They'll hang

them over the fireplace in their drawing room and others like
them will recognise them. (More gin.) Oh, yes, they're so sure:
life is good for the man whose image will outlive him. God willed
it – he who has possessions is one of God's chosen.

Later, in the silence and echo of their words, alone so you
can finish the painting, you struggle with them for months at
your easel. Fighting the pride that purses their lips and darkens
their looks. Fighting the certainties eating their faces away. (You
pour yourself another glass.) They're passed on by their parents,
predigested, unthinkingly repeated. Alone at your easel, you
drink too much gin, you tell the portrait of God, death and
kindness. Later your brush sets paint and life on their faces.

Geertje has gone. In the house, it's easier to breathe, the air's
less dense. I've got more work, of course I have, but I've
learned a lot. Judith comes every day. On Thursday, she'll
get help from Geertruid (who lives on the same canal in the
Jordaan) to clean the kitchen and cellar, and then again on
Tuesday afternoon to polish the bedrooms and the big rooms
after market. Geertruid will kneel on the floor and look for
eggs and droppings left by the cockroaches and lice. If she
finds any, she'll spread a mixture of lime and turpentine along
the walls to suffocate them. And I'll show her how to recognise worm and termite tunnels in a beam full of holes. Tell
her that too many tunnels and spaces in a beam can make
the house roof collapse with great clouds of dust and the
roar of death. That's why the Lord sent a plague of lice to
Pharaoh's house.

Geertje has gone, slamming the door in a cloud of dust; when
I think of it, the roar still echoes in my chest.

There are people who are blind, and there are people who
know, but Rembrandt won't even tell them what he thinks.
There are friends and former friends. It was years since you'd
seen Constantijn Huygens. I opened the door to his messenger.
After he'd made peace with the Spanish, our Prince Frederick

Henry died, and he just had time to see his country reborn after that long war; his secretary Constantijn Huygens was in power for a very long time, but not any more.

He'd come to Leiden to visit the studio in your father's mill. He looked, he even turned over paintings you'd leant against the wall. He said you'd soon have a court commission. He was twenty-five, you were twenty-seven.

I've opened the door, he's come in; he's still young, with a few frown lines, and a wide brow, puffy skin round his eyes. He's smiled, I've stepped back, burying myself in the shadows. A throbbing under my breasts. It's Constantijn Huygens the Prince's secretary, even though the Prince is dead.

Rembrandt found the little painting in a box – the study for the large Descent from the Cross. I've seen desolation, the death of the world, I've felt the weight of Christ abandoned, escaping the panic-stricken arms, I've seen His thigh, useless now, fragile, and His too-heavy head which the Earth sucks down. The earth which will never be His tomb. Huygens liked it. He'd commissioned three paintings of the Passion for the Prince that a Flemish painter* had just refused to do. He liked it but he had power. And you, who aren't good at keeping money, you've written him seven letters, seven, asking the Prince to pay you for the paintings and your work.

A man eaten alive by his lice.

Your lion's rage is beautiful and joyous. You speak low, very gently, you kiss me and you sigh. The rich always think the poor spend too much money. A poor man has to stay poor. (You murmur.) And if through his work he becomes a bit richer, don't dare give him a helping hand. He has to learn that talent is something he's been lent and that, if he has it, it's only because some rich person let him have it. The rich are always jealous of an artist's talent, they know that an artist could earn money by his talent but that a rich person will never have the talent of the

* Rubens.

artist, he won't ever have the artist's riches. And they know that a poor person doesn't know how to keep money, he likes spending it and buying what the rich have had for a long time, often since the time of their parents. Whereas a rich man knows that you're rich if you don't spend money. He always has to remind the artist of the difference between a rich man and a poor man who becomes rich, and above all leave him in difficulties (you say without murmur); it's up to the artist to claim his due; leave him in need, make him wait, make him beg. Even Huygens, who composes music, writes Latin, reads French and reads an English playwright, who draws and is friendly with doctors and a French thinker* (you say with your sad laugh), even Huygens had made you wait and write to ask for money. Seven times.

Huygens has visited your studio. Since you first met in Leiden, he's always advised you to adopt the Italian style of painting. He criticised your shadows, but you said nothing; if your painting didn't give him an answer, words wouldn't either. You wanted me to stay by you, you wanted to introduce me: my servant and my woman. 'Not yet,' I thought, but I thought it was because you were good. It's too early, people aren't used to me, and neither am I, for that matter, to myself or them. In the city, Geertje Dircx is still shouting, 'His servant, his whore.'

She's gone. I can think of it without fear now. She was crying and shrieking, stretching out her arms to Titus, who ran to me. Her cheeks were sticky with red tears; she wept for Geertje Dircx, weeping from her eyes, but also from her nose and mouth. She slipped to the floor, her mouth twisted, and she stopped moving.

That was the night Rembrandt put out the fire in her room, that was the night a fire caught alight in her. Quickly, we filled buckets from the pump in the courtyard, Judith, Geertruid and I.

---

* Constantijn Huygens composed a great deal of music, wrote Latin, the cultural and academic language, read Rabelais in French and Shakespeare in English. He was also Descartes's friend and publisher.

Quickly, we carried them to Geertje's room. That was where her portraits were hung, on the walls of her room, the eight Rembrandt paintings she'd posed for. Eight in seven years; three were hers, the three he'd given her. Maybe she didn't want to abandon her living image in the house she was quitting, maybe she couldn't leave that face that hatred was destroying and that her mirror detested a little more every day. Maybe she wanted to wash away her pain in fire and kill a bit of Rembrandt by wiping out his works. The painted faces of Geertje Dircx were already streaked with black from the flames, she'd already burnt several portraits.

Your work, Geertje Dircx and her screams. You put the fire out, you're shouting too. You're beating and shaking the madness and sickness that's got hold of her. I'm leaning against the bedroom door, I can't breathe any more, neither can Titus in his bed, nor Judith and Geertruid in the kitchen. After too long a silence, gently, words return.

I knew how grateful you were and how you wanted to take care of her. But she can't see, can't hear you. She stares wide-eyed into the distance, it's frightening. Rembrandt keeps saying he'll give her 160 florins a year for the rest of her life and, if she's ill, he'll give her more, as necessary.

Geertje groaned: 'I'm old and sick already . . .' Her left eyelid slowly lifts, the other eye's still weeping. Her breathing had become a rattle. She bent her head on one side, smiling out of the corner of her mouth, her voice grating: 'D'you think I'm going to leave you in peace, Rembrandt, to sleep happily ever after with your whore? . . . I've had no children, but I loved your son as if he'd sprung from my own womb. D'you think after giving you both, you and him, my last woman's years, d'you think I'm going to quit your life because that's what your whore wants?'

That word – it hurts so I'm paralysed, I can't answer; just clench my teeth to hush what's inside. Rembrandt's gone up to her, tells her how much he cared for her even if he never loved her (men don't always know how much words say). She had his affection, and he'd prove it to her. She turned her face towards him, twisting her mouth, half flesh, half flower.

Rembrandt said again: 'That evening, it was late and I was sunk in despair after too much gin, I wept on your breast. You were a mother to Titus and I didn't know how to say thank you, to tell you that, even though you've not got time to be beautiful, you're good. And I gave you a ring with a diamond, it's the best stone for warding off the Plague, a ring I still saw on Saskia's pretty, dancing fingers, the living fingers of the mother who never saw her child grow up.'

Geertje shut her mouth and the rattle was quiet. She almost smiled in spite of herself. 'In your will you want to give Titus back the ring when you're no longer here, you want to give him his mamma's ring. You're giving him all you've got, the little you have. You're a kind woman, Geertje Dircx, don't change anything in the will and I'll take care of you.'

Geertje was breathing without the noise now. I left the room, I left the house and I walked in the night, looking at the stars in the depths of the canal, where the rats eat the worms and the miasmas.

I wondered if I would live long enough, if I'd live till I was forty and an old woman. I told myself that, away from you, my life would be like a quivering candle flame, alone in the pool of light it casts, with nothing but darkness around and no one to see it go out, to see that it snuffs itself out. That was what my life was before I met you.

That night, in my dreams, before they opened their tiny jaws with their minute teeth, the worms formed ranks, an army along a straight line, squirming with impatience before the attack.

Very early next morning on the Breestraat, Geertje Dircx pulled the heavy door closed behind her with a noise of thunder.

Today, they're starting the inspection of fire-fighting equipment in the city. The city employees knock three times on the door of each house in each street. They ask to have a look. In the little Bradevoort house we had to have a bucket in good condition. In the big house on the Breestraat, I show the two ladders and the two buckets. The city employees lift them up to see their base in the light. If they've got holes in, they'll demand a fine of florins. They pull and lean on each rung of the ladders. They'll come back next year. Let's hope we don't need to use any of this between now and then. (And yet we all know that in a year there'll be fires to put out, especially if torches are lit in the city to burn the air and the miasmas of the Plague.) Let's hope, that's what they say as they leave every house in every street.

Every morning, I take Titus to the Oude Kerk school. The teacher is a friend of Ephraim Bueno. He says that Titus is a hard-working child who likes to understand and that, in his gaze, he can capture the light of immaterial things. On Sunday, in his father's studio, while Rembrandt draws and paints, Titus learns. The pupils like Titus, he laughs a lot with them, especially with Nicolaes.

I've opened the door on the Breestraat. Two sharp knocks the man gave, he's dressed in black with a little white square collar. The rain's falling on him, dragging his glistening hair down to his shoulders. He's not smiling as he looks at me, avoiding my eyes. Holding a letter sealed with a drop of wax, he says, 'Town Hall, the Chamber of Marital Affairs.' And the black messenger moved away in the rain. I hadn't grasped the words he uttered, but the threat stuck at the back of my mouth, where my tongue had suddenly gone dry.

The letter and the red seal. I turn it over and over. As if the yearning to know and the force of my eyes would make me understand. For the first time, I'd like to recognise the letters and words. Quick, into the pupils' studio to see Rembrandt. I quietly open the door, don't go in. It's not shyness, I know now they're kind, especially Barent and Nicolaes. No, it's just habit, so I don't interrupt their work, their conversations or their laughter. Leaning on a column, Daniel the apprentice was posing half-naked, a cloth round his hips, his arms too long, too thin. Master and pupils were seated around him drawing, encircling him with the strength of their gaze; each drawing would be different.

Rembrandt's pencil is what teaches them but, more than that, it's what he says: 'You've got to look properly. You have to love life, accept it as it is; understanding is seeing the truth before your eyes . . .' He's turned his head towards me: 'Come here, Hendrickje, my pretty one, come closer to me so I can see you and understand you and your beauty properly . . . But what are you hiding behind your back? Yes, yes, I can see you're hiding something . . .'

The red seal bursts open in Rembrandt's hands. His great brow furrows in waves, then two lines are etched in the other direction. His lips part, his unblinking eyes can't believe what they're reading. Finally Rembrandt recovers the roar of his ancestors, the lions, but it's mingled with his sad laugh. Daniel hasn't moved, nor have the other pupils. A breathless stillness. Rembrandt lifts his face, his lips breathe a smile around him, and slowly, very slowly, he tears up the paper.

'I've been summoned. Yes, Geertje Dircx is issuing a writ against me! Of course I won't go.' From the back of his throat there's a laugh again. 'And you know why? . . . I'd like one of you to guess.' No one dared guess. In the silence, Rembrandt has spread his fingers, dropping the weightless squares of torn paper to the ground. 'For breaking a promise of marriage . . . Yes, for breaking a promise of marriage!' His laugh again, hesitating between laughter and anger.

That evening, held prisoner in your arms and your legs, I bit the grey hairs of your chest in anger and I didn't cry out.

And that night, the little white worms in my dream attacked the great chunks of wood, gradually digging tiny burrows with barely visible teeth.

Uylenburgh comes to see you unannounced. When you left Leiden for Amsterdam, it was to lodge and work with Hendrick Uylenburgh. It was a good choice for both of you, you were sure: you even lent him a thousand florins (which your mother had taken out of its hiding place for you) so as to get started in the trade of his Academy. Uylenburgh is a famous art dealer, he knows the city's dealers who want, and say they love, painting when it answers to the tastes of the day. He was also Saskia's cousin.

He hasn't sent a messenger, and he knocks at the door, laughing and talking loudly, he bows low as he passes me, then heads for the stairs. He opens the door to the pupils' studio and hails the company (as he calls them). Then he strides towards your studio, without listening to my 'Wait, wait, I'll tell him you're coming.' He often goes away empty-handed. He says he knows the buyers, and that your painting is getting darker and darker. You pour yourself a glass of gin, you tell him he'll never see any other painting on your easel than Rembrandt van Rijn's.

Uylenburgh disappears along the Breestraat, his figure dwindling into the distance with every step. You cried: '. . . or try knocking on Govert Flink's door. That good pupil is striving to forget everything I taught him these days. He can do what he's asked, he'll be able to cater to your blind, ignorant men who can't see for themselves!'

You hugged me to you and very quietly said again that a man who sells his soul to fashionable taste like Hendrick Uylenburgh may one day go bankrupt, in spite of all his fears and precautions.

Rembrandt wants Geertje Dircx's good; he knows that, sick and without work, she won't live long on her own in her little room in the Jordaan. He wants her to have a decent life. He's torn up the writ. 'Too ridiculous,' he kept saying, and 'lost dignity never comes back.' He won't go to court on the 25th September, he won't even reply. He'll buy his absence with a one-florin fine rather than waste his time when Geertje Dircx has lost her mind.

You can't just wipe out seven years of someone's life. In the house, we all know that Geertje will come back. I believe she doesn't know the harm she's doing: she's shrinking the timespan of memories so that they come crowding in. As if the death of the babies Rombertus and the two Cornelias, then Saskia's death, as if all these sorrows which had hidden under the lid of life which always goes on (especially with a newborn baby crying every time it's hungry) – it's as if all these misfortunes were now being born again behind your eyes, as full of salt tears as the day after the deaths. This woman who'd helped you survive wanted suffering to enter you again, she wanted revenge.

Your work every day (and you've done so much of it since you've been older) is like a prayer. Every day you give back a little of God's gift to you. Every day till now. Geertje Dircx has gone, but her silence isn't an end, it's a threat. And I tell myself, even if it's not sickness that's stopping you painting, you might get sick if you don't paint. So when I see your palette and brushes going dry and a servant who's fallen prey to melancholy and spits sickness and poverty every time she opens her mouth, that's when I decided: I'll go and see a notary, I'll tell him what I've heard, all about the 160 florins and everything; the notary will write and I'll sign with a cross. It's for your good, so no one thinks you've just ungratefully abandoned her.

You say no servant-girl would give evidence, and that it could only be the whore that lives with Rembrandt, the one Geertje Dircx talks about. I reply that if you're still summoned, my signed words will help you with the Chamber of Marital Affairs (what's to stop things going ahead now Geertje Dircx has started them?) and you've got no good reason to stop me. In my heart of hearts, I also say quietly that by giving evidence I'll be telling the whole world that the little servant-girl is sleeping with the Master. She's not a whore, but she loves him and is happy and wants to do him good. I don't know how to tell you this, so I'll give evidence.

In the ebony-framed mirror in your studio I carefully arranged my free locks of hair under the hood of my *huik*. I kissed you. We kissed a long time. Then I picked my way between the puddles to the notary Jacob de Winter's office. Standing before him in his office with its lightless leaded windows, I said I didn't know my letters. He told me how much his time would cost. I'd brought some money with me, and I paid and he listened. He asked, I answered and his quill pen went scratching over the paper. I told him about your offer of 160 florins a year, and said you would help more if necessary or if she was ill, and that Geertje Dircx wouldn't take anything, didn't want your generosity. I didn't say anything about breaking a promise of marriage or about the summons, her lie.

The notary wrote, then he read what he'd heard and transcribed. It was like a contract that Geertje and you could sign. I took the pen the man in black handed me, and underneath his letters I drew my cross, two neat straight lines from top to bottom and left to right.

I came back with my hood down, my face raised to the grey sky. The rain bounced and trickled down my cheeks, cleansing me of the filthy word Geertje Dircx had used. I'm going to forget it. Taller than the roofs of the houses, a ship's mast ran its shadow over the gables that matched it for height. In the hissing rain, a few canals away, the wheels of the golden carriage and horses' hoofs belonging to the man in black struck the wet bricks. They came too fast, then they took a different road, and their clatter faded into the distance.

Jan Six likes artists, he's an art lover, you tell me, pursing your lips to make me laugh. He even thinks he's an artist himself, and he's written a play about Medea. Think about the fatal flaw, you say. But that woman, who cut her children's throats when her husband left her for another woman, even though, before and after, she knew the worst fires of grief and hell, that woman . . .

Jan Six has asked you as a friend for two engravings for his play. The burin dug noisy grooves in the copper's polished surface, clawing right down to the golden metal. Out of the shadowy dark, Medea appeared, clasping a shining dagger in her hands. Uylenburgh calls Jan Six a collector in spite of his youth. He's already bought paintings from you. So a collector is a purchaser an artist makes presents for and who accepts them. In spite of his friends in the city, Jan Six's *Medea* has only been put on three times, but three times has been enough to make his talent known. You purse your lips to make me laugh.

If the little worms turned round, all they'd see behind them, as in front, would be darkness. The tunnels they dig aren't straight, you see, they twist and turn, like the worms; it all depends on the shape of their bodies at the time. That's why it takes them years to eat through the great wooden beam and reach the other side.

Jan Six knocks at the Breestraat door. I open, but I no longer step back into the shadow staring down at my apron. He wouldn't even see me in broad daylight, he doesn't see servant-women, and hardly notices me when I put out my hand to take the tunic he's holding out into the void. He doesn't ask if you're there, he knows you never put down your brushes from morning till night unless you're selling a painting. He walks towards the stairs, goes up to the studio. I stand in the hallway, his tunic draped over my arm, watching him disappear, he's young, lithe and handsome.

He thinks you greet him out of friendship, he doesn't know it's because it's polite and because you're kind. In your presence he's suddenly a protector, and he squares his shoulders; he calls himself a Maecenas. And you play along with his game. You forgive Jan Six a lot, too much, I think, but I don't say so out loud. I think you feel for him a bit: he'd so much like to have made his life through art and left his mark on life after he's gone. You often say it's not just their portraits purchasers want, they're buying eternity. Even though the sun no longer moves round the Earth, nothing can threaten that sort of eternity, the eternity of art as long as a painting lasts; with a good animal-skin glue to prime the canvas, hundreds, maybe thousands, of years.

*　　*　　*

You tore up the second summons from the Chamber of Marital Affairs, same as the first, maybe a bit quicker; and you paid the new three-florin fine.

I'm settling into this new life that's both yours and mine a bit more each day. I've rearranged the kitchen to suit myself, put the honey and preserved fruit in the spice and ginger drawer, and on the empty shelf I put my earthenware jars of potions, and medicinal powders and unguents. The Bradevoort midwife taught me. I was brought out of darkness and my mother's womb in the breech position. Without this woman I might have been born dead. And my mother would have died too, she would. Without her, I would have killed my mother without knowing.

There's no writing on the little jars; but they're all different sizes, so I won't make a mistake. I can cure everything but the Plague. The Plague's treated with quicksilver,* but mostly prayers.

You can also air the place if there's still time, but once you've seen buboes on the dying man, it's too late. The night before I left, my mother blessed the biggest earthenware jar, the one with the four-thieves' vinegar in it. Mix a handful of rue in a good-quality vinegar, a handful of mint, a little wormwood, a pinch of rosemary and a handful of aspic. Infuse the mixture for eight days, then dissolve an ounce of camphor in this liquor. Dab a sponge in it and rub it on the mouth, nostrils and all the body's extremities. Everyone used to use this vinegar when the Plague was raging and, at the same time, the four men who'd sold the remedy were stealing in the other rooms.

I place the jars in a straight line in height order, smallest first, saffron, Chinese wine, aloes dye, gentian syrup, myrrh, juniper oil. And the vulnerary which heals all wounds and is known to all (even city dwellers), the ball of moss washed on the skull of

* Old word for mercury.

a hanged man, then mixed with two ounces of human blood, and a dab of lard, linseed oil and saffron.

I put down the great copper dish on the table. Steam was rising from it, giving off a fine smell of veal trotters, tripe and peas. Titus talks seriously to his father. He keeps saying I must learn to read. He wanted to show me the alphabet, but the letters dance on the paper as soon as I look, and sleep slides down my eyelids into my eyes. Titus gets cross on the words' behalf. Rembrandt laughs because he doesn't believe in any of this, and says that words will never understand, not like painting.

Titus gave a cry. We hadn't heard her let herself in with her key – there she was, Geertje Dircx, her fat hands planted on the table before us, leaning forward. Wickedness and revenge have aged and discoloured her face. In the flickering candlelight, her sticky nose and chin are quivering, her skin's scratched and flaking off in bits. The flab around her head hangs heavily where the bones no longer keep it up. From where we sit her face looks like it's been filled with air, especially under her eyes. You can't make out her eyelids any more, and her right eye is half shut. But her mouth is full of words; that's the only part of her still living. Her lips smack open and shut and her mouth twists into knots.

'. . . I see you're eating well and are happy here . . .'

'Will you sit down and . . .'

'No, Rembrandt van Rijn, never again in your house.'

It's like she's laughing, Geertje, or groaning. Maybe it was a belch. She brings her flabby face nearer, she stares into Rembrandt's eyes.

'. . . Saskia's ring,' she says getting her tongue round the words. 'The engagement ring with the diamond, the stone that wards off the Plague, your promise of marriage . . .'

'Ridiculous,' says Rembrandt. 'No one's going to believe you.'

'The ring that belonged to the dead and grieved woman: would you really have given it to a servant just to thank her for her work? . . . It's you no one's going to believe, Rembrandt van Rijn.'

'Where is the ring?'

Geertje gives a smile. Just one. 'Nothing can happen to it.'

Her laugh breaks behind her teeth. Rembrandt waited, asking no questions. Titus came to sit on my knee, hiding his head in my apron so as not to see Geertje's puffy face which he didn't recognise. On the table rug, the copper dish had stopped steaming. One after the other, Judith and Geertruid had got up as though to go to the kitchen, and they hadn't come back. Barent and Nicolaes looked at one another across the table; together, they pushed their chairs back and left the room.

'How do you think I'm surviving, Rembrandt van Rijn? All those years I devoted to taking you by the hand out into the sun, cutting up the meat and vegetables on your plate and practically putting them in your mouth so as to chase out the death in your head; feeding your son, chewing his food for him, wiping his body of what came out of it, sitting up whole nights blowing on the nuts filled with spiders' heads spread on his chest to get rid of fevers . . . All those years, and now I'm on the street, old and sick as you see me now and out on the street.' And looking at me out of her one eye, she says: 'That's how the painter Rembrandt treats his servant-women, when they aren't whores.'

My silence is strangling me, I'm going to faint. I said nothing, I won't say anything. I fixed my gaze on Rembrandt so she'd know that by not seeing her, I couldn't hear her, maybe I'd become transparent and wasn't in the room any more. But I didn't disappear and Geertje Dircx's eye didn't forget me.

Her mouth and body were writhing. 'Yes, I've pawned Saskia's ring. It's she who's supporting me now, not you.'

You don't let the anger in you grow, you mustn't. You say you'll reclaim it and that, when she's dead, Titus will get it back, his mother's ring; it's got to stop, all this nonsense, and you'll go to the Chamber of Marital Affairs. You ask Geertje to give back the key to the house, she no longer needs it and she can't just come in like it's still her home. She shook her head, so you got up and went round the table, moving slowly so as not to lose the calm in you. She's wide and solid, Geertje Dircx, ugly and fat, but the closer you came, the more you grew and the stronger you got. You put out your arm to the pocket her hands were shielding. She gave a great cry.

Later that night you took my head in your hands and looked at me gravely. You asked my forgiveness, but because there was nothing to ask for, I quickly kissed you. You told me it was a secret, a double secret, you said. But that you wouldn't have any secrets from me.

'You know Geertje Dircx keeps house well, but she never looked at my paintings and she's no woman for me. Because you know her and you know me, you know I never asked her to marry me. I didn't, and I never would for a reason you don't know about. The fact is, I can't marry again.'

My ears, maybe my insides, are filled with the buzzing of insects. It's not Geertje Dircx, it's me Rembrandt's talking about, it's my life. I love him, I know I do, and I don't know how to tell him. Some days I stand quite still, listening to the ceiling, which is also the floor of his studio. When it makes barely a sound, I know he's sitting on his chair with one leg bent, hugging the other to him. These silences can last till the sand-glass has run out and run out again, before he'll get up, and I'll hear his heavy tread as he goes to the door. In a few steps it'll open and he'll call my name – perhaps he's hungry or thirsty or his back aches. Or he just wants to see me. Or maybe he'll come downstairs. In a moment I'll see him; there's a different throbbing under my breasts. Yes, I love him. I shut my eyes; a great void sucks my belly empty and my fingertips itch.

'In her will, Saskia asks me to pay 20,000 florins to the Chamber of Orphans for Titus if I marry again; that's half of what we possessed then. It's been years since I've had that much, half of that much, even. It's because of the shadows in my paintings, and because of my purchases, because of money, fearful money, and the way it hides away. Which proves I couldn't have promised to marry this wretched madwoman, but I can't tell her, I can't admit that money's become a problem, it would stop me being able to sell my paintings at the same price. Do you understand?'

I said, yes, I understood. Mostly, I just understand that Rembrandt can't marry again. I look at this man's face next to mine, already lined and puffy from life and life's sorrows. I look at his eyes, his kindness. I know this is where my life is.

Then, a week after the second summons, there's a third. Rembrandt says he's got to end this once and for all. He walked to the Dam and along to the Town Hall, and from there, up the old worm-eaten staircase to the Chamber of Marital Affairs. He might shake his head over the absurdity of it, but all this hatred and revenge are wearing him out. He couldn't work, couldn't love me either. He would go and sign. He'll tell me all about it when he gets back.

With trembling chin, her mouth caked with salt tears, Geertje told the notary, Laurens Lamberti, that Rembrandt had asked her to marry him, and the ring with the diamond which protects its wearer from the Plague was proof. And he'd slept with her several times.

Never any question of marriage, Rembrandt answered, and there was nothing to make him confess to having slept with this woman either but, since she said so, she'd have to prove it. He could just as well have said, 'No, I never slept with this woman,' but that might have hurt her more than her sickness, and him a bit too, when he looked into his mirror.

Then he said 'yes' to everything. He didn't want to talk about the money. He wanted this to end and Geertje to get over her sickness. He'd give 200 florins for now so she could live decently and reclaim the ring that was to go to Titus one day. And not 160 florins, but 200 a year till the end of Geertje Dircx's life, but not longer than that. And if she got sick or was in any other need, Rembrandt would give her whatever she needed for the rest of her life.

Laurens Lamberti said the offer was generous. Rembrandt said it was gratitude: for seven years she'd helped him survive, and his son to grow up. Seven: today was a new life. The notary dipped his quill in the ink, then handed it to Geertje.

She takes the pen, her arm hovers a moment in the air. Her hand drops the pen on the table. Her mouth twists and says that Geertje Dircx won't sign. Rembrandt must keep his promise and marry her. Silence. Her eyes are white, she says it again, louder. There's a sigh. Rembrandt bows his head over the table, the notary tries to speak, but Geertje Dircx repeats it, red in the face, her eyes running into her mouth. She'll never sign, Rembrandt will marry her, it's not 200 florins she wants, but marriage.

The notary's seen and heard how jealousy has fried Geertje Dircx's brain. Maybe the Devil's fire, too. Heard all about the marriage and the broken promise, and that she wouldn't leave Rembrandt in peace, she'd never leave him in peace with his whore. Rembrandt placed his head in his hands, the notary stood up. Geertje's red face couldn't see or hear anything any more.

The two men from the house of correction have taken her under the arms, she's screaming like she's been bled, like she's a pig about to die. They're taking her away. At the end of the long corridor, she's still screaming that Rembrandt will marry her, she won't leave him in peace with the ring, she'll force him to marry and he'll never live happily with his whore.

1650–1654

Bathsheba is sitting on a cushion, her face tipped forward, King David's letter in her right hand. She's wanted as soon as possible, she must go to him, it's an order. Maybe King David also tells her that he has desired her ever since he saw her bathing, such beauty. She has read the fatal letter, and already her gaze is elsewhere. Just inside the frame, crouched over her feet to her left, the old servant-woman purifies her before the sacrifice. Bathsheba's eyes are lost in the future, she looks at nothing. I am looking at nothing. There's no writing on the white sheet clasped in my right hand (and if there were, I wouldn't be able to read it). You've pulled a few locks of hair from their fastening behind my neck; they frame my face. Behind the canvas, I can hear your brush stroking the painting and stirring the paste. I raise my head, I smile at you. My arms rest on air, I settle back into my pose.

Rembrandt has a big stretch in the warm bed. In the silent house he's still resting, later than most days. Titus and the pupils are still asleep. Every seventh day at eight o'clock, I go alone along the cold canals to the Oude Kerk. Before leaving the Breestraat, I massage Rembrandt's back and shoulders, I count the little bones of his spine, working the way the flesh moves. Because he keeps his arm up (always the same one) for hours on end all those long days of painting, because painting's suffering. I tell myself I'm just giving back a little of the good he does me every day.

On the kitchen table I've put out the bowls, plates and tankards for breakfast. Rembrandt will find milk, beer, bread, cheeses and herrings. If Titus comes down in time, his father will serve him. Together they'll play with the light from the coloured window panes. Then they'll go up to the studio. If he screws his eyes up at his easel a little, Rembrandt will see the unfinished painting as though he'd never set eyes on it before. He'll choose the day's first brush. He'll make the bristles spring between his fingers, he'll smooth them down, check they're glossy and pliant. He'll hold the oils up to the light to check their transparency, then he'll squeeze the bladders of colours.

His brush will search the palette and transfer the paste onto the canvas. Palette to canvas, palette to canvas, till evening falls, every day of his life. He doesn't go to church. But he speaks with the light and answers to God. When he screws his eyes up. Every day.

The man in black is preaching from the pulpit. Beneath him, the men and women stand with their backs to him, muttering together in circles. The women hold their heads up; they've got nothing to be ashamed of in their colourful dresses, whispering behind their earrings swaying and sparkling in the light. Red-faced, as if they're strangled by their ruffs, the men wear velvet and black satin, and survey their bloated bellies, as swollen as their purses, with the flat of their hands. I see the fat on the outside, and I guess it's there on the inside: I turn away so I don't vomit. The richer they get the fatter they are. Over by a pillar, a baby screams for milk; quick as she can, his mother passes him from one breast to the other. And behind her, where the shadow's darker and a stone's been overturned by the gravedigger, deep in the bottomless blackness of an old tomb waiting for a new corpse not yet eaten by worms, behind the spade, behind a fleshless skull that's rolled on to the next stone, two dogs are picking at the bones. A rat runs by. The dogs growl. Maybe with their barking and their hot breath they'll wake the worms lying dormant and replete in the dust of men.

The man in black leans down to the rich and poor, the healthy and the sick who've gathered in church to hear him. In a moment of fear, they raise their eyes to the preacher and the wrath from his toothless mouth.

'How can the people of God adorn themselves like this? How can they come to church wearing satin, brocade and leather worked in silver and gold? . . . Howl, inhabitants of Maktesh, for the merchant people are cut down; all they that bear silver are cut off.'

The two dogs are barking, their lips drawn back as if they're swearing at each other. They sink their teeth into a dead bone, one at either end of it, legs stiffened, bracing themselves in the void before them; they pull, shaking their heads madly and leap from side to side, fixing each other with wild staring eyes. Their lips tremble and steam, their fangs bared threateningly either end of the bone . . . until the congregation forget the wrath of God and burst into merry laughter.

Four carriages drive through the streets of Amsterdam. They're made in France for princes. The man in black whose golden horse gallops through the city's winding streets is Doctor Tulp. He's the man who cuts into and opens corpses. Rembrandt told me. His name's stolen from the tulip* and he goes to visit the sick rich in his carriage; it's quicker than walking, and he doesn't get so soiled from the bricks of the street on the way.

Rembrandt has placed last year's unfinished paintings on his easels. His knife chips off the crusts from his palette. When the trial was over and Geertje Dircx had been taken to the hospital in Gouda, he slowly came out of the sorrow that hatred had revived. He slowly forgot. He tells himself that the mad are cared for in Gouda. But no one says they're cured.

Market days on Tuesday and Thursday were the only days I left

---

* Tulp's real name was Pietersz (which means 'son of Peter'). Surnames, with all their bureaucratic significance, in fact, did not come into being until the time of Napoleon. The vogue for tulips was undoubtedly what influenced the choice of this name.

the house and then again, on the seventh day, when I went to church. Judith's the one who takes Titus to school and fetches him at four o'clock. I fix my eyes on the street straight ahead, mustn't meet the gaze of anyone I pass. Behind my back I hear or I guess. Little shakes of the head, and that muttered word in their smiles; it bounces off the bricks and trails behind me in the folds of my dress.

Rembrandt hasn't married me. He won't marry me. He talked about it sometimes, but nothing's going to change now. I knew that very early on.

One rainy morning, weighed down with a heavy basket of turnips and cheese, I was slowly making my way home. Slowly approaching the rain-bedraggled man who was waiting for me at the door. He opened his mouth: 'Do you know what they say about a widower that becomes infatuated with his servant-girl?'

Even if I'd known what to answer, I couldn't have. The breath or my voice were missing, or maybe both. The word sizzled in my ears, with the sound tripe makes when it spills into boiling oil, bursting open like a poisonous flower and letting out its stench. I'd never seen the man before. He was the same age and the same ruddy colour my father was; he'd stewed too long in beer. He had a Frisian accent.

'They say he's shat in his own hat before putting it back on his head.' He leans back to laugh, showing all his teeth.

A rap of the door knocker of the house I now call 'my house'. Mustn't take the key out, even though it's hanging on the chain round my waist with the keys to the little courtyard and the cellar. Fear gripped me. At last I shaped some words in my mouth, I asked the man why. He wanted to see Rembrandt. I asked why, and the door opened.

The man's called Pieter Dircx, he's Geertje Dircx's brother. He's talking about arrangements and what the Gouda hospital costs. Says they've got to be paid, and that they're keeping her. Yes, of course, so they can cure her. Says Rembrandt should give the money to her brother, it's easier for her brother to organise his sister's money, easier when she comes out, when she's better. I can see from his smile he doesn't believe she'll ever come out, maybe doesn't even hope so. When he'd gone, you hugged me to you. No more grimaces, no more ugly words, no more mention of Geertje Dircx or her family ever again.

The collector, Lodewijck van Ludick sometimes comes to supper. He knew you when Saskia was still alive, he's a friend of both you and your painting. He says that paintings pass between hands, which are only fleetingly on Earth, and that these hands never possess them. And he says art always outlives the collector and that it's the art that possesses the collector. Because he likes collecting (whilst in passing on this Earth), he wants to become an art dealer. In answer to his wish, you tell him that the art that'll survive longest never answers to today's taste, that the art he likes isn't art that pretends and that the threat of bankruptcy always hangs over honest souls like him.

When the evening meal is over, like all Dutchmen, Rembrandt reads the Holy Book in the flickering candlelight. I watch and admire him. God has chosen him to paint His light. And Rembrandt has chosen me. Judith says it's my fate. And I say that if God has destined me to accompany Rembrandt and his work, I shall be with him all the days of my life or his (depending on who dies first, Lord spare us), to do all I can for his good, for Titus's and for the good of our unborn child. And pose in the smell of turpentine.

In the vaulted church that seventh day, the table was brought out and covered in a cloth with red brocade, same as it always was two or three times a year. One by one, we sat down at the Lord's table, one by one, we took the bread the preacher broke. Take, eat. This is My body. The sacrifice Christ made is unique, it's timeless. He made it for our salvation. It's the living bread that was sent from Heaven. He gives it for the life of the world, it's His flesh. He who eats of this bread will live forever.

I don't eat this bread, I chew it over and over. It turns sweet and melts in my mouth. My body receives the body of Christ and is fed by it. Then I take the pewter goblet from the hands of my neighbour on my left, I tip my head back and let the wine of my Church add flavour to my lips. I hand the goblet to my neighbour on my right. The Blood of our Lord Jesus Christ, which was shed for thee, preserve thy body and soul unto everlasting life. I swallow.

I've opened the door, and I know who he is. You'd told me about your brother Adriaen, but not about his face. His ways that never changed, especially since the death of your father and then your mother. The life of a miller from Leiden is full of the changing seasons, humble accounts, poor harvests and diseases. Not like the life of a famous young painter in Amsterdam. So, ten years ago, with his moods and his ways, when he found himself in difficulties, you asked your sister Elisabeth not to include you as a brother in her will.

Adriaen it was. I knew straight away. His eyes lost in the distance, his lined brow, his drooping mouth, the sadness at its corners. He murmured his sentences as if he was sorry for what he said. You laid aside your brush, came downstairs. Opened your arms, asked what news. Your sister Elisabeth is growing a little further away each year; all her life she's smiled, she never thinks of sad things. You introduced me as Hendrickje, and I kissed Adriaen like you kiss a member of your family. You promise to help him in his hour of need, you'll give him some money. Not much, because business is slow for you too.

Suddenly, in mid-sentence, you take a step towards your brother. You pull his arm so he steps forward and turns towards you. The light from a leaded window falls on his face in an orange glow, the light in your eye burns clear. You've forgotten me, already you're dragging Adriaen with you up the stairs to your studio, feet moving faster than usual. I know that look, I see it sometimes; time stands still, like the first day of the first painting. It's a white flame burning in your eyes, it's a vision.

Already you can see the painting, already the brush daubing the canvas can recognise it.

The sandglass shows two hours have gone by, and I've come up to the studio with rolls, herrings and warm beer. Very gently I open the door. Adriaen's eyes wander over the floor between the spots of paint; they always trace the same path. In his closed face, his lips are parched with thirst. On his head he's got the copper helmet, the one with engravings and carvings, a gold looking-glass that draws the light, sets it ablaze in a thousand points of fire before reflecting it back to the windows. Adriaen asks when he can leave his pose.

The whale is a big fish that swallowed Jonah. Then, on the Lord's order, it threw him up on dry land. And the sea has thrown up a whale on the banks in front of the port of Amsterdam. The city children stride about on stilts knocking at people's doors. They beat their drums, run and shout and sing. A whale that offers itself up to men is a messenger of God. I know this. On my knees I know, may God in His mercy have pity.

You said to me: 'Come, let's go down to the harbour. I've cleaned my brushes, it's not every day there's a beached whale in the port of Amsterdam.'

And it's not every day you go out into the port's rosy light. Or tug gently at my timid hand, and slip my arm into the crook of your own. We're walking along. You hold your head up, you're telling everyone wordlessly: 'This is my woman.' And I, who still don't know how to look passers-by in the face, I see only you. I smile at you, I am your woman.

As we get closer, there's already a stench coming from the monster; it burns in your nostrils. The crowd is thronging around. Lepers' clappers rattle in the shadow of the porches. Men in black and women wearing earrings run across the great bricks of the harbour streets; people lose their footing and twist their ankles. I can never hold in my giggles at the sight of them.

Beyond the bobbing boats, behind the masts that pierce the

orange sky, beyond the pebbles on the embankment, behind the black and colourful crowd (rich and poor alike have left the city to have a look), there it is, there it lies, the whale. Bigger than anything you could imagine. Bigger than anything the mind can stand. A creature of the Devil. I fall to my knees, like others around me. My face in my hands: forgive us our trespasses, oh Lord, grant us Thy mercy. Lead us not into temptation, but deliver us from evil. Like the city of Nineveh, Amsterdam will repent. I spread my fingers a little to spy the monster through them – bits of whale between a fan of great pink pillars. In the mouth of the prophet-eater, in his mighty jaws, the Devil has sown huge pointed teeth.

Jonah wanted to escape the Lord's order, then in the darkness of the fish's belly he prayed, calling on Him with all the strength of his soul, and the Lord saved him; Jonah travelled from sin to the redemption of his soul, from darkness to light, from water to dry land. A beached whale is a sign from God. A stream of frothing mud dribbles from the gaping mouth, vomited up from the innards in a long deep gurgling sigh.

Rembrandt walks towards the monster. I get up and follow him. Men and women, rich and poor, even the lepers laugh out loud. Little men have climbed up the great sticky body and skate about. They're feeling the animal's fatty flesh with their feet as much as with their hands, already they're holding their noses and slapping their thighs. They're as fat as what fills their purses. On their bones they make food that one day the little worms under the earth will gorge on. Rolls of fat. Their red faces show all their teeth; acquiring so many possessions is the sign that they have been chosen by God, of course it is.

They've not even got the boats and fishermen ready, they've not risked money nor human lives, they've not known the danger of hunting out at sea, but today, once again, the whale-blubber merchants have become richer. So rich they're ready to burst like rubber balls. God is good to them, unless He uses them and their sins and innards to swell His revenge, the Flood that one day (outside time, not near and not far) will wipe out the United Provinces and their inhabitants.

The fat-melters will be cooking day and night. The whole city will be full of the stink of the Devil. As we pray, we will know that the rich don't believe it will be hard for them to enter the Kingdom of our God; we will know that God's sign is melting away. And maybe His wrath and our sins too.

Shouting and laughter all around the monster. Two men in black hats are measuring the whale's penis, and it's so . . . so incredibly long my eyes don't believe what they see. The figure rises, muttered about from person to person, swelling towards us. Fourteen foot of penis! Fourteen foot, a man in black repeats in front of me. He speaks between clenched teeth. Slowly he turns his knife-like profile to his neighbour. He hasn't seen us. In that instant I recognise the man from the golden carriage. Rembrandt bends down to my ear: 'That's him, Doctor Tulp.'

Jan Six pays you a visit. He still doesn't see me, even though I've got my face in the sun and I'm holding my arm out for his doublet. Did he know that I would hear? Did he want me to? The studio door was wide open, Jan Six already on the first step.

'. . . I'm sorry, too, believe me. But art-loving society will turn its back on you if you mix with people of low birth. Because polite society always finds out what it ought not to know. (He laughs.) Sleeping with your servant doesn't offend if there's no trial or scandal. (He laughs.) Look at Descartes, he was happy with his servant and their little Francine, and yet he never married her.* (He laughs.) Mark my words, Rembrandt, this broken promise of marriage the city has been talking about for months is damaging you and your art business. But (and his voice becomes too soft) gradually it will be forgotten. Time will erase the misjudgment.'

Jan Six comes down the stairs. A misjudgment, I'm one

* Descartes had a relationship with Helena Jans, a servant to the bookshop owner with whom he stayed in Amsterdam in 1634. He was deeply affected by the death in 1640 of their daughter Francine, born in 1635.

too and I dissolve with shame. Without seeing me, he unerringly catches hold of the doublet which I'm not holding out to him; he swirls it around and places it on his shoulders.

Judith says that the whale's raw sperm protects one's skin against wind and time and stops you getting wrinkles. Every morning, when I've got dressed, I do my hair in our bedroom mirror. As if time passed quicker each year, from the other side of the mirror my eyes glow like dying embers deep in their sockets. It's time and tiredness. I push my lips forward in the shape of a kiss, they crack when they touch the glazed surface. The hollows in my face have sunk, my nose is sharper, more pointed. In spite of Judith and her whale's sperm, these lines on my skin aren't grimaces and smiling doesn't get rid of them any more. My chin and cheeks are less transparent than I remember, there are pink blotches on them. Time must be passing quicker than when it didn't notice me.

When Jan Six had left, I waited till the end of the day, and went up to your studio. I said to you: 'Keep me. I'm so happy by your side, you've taught me about life and what's important. I want to help you, if my help is any good to you. But if I become a burden, if your life gets complicated because of me then . . .'

You come up to me, gently place a finger on my lips. The other hand strokes my cheek, moves down my neck, I feel its weight on my breast, then it turns flat on my belly. In spite of your finger and your hand, no laughing, no grimacing, I go on.

'We won't publish the banns three times in a row. You won't say "yes", you won't put a ring on my finger, I won't wear two during the ceremony, one on my big finger, one on my thumb. We won't invite family, pupils and friends to the wedding. We won't drink *hypocras*,*' we won't eat peacock confit or capon stuffed with Hormuz apricots.'

---

* An infusion of sweet Rhine wine with ginger, cinnamon and cloves.

Gently you shake your head and smile. Your hand revolves around my navel. Then it glides lower, wanders among my petticoats and loses itself in the hairs, a struggling captive.

'Saskia decreed it in her will, but she was too young to know that life changes, and that the 40,000 florins you then had between you would no longer be yours in ten years' time. Not even half that much, the 20,000 that was supposed to go to the Chamber of Orphans for Titus if you married again. Saskia always wanted what was best for you but, when she was dying, she thought she was being wise. For the first and last time in her life.' Your hand has found its resting place; it's warm and firm against me. I kiss you with little breathy kisses that burst like bubbles.

'You talk of marriage, you say it hurts you not to keep a promise you've never made and which I would never let you make.' Your hand lingers, enjoying what it's searching for. 'Even if you had 20,000 florins today, Rembrandt, I'd never want you to part with it for my sake (bubble kisses), I'd be ashamed to be the reason you did.' Your index finger feels for the pleasure that's quick to flood it. I spread and bend my legs, put my arms quickly round your neck so as not to fall, so as not to slip. Always deeper your finger, burning. I moan and close my eyes. I hang round your neck as if you're carrying me with one finger, not even the ends of my toes touch the floor any more. My lips in yours.

'I don't want any other life but the one you've given me. Happiness beside you, Rembrandt van Rijn.' You were kissing me, swallowing me, my tongue, my saliva, pressing your whole body to me, the whole of it for me. There, as we stood.

On the seventh day, the last day of a moon, a comet crossed the sky of Holland. Another sign. Old toothless folk who never leave their houses opened their doors to remember. In their long lives they've seen other warnings. They know them when they see them in the sky. They pray together. God always takes revenge with pestilence and floods.

*   *   *

In the mirror in your studio, in the great ebony-framed mirror that watches you growing old, your finger traces the marks time has engraved on your face. You wear a black velvet beret. You've truthfully revisited past sorrows. Your face stares straight into the future with a new courage in your new life. Your brush plunges into the linseed oil (for a long time your portrait my love will smell of the garlic which gauged the heat of the oil), then hovers over the palette and, like a spade, picks up the cerulean blue paste and beats it furiously to a dark mixture that will look light against the painting's shadowy background.

You're no longer like a drowned man brought back to land and then to life. With your arms round me, you don't need gin to help you fall asleep. In the great studio the frozen smells and the silence have been swept away by talk and laughter. Once again, the house is filled with the steam of the vats of rabbit skin and bones. There's the sound of the models running up and down stairs (and their smothered giggles) escaping from the pupils Bernhard and Willem,* with their sometimes unwelcome jokes, especially when they want to get a closer look at how the flesh sits on the body.

On the night of the 5th to the 6th of March, water fell from the sky and swelled the rivers and canals. The Saint Anthony Dyke was plugged in time, just before the lands were flooded. Men and women worked through the night in the wind and rain. And all night long women who had no cart carried clay in their aprons. God will punish us, He will cleanse us of our sins.

Together we'll go by canal to where Jan Six lives in the country. I'd rather not have come. Especially on a Sunday, especially when it's time for church, and the city gates are shut. Titus can play in the fields, and I, the servant-girl, I'm going to play with him. It's not how you would have wanted it, but I'll never be your woman

* Bernhard Keil (1624–87) and Willem Drost (c. 1630–87).

in this man's eyes. For Jan Six, I'm your servant, I'm not visible.
I prefer this lie – it hides me and it's better than feeling his gaze
cut through me like a knife.

I lived in the country for twenty years, I know you can catch
the sickness of melancholy there. It's a green fog that gets into
your body through all the little holes in your skin and rises up
to your head and turns it to rust. That's why everyone does more
washing in the country than in the city. They rub, scratch and
scour the rust that bubbles up everywhere. If it gets stuck for
good, it forms little lumps that get all tangled up like a family
of little brown worms.

We got on to the barge. On the bank, the horse walked
painfully along, its hoofs sinking into the mud. Amsterdam
receded and, behind us, the ringing of the Westerkerk bells
slowly grew fainter. Around us on all sides, stretching away to
the horizon, the great green sea was split in two by the canal. In
your box were three copper plates, drypoints and burin, varnish
and brush. In those years between the two wars, you used to
say that the sight of the country was restful to your eyes; the
silence of the horizons at the furthest point you could see, the
web of canals disappearing to the edge of the flat land, the vast
skies and the quick-passing clouds casting their shadows about
us, then abandoning us to the early sunshine.

You never take your Bible out of the city. God is everywhere,
you say. In the canals where the swans glide, their heads held
high on their long necks, in a bridge, a sailing boat, a fisherman,
in the whole of this untroubled life, you say, and your drypoint
captures it in copper. So that we, too, can see it as God made it.
You know the truth of things that others never will, I can feel
it right beside me here. I am in your life, and slowly, your life
enters me.

Jan Six puts his arm round your shoulders. I don't know why
but I'm embarrassed by this gesture and look away. And yet I
shouldn't still be listening to what I feel, you're always saying
so, and you're right; it's not because I feel that I'm right. He

believes in friendship, he says. He who doesn't love women and doesn't know what love is. You've been in his house already, a few years ago. You engraved the portrait of the man who offered you so much friendship. He posed in his drawing room, his back to the window, the dog snapping and jumping around him. Jan Six didn't like the preparatory drawing for the engraving. Too different from the unsmiling image his mirror shows him, and too different from the artist he wants people to love and from the great works that will survive him into immortality. (You purse your lips to make me laugh.) Too rustic, all those trees and that birdcage, too natural with the dog and the boots. Jan Six changed into different clothes, the dog disappeared, banished from the drawing room. He bent his head over a book. He closed his mouth and furrowed his brow. He was pleased, he liked the engraving, he'd become the scholar, the friend of the arts and artists, here was the talented author of a *Medea*.

The dog snapped and jumped after his master. In the maze in his garden, Jan Six was talking to Rembrandt, staring straight ahead, changing direction unhesitatingly at every turn the path took. Maybe, with his great strides, he wanted to lose me but, far behind, I held Titus's hand; I held him back, he was tugging at my arm, he wanted to stroke the dog. That's why I stayed a long way behind: the fur of cats and dogs is a carrier of the Plague. Then Titus cried so loud I let go his hand.

Without declaring war, the English have attacked the Dutch fleet. Peace hasn't lasted three years. First the Spanish, now the English. This war's going to be on water – their sea trade against ours. The old folk who opened their doors when they saw the comet are gathering in the street. With their toothless gums, they chew over the harm the war will do to the port of Amsterdam if it goes on.

Each of the squirming little white worms follows its own path and digs its own tunnel. Slowly they nibble away at the wood, digesting it, then leaving behind them narrow trails of grey ash. On and on they go, along their quivering path. They can't turn back, they wouldn't know how. They dig very slowly, then curl into a ball and sleep, stuffed with work and wood shavings, in no hurry to continue. The females lay eggs. They leave them and go on. Later, a new army wakes up behind them, and every baby worm emerges from its transparent cocoon to dig its own new tunnel beside the one where it was born. It takes more than ten years for each worm to get to the other end of its tunnel.

You say, and you keep saying, that I'm ready for other people (except Jan Six); that I already was when I held your arm on the beach and wasn't afraid of the whale or the other people; that I'm not married, but I'm your woman and I'll go with you to the auction. I hold your arm and look down at my feet walking along between the benches. I can feel people looking at me, hear their words judging me. At last, when I'm sitting down with your hand a prisoner in my playful fingers, I raise my head. They're all there, Jan Six and Doctor Tulp, all in black in their close-woven velvet, Uylenburgh and Huygens. They're not judging me, they don't know me, they've not seen me, not they nor the women in their heavy, brightly coloured satin. Looking straight ahead, all they see is the platform at the end of the hall, the insolvency auctioneer and the paintings held up by the porter.

This one's a big landscape, a storm of blue shadows by Hercules Seghers. The auction starts low and the bids are small. The eyes of the auctioneer dart from person to person, from bid to bid. Your leg judders on the floor against mine; now your whole body's shaking as if you've got a fever. You shake your head, the hand I was holding breaks away. A kind of groan escapes your lips, repeating words, louder and louder. Shame, shame, you keep saying.

'150, 160, 165 florins,' the insolvency auctioneer's eyes sweep the rows and flutter over the white ruffs.

'250 florins.' Rembrandt's voice. The figure burst from your lips, and all heads turn to look. Red faces with round eyes, frowns as well but no smiles, no, you've no friends here.

Rembrandt's hand seizes mine again, conspiratorial, wanting to share the fun of the moment. Unabashed, you face the hollow cheeks, hard mouths, reproaches and judgments. You spread your legs, your chest swells, you turn to right and left, smiling at everyone. You take a great gulp of air: 'For the good of my profession! . . .'

It's too much for the local grandees, who screw their heads round on their necks. I look at you, you're joyous and beautiful. You're thinking of Hercules Seghers, snatched from your friendship by death; you're thinking of his attempt to print colours on cloth; of the price he used to ask for details of his engravings which he'd cut up. So he could eat. And how, one evening when the affliction was too great, it was the gin that cast him head first down his stairs. I tell myself he's proud of you. And so am I.

You've insulted the law and accepted behaviour, money doesn't grow on trees and should be respected, and you've insulted that, too. It buys for the lowest sum (and sometimes well below that), lends itself with interest and, of course, always acts with reason. That day, the stern faces strangled by their ruffs condemned you. As expected, I pretend, and cast my eyes down.

Later, we'll laugh at home with Titus. I'll keep kissing your face; I'll tell you how much I loved you that day, how happy I was and how proud of Rembrandt van Rijn, my husband.

The sun has warmed the earth. On the cherry tree in the little courtyard the hard new fruits have seen off the flowers with their white petals. Judith hangs cloth devils on the tree so the birds will be frightened and fly off. The cherries will ripen, shiny as buboes, and so full of black, black juice their skin looks ready to burst. I've never told her cherries carry the Plague, she likes them too much and she wouldn't believe me. Not even a cloth devil will get rid of the Plague. I turn my face away.

*   *   *

It's a groan, more than a sigh, that escapes me. My face crumples and I bend my left leg. Your face leans round the stretcher. I yawn. It's that hour in the afternoon when sleep takes over and I can't hold it off any more; that's how it's been since our child's been feeding off my life in my womb. You put down the palette and brush, you leave Bathsheba on the canvas, you come to me. I bend my right leg, huddled over, gathering my life about this second heart that beats within me. You lift up the red drape that half covers me, slowly you crawl under the velvet. Slowly, you come towards me.

The war against the English will be long. Uylenburgh pays you the odd visit. When he leaves with a painting, he hasn't bought it, he's not even paid you an advance. As if it's risky for a merchant to buy a Rembrandt these days. Van Ludick is more generous but does less trade. Fortunately for everyday living, the collector and engravings dealer, Clement de Jonghe, often comes to the Breestraat. You help him choose a Christ, he looks at the drawings and sketches in the boxes, he's always got the florins in his pocket and a pen for your two signatures.

Rembrandt gave me a cupboard with a pretty carved frieze of tulips; it's better than a wedding present. He won it along with twelve sabre handles and ten silver dagger handles on the Dam. It was at a lottery to help the city of Veere and its poor (all of them widows and orphans) after the flood and the Plague. The cupboard wasn't empty. Carefully folded on the shelves were fourteen pairs of sheets, thirty towels, a dozen handkerchiefs and ten scarves. I'm Rembrandt van Rijn's woman, mistress of his house, and I hang the key to the cupboard on the chain I wear round my waist. It's as if my husband has given me a dowry. I hold my head up in the mirror, then stick my tongue out so I stop believing all this. I run my fingers over the dark carved wood, listen several times to the squeaky left-hand door, put my nose to the greener wood of the shelves. I'll scent the cupboard and its linen with woodruff. Now I own a cupboard, I feel like I've really grown up, I'm a woman now, perhaps I'm growing old.

*   *   *

We all heard the fire before we saw it, we heard it in our sleep. The bricks were the first to fall in a flood of hail. The watchmen's clappers clattered their warning. Wood and metal were torn away, and the flames licked at them as they swung free before they were completely disfigured. Then the flames went for the beams, which groaned and fell out of their sockets. We leant against the windowsill and saw the old Town Hall go up in flames. The fire sprang up to the moon, outlining a second building bigger than the real one which stretched to the stars.

The old Town Hall (already condemned by the new one being built) shimmers against the sky in a festival of lights such as it has never seen. Draws its last breath. Through the open window, the flames paint rose windows on my face. Rembrandt says he's going to draw what's left of the building's deafening death throes at the first crack of dawn, just before it goes out so we don't forget the dying embers of this charcoal skeleton.

Rembrandt's sad laugh right beside me, shaking him, shaking me a bit. The wind is fanning the flames across the Dam, like a wall of fire threatening the new Town Hall being built. The city grandees call it the 'eighth wonder of the world'; it's going to house the city administrative offices, the court, the treasury of the Bank of Amsterdam, and in the cellars there'll be prisons – the ones at the city gates aren't big enough. It's built on more than 13,000 piles, it's our Temple of Solomon. If the worms gnawed their way into the wooden piles, the squares of Bentheim stone, those fine black-and-white stones, would crack, the flat earth would rise up, like a sea shaken by its waves, and the walls would slowly crumble in a black-and-white cloud. Maybe this evening God's starting to take revenge on His House. In the flames and smoke, men and women are running about, weighed down by their heavy buckets.

The new Town Hall felt the heat of the neighbouring fire, but not its flames. Three weeks later the city found out (news spread by word of mouth from door to door) that silver coins had melted in their coffers in the cellars of the charcoal skeleton; it's a shame. But also, a large part of the archives had been burnt. Is bad news for some good news for others? Does the old world have to disappear so the new world can live? Judith is whispering; she doesn't want to disturb anyone, but asks if it was a man's hand that kindled the Devil's flames.

Judith has bought a handful of Chinese tea-leaves from a sailor on the shore. Further along, she saw whores selling their bodies for a few leaves. Perhaps they sell them on again in the city. You have to boil a few ounces of the precious plant in water for a long time. Then add honey, at least four small spoonfuls per person. Ephraim Bueno says two or three cups a day can't hurt anyone. But Doctor Tulp says up to fifty for women suffering from irritability and constipation; he'd put their lives in danger. I tried it, and spat it out, too bitter. And anyway, I'm not constipated.

Bathsheba and David's child is sick, the Lord willed it. To help his prayers and supplications, David has stopped eating and no longer sleeps in his bed; he sleeps on the tiled floor. The damp paper smells of ink and linseed oil. In his nightshirt, on his knees, leaning his elbows on his Dutch bed with its thick hangings, the man prays. He is King David; on the seventh day, his child will be dead. Seven, a phase of the moon. It's all so close to us, so Dutch. David won't stretch himself upon the child like Elisha, the child won't sneeze seven times and open his eyes.

And I'm posing as Bathsheba, Uriah's wife, I who have never committed adultery, who have not been desired nor offered by any king other than my own, but I still know that there's always a price to pay. I've taken up the pose again today, and under the cloth I uncover my belly swollen by the child that will soon breathe the same air as us. You remember the three little lives that ended so young and, for a moment, behind your brush, fear extinguishes your eyes. King David's letter tells me to go to him, a few words, an order on a square of paper. With my child kicking inside me, I'm happy; I shut my eyes and feel my face smiling. I open my eyes and remember Bathsheba's fate is already sealed.

My dream smelled of burning pork. The new Town Hall was in flames. In their cages beneath the ground, the prisoners writhed, caramelised mush around a great scream. Stakes pierced their bodies. Smoke billowed from their cracked and blackened mouths.

A letter has come all the way from deepest Italy to Amsterdam. All the way to the Breestraat. The letter is signed 'Don Antonio Ruffo'. It's written in Italian by the merchant Isaac Just, who sells to dealers in other countries and who knows and translates their languages.

Don Antonio Ruffo desires paintings for his new library, portraits of men of thought and men who have helped others think. Philosophers and poets. A collector, that's what Don Ruffo is, an art lover, Isaac Just says. Rembrandt says: a cultivated man of taste, a man of quality. And when a man of quality crosses vast countries and aeons of time (so many years since our moment of glory) to meet him, him and his painting, it restores his faith. Yes, I think it comforts him in all this war, when money's uncertain and grandees with no memory can't think or choose for themselves any more. He wants to paint a wonderful painting. He's taking his time, he's thinking about it.

Rembrandt asked me to, so now I take off my apron before I open the door (except when I make out Jan Six's long figure through the hole in the wood). That's how your visitors know I'm not the servant and that we're expecting a child, very soon, nine months, brand new. Doctor Ephraim gently taps my cheek, he asks if the winter is tiring me, with my great belly.

Rembrandt has learnt the stories of men in the Holy Book.

He's wary of words and other books. But, for the painting for the Sicilian's library, he opens his door to his friends Ephraim Bueno and Lodewijck van Ludick; together they remember and consider. I listen with Titus and I learn the names of those who have thought and worked, and who have loved enough too, to share their knowledge: Homer, Socrates, Plato, Aristotle, Leonardo da Vinci. Unlucky, misunderstood or betrayed, their names ring like music from warm seas where the mermaids swim.

The English are winning battles. No Dutch captain ventures to bring his ship and crew into the estuary of the IJ any more. In the city, we no longer hear tell of the joyous return of sailors, full of the colours and spices of the East Indies or the peninsula of Manhattan. Amsterdam's port is empty, its trade dead, 'dormant', according to the local grandees.

The city's merchants no longer meet in the Amsterdam Exchange. Money has stopped going out of the Bank, from hidden safes or house walls, or beneath floorboards or stone slabs. As if life had stopped while we waited. 'What are we waiting for?' You shake your head and your lion's mane of long hair: 'For there to be no more war ever again, for the sails of the mills to cease turning, for no tulip bulb to yield a tulip in the soil of our United Provinces, or else for our neighbours to set the first example?' It's fear of the grandees, fear. You say it again, you laugh, you're anxious. About debts, about your art too, about Titus, about us and the baby, clamouring to be born with his little feet.

Ephraim Bueno says he always smokes a pipe in a room where there's disease. Torches in the street burn the miasmas in the air, and tobacco smoke stifles the Plague in a house before it can infect him.

Rembrandt hardly ever goes out of his studio now. Auctions are rare and there's no money to spend 'for the good of his profession'. He says war and power are the work of man's vanity. Says he's waiting for peace and that, between two wars, there's always peace.

Clement de Jonghe often comes to share our evening meal with us. Engravings are much cheaper than paintings and they travel more easily. You often thank him, for his friendship and the advances he sometimes makes (and without interest) for commissions and unfinished plates. You even engraved his portrait for immortality. Etchings, aquatints, mezzotints. I listen, I like learning.

I opened the door, the man entered. I went quickly up to the studio. I don't know why, but fear was beating in my breast. I saw your face fall and noticed the rings round your eyes, suddenly hollow.

'Christoffel Thijsz,' I repeated.

I showed Christoffel Thijsz up to the studio. He bowed before you and held out his hand. 'Master Rembrandt, forgive me, I'm disturbing you. I've not been importunate till now.'

Pressed against you, protected and supporting you, I look closely at the man to understand what I'm hearing. I look at the short hairs on the thick skin of his nose, his little grey beard, neatly trimmed and brushed, and his dry lips around his yellow teeth snapping open and shut on the words he utters.

You must settle the debt on the house. The fact is that for years you haven't paid as you should. And the 8,000 florins still due, not including the interest, are badly needed by Christoffel Thijsz in these times when business is slow (but he doesn't want to disturb you). You reply to all this that you understand, yes, you've understood perfectly. Christoffel Thijsz thanks you and goes away, confident because you've understood. He's gone away confident.

The light has gone out in your eyes. I cross my arms round your neck, lay my head on your breast. Frozen inside, the beating's slower now.

*   *   *

The dark streets echo with the word of fear. The Plague doctor walks through the city's fear, holding the white stick of disease at arm's length. Those who live in healthy houses turn their backs and run away, those with a sick person in the house call to him. Twenty-two dead in four days in the Jordaan, none on our side of the Breestraat.

I like learning and I listen. The Trojan War, the Republic, Alexander the Great. Leonardo da Vinci, who only painted thirteen paintings, wanted, above all, to understand the inside of bodies, the sky, water and machines. He cut open more than one hundred corpses. Ephraim Bueno says, of course, he died unhappy from so much work and thought, and because he left the living with nothing but a great mass of confused writings after his death.

Rembrandt has decided on the man he's going to paint for Don Antonio Ruffo. He also had a great library; Aristotle was Plato's pupil, and he tutored Alexander the Great, but Alexander didn't listen to him when he grew up.

Judith has seen a comet with a tail in the dark sky. It's a portent of many deaths or the coming of a prophet, that's what the toothless gums of the old folk say to one another. The screaming goes on through the night, but in the morning it dies down. The living abandon the dead. For the living know that they shall die; but the dead know not any thing.

A gloved hand knocks at the door on the Breestraat. It holds out a letter sealed with red wax. Christoffel Thijsz has waited patiently for ten years. But he needs money immediately. The law is now claiming the 8,000 florins and interest on his behalf. If you don't pay your debts, and pay them quickly, your house will be put up for auction. Your house, your life. Your happiness with Saskia, your more troubled years, but always your studio and your work. And the paintings on the walls, and your collections, your life. You've got no money, all you've got are debts. Like you, I can't believe it, I clasp you to me, try to warm your frozen heart.

This morning they've been killing the bulls in the meat hall. One by one, they come into the great building, their heads lowered in the face of death. It smells of death, it smells of fear. The steam from their nostrils is really a sob. In the afternoon, Rembrandt, Titus, Judith and I go to choose our carcass. Like every November. We feel the meat with our fingers, pressing along the muscle; we squeeze the flesh to see the colour of the still-warm blood that spurts out; with our noses we sniff for smells that must be neither strong nor insipid. Rembrandt, he doesn't go near them. He goes from carcass to carcass, screwing up his eyes, looking at them from a distance, then close to, framing them with his hands, like they're a painting. It's always Judith who chooses. She'll take a large knife with a good sharp point, and cut the animal into pieces. And for two days, we'll eat fresh meat grilled over the coals of the hearth. Just two days a year. Afterwards, the little white worms will come out of the eggs already laid in the carcass and they'll devour it, infecting it with their stink.

All the other pieces will then be scrubbed, dry-salted and placed in a couple of great earthenware jars. Two months in the freezing courtyard. We'll take the meat from one of the jars and wash the salt off. Then, like each year, Judith will take charge of them being smoked in the hearth. But today, in the meat hall, all these carcasses of bulls hanging up with their legs splayed out to the four corners, burn the tunnels in my nose. Life and death are in that stench. What's on the outside is suddenly making the inside sick. From tomorrow, I'll eat nothing but vegetables that have come out of the earth, never again make my body a receptacle for carcasses. I say that every November. And then I forget.

You walked about the city for a long time. Mustn't let the law get hold of your house, money must be borrowed, and fast.

You knew where you were going, but your feet didn't. They went right out of their way along the Leidesgracht. There you passed the fumigators who protect houses from the Plague; they scrub the walls and around the doors and windows with a good-smelling mixture of herbs, sulphur, nutmeg, camphor and some secret of theirs.

Then your feet turned on their heels. In one of the harbour taverns, you threw back your head and drained a huge pitcher of beer in one gulp. With your head heavier and your belly full of bubbles, you walked down the Kloveniersburwal to the beautiful house where Jan Six lives. Your hand's tightened round the gold knocker, and you knock twice without thinking (were they sharp knocks, shy knocks?). His man-servant opens the door, he's wearing a suit that shines with rows of golden buttons. He looks down at you, down at your purple jacket. In Jan Six's house, no one is humbled by anything less than white ruff and black velvet.

A stork has landed on a house-top on the Breestraat, on the last step of the gable. Maybe she hesitated a long time before deciding and gliding to that particular house. It's because she was going to build her nest here and watch her family hatch. Maybe it was that very moment she chose to land, flap and beat her wings, and finally get her balance.

With open arms and the smile of friendship on his face, Jan Six leads you into the great rooms of his vast house. You admire his collection of China porcelain with him. He frowns, suddenly worried, and asks if you've been visited by dealers for your paintings since the trial. Then he falls silent. You've left your studio during daylight hours, you've not just called in because you happened to be passing. He knows money is hard to come by, he's one of the one's waiting to get it out of its hiding place. He knows you're in trouble. But he listens without interrupting.

Later you remember he listened attentively. 'It's no small sum,' he said. Then, after a long silence, like he was mulling it over. 'I'm not promising anything, my friend. I don't have the means myself at the moment, but I can think of a few who might have.'

You thanked him very warmly, even though, with the high-and-mighty Jan Six, you've lost your sincerity. I think that since he left the world of art which didn't want him and went into the family business and the City, knowing that an artist he still admires is in trouble gives him confidence, maybe even pleasure.

The stork never stopped as she came and went, carrying sticks, dry leaves, yellowed moss and peat dust that the chimneys had coughed out onto the roofs. The stork was building her nest.

Leaves were being torn from the trees and whipped up by the wind. Rembrandt had been watching the wind since midday from behind the coloured window panes; he kept saying between his teeth that he wouldn't go out in the evening. He wouldn't go to the honorary dinner. He'd keep his own honour untarnished. I said nothing. He said that just the thought of meeting and greeting all those people wore him out. Said he wasn't one of those artists who spend more time bowing and scraping in people's drawing rooms than hunched painfully over their easel. I said nothing. And, while I was quiet, the evening put out the light in the window. Titus had his dinner in the kitchen with Judith. I went to find Rembrandt, he was in his studio in front of his easel, no light burning.

Aristotle studied, he also admired the poet Homer. Then he gave his knowledge to his pupils. He's looking at a plaster bust that Rembrandt bought some years ago in a sale. The beard and hair make it look like Homer. Rembrandt decided: it was a bust of Homer. Sorrow has already burnt Aristotle's eyes as he looks at it. Worn out, he looks, his eyes made with great brushstrokes with no paste on, like a man who's seen and believed, who's judged men and emperors, who still hopes.

Homer's voice carries across death and time to Aristotle, and Aristotle hears and answers him.

I come up behind Rembrandt's back. They can't have an evening in honour of St Luke, the patron saint of painters, without Rembrandt van Rijn, Amsterdam's most important painter. He places his hands over mine.

He says very quietly: 'Thank you for your confidence, but I'm not called that any more . . . if I'm not forgotten altogether.'

'The best people know you are.' And, spreading one hand over the full moon of my belly, I say to him (I know he won't resist this): 'And our child shall know too. Go, you're already very late.'

The stork hesitated before flying off again. She bent her head, looked at the nest, considered it. Like a crab, she put one foot over the other, walked round it. She was thinking that her work was well done. Faltering, fluttering her wings, she settled. For a long time she'd get up and turn round, a long time before the hollow was perfect.

Rembrandt came back two hours later, exhausted by the evening, by the approaching winter and by life. He came straight back to the Breestraat without going to the tavern, hurrying to get back to the warmth of his house, the studio, the even breathing of Titus as he slept, and me. No one but us now, and the glass of gin I hold out to him before the flames of the hearth.

In the cold, you walked to the St Joris Doelen, to the archers' great meeting hall. You pushed open the heavy door. In the hesitant light of hundreds of candles at the huge table, sat the worthy gathering. They sought each other's faces, greeted one another, cast furtive glances between the points of flame. Some leant over their neighbour's shoulder and poured wounding venomous words into his ear, their eyes never leaving their victim on the other side of the room. And in the seat of honour, smiling puffily the city's Great Regent, Joan Huydecoper, counted those who'd turned up. He knows artists are the natural companions to glory, gilding it, making it eternal. Maerten Kretzer, Bartholomeus van der Helst . . . he tries to remember the names, Nicolaes van Helt Stockade, but loses interest almost immediately. Govert Flinck, Emmanuel de Witte, Philips Koninck, Jurriaen Ovens, they're all there, all hoping to be included in the city's next commissions. They're all thinking of the paintings for the new Town Hall. One man will be chosen: the greatest talent will have the honour of glorifying the Great Regent the most.

Rembrandt van Rijn is the only one who's not at the table. No one's said a word. Hasn't his absence been spotted? But his presence hasn't been noticed either, there in the shadow, near the door. As if you're attending the dinner after your own funeral, stop it, my love, don't say such things. A choking laugh in your throat. You shake your head: sure there'd be fewer of them on that evening of the feast of St Luke if they were saying goodbye to you, before the flag stone is put back over your coffin. I pour some gin into your empty glass.

Further away, in the middle of the long table, Govert Flinck is applauding Joost van den Vondel, the guest of honour sitting opposite him. You describe the poet to me, the glory of Holland, the great Vondel. Sitting very upright in his chair as high as a throne, in his crown of laurels, he listens to the words that come out of his mouth.

Rembrandt doesn't move, he still hasn't decided whether to share this supper (how much richer than the Lord's!) with the gathering. He brings to mind some lines by Vondel that mocked his portrait of the preacher Cornelius Anslo, verses that condemned the painting, and which he thought too weak to capture the strength of the preacher's words. Four lines, the only meeting Rembrandt and Vondel ever had.

Everyone here will remember others who've been chosen like them by this great evening; they raise their elbows, weighing the tannin of blood in their large transparent glasses. Do this in remembrance of Me. They laugh and drink noisily.

*   *   *

The very moment when the stork laid her eggs in the nest she'd finished.

In the shadow behind the door, Rembrandt listened. It's Govert Flinck's turn to speak. He's standing up, he turns to everyone, all smiles. He reminds everyone that in the presence of Vondel, who rose from our Land like a phoenix, a new confraternity of painters has gathered to be elected this evening. Joost van den Vondel himself set the example with a Poetry Academy. Old and new poems will now be judged by those who know; in the search for beauty, there will be no more of those mistakes that creep in where there's no noble ambition. Govert Flinck is speaking up, he hopes, for a similar Academy for painting in his country. The beauty of art will exist at last, recognised by those who know. Who alone can say. Everyone claps.

Vondel again. Attentive silence. He reminds them that painting and sculpture are not created without measurements and figures. They can't do without geometry, which brings them closer to God, for didn't God arrange everything by weights, measurements and figures?

Rembrandt has gone out. As he came in. No one saw him come in and no one saw him go out. His place is elsewhere. For sure and forever. These dabblers in art, these self-satisfied men with their figures and measurements, these dealers who only ape art, they've forgotten Rembrandt van Rijn and his work. Not even noticed his absence. That's the last time you'll leave your studio. Your solitude in the light. Titus and me, and our child soon. A few friends, a few pupils. You'd rather always be alone, travelling further away, further down. You'll search souls and shadows with the hairs of your brush.

I'm stretched out on our bed, peering into the night, through the ceiling and the floors to where the stork sits on her eggs in the dark. Right on top of our roof, with her straight body pointing up to heaven like an arrow. A stork on a roof is a sign, a good sign.

*   *   *

The shepherds are visiting Mary and her child in the stable. Joseph greets them with open arms and hands outstretched. You wipe the ink from between the grooves with a cloth. The law forbids the young mother to enter the temple before the forty days of purification after birth are over. So the child was circumcised in the stable. Joseph takes the child on his knee, Mary folds her hands in prayer. The press makes a grinding noise. Clement de Jonghe comes and goes away again. He comes with money, he goes away with the prints.

Jan Six has brought the dealer Hertsbeeck to the Breestraat, and two days later, the councillor Cornelis Witsen. I ask questions, but Rembrandt wants to spare me the disagreeable parts of life, what he calls 'details'. My poor love, I'm the one who ought to be comforting you. Saving you from everything that holds up your work, the most important thing.

It's his decision, I'll only know what he doesn't keep from me. Contracts with money-lenders have been signed in the presence of a notary. The merchant asked for interest, the councillor chose reimbursement without interest. To be sure of being the first to get his money back, he pays the 180 florins for the record, which you'll reimburse him. And to be sure you'll be able to thank him with paintings and engravings as well, of course. Now he's seen the two men lending you each 4,000 florins, you whom he calls 'his friend', the patron Jan Six has made an effort and come up with 1,000 florins. With interest, and on condition of a guarantor. You were right to sign, there are a lot of debts and money is too scarce; but friendship is very suspicious. Not like your guarantor, though, Lodewijck van Ludick signed, no questions. Because he's your friend and he loves your work. You'll pay Christoffel Thijsz's debt and you'll keep the house. Later, when the immediate danger is long over and we're pretending we've forgotten, I'll tell you what the money-lenders and Christoffel Thijsz don't know: a house with a stork on its roof is worth twice its price.

*   *   *

In his gold silk, Aristotle is a prince among men. A light from nowhere burns around him. It comes from him, it's his face illuminating the painting. It's his love, his compassion for humanity and even for its faults. I massage your shoulders, I look at the painting on the easel, I know it's the light inside you that kindles such life.

The Plague claimed fifty-two lives last week in Amsterdam, thirty-nine of them in the Jordaan. It's the damp air from the canals, that's what it is; the miasmas settle on the air, level with people's mouths. I tell Judith not to go out any more when it's raining or foggy, she's to wait for the sun to shine before she comes back to the Breestraat. She dug out a filbert – just took a little time and a pin, that's all – and scooped out the kernel. Then she poured quicksilver, which Ephraim Bueno bought from the apothecary, Abraham Francen, into the little hole. She plugged it with animal-skin glue. She wears the filbert round her neck day and night to ward off the Plague. Every morning, she and her husband wash their mouths, nostrils and the extremities of their bodies with *oxycrate** mixed with rose water. She carries a sponge dipped in vinegar so as not to breathe in the miasmas of disease, then she can cross the city.

Rembrandt has offered Jan Six a drawing. Homer is reading his poetry to a spellbound audience, he tells of Helen's loves and of the Trojan War. Jan Six refuses, hesitates, he understands that Rembrandt is thanking him for his help, the two money-lenders and his 1,000 florins. But he can't accept, you shouldn't give thanks for help that's given in friendship. No, he's only accepting the drawing as proof of their good relations and, above all, as an engagement present. Yes, he's going to marry Margaretha Tulp in the first days of spring, yes, their relationship is good, and so is his relationship with his future

---

* *Oxycrate* is a mixture of vinegar and water.

father-in-law, the affluent, powerful Doctor Tulp, the recently elected city Regent.

Geertruid is never unkind. But she laughed, she laughed with all her heart for days on end. About Jan Six, who likes men and books better than women, of course he does. Rembrandt thinks that Jan Six is the best husband this abandoned fiancée could hope for:* he doesn't like women much, whether they're for show or to be hidden away, so he'll be faithful; he prefers honours to rowdy dinner parties and good wines whether his ambition today is to be a poet or in a few years – for sure – to be a city Regent. As for Doctor Tulp, he's finally marrying off his daughter, he's marrying her to a son-in-law who bows low, makes fine statements and has his own fortune (although Tulp's is worth ten times as much).

Geertruid was still laughing about Doctor Tulp, driving about in his golden carriage to visit his gilded sick, but who, now he's Regent, wants to forbid banquets that are too rich and wedding presents that are too expensive, because they're sinful. She laughed about his daughter as well; Margaretha Tulp doesn't bear looking at except by those who know possessions are an enhancement, with her wobbling chin, eyes that bulge like marbles out of her head and who . . . I flick my cloth at the wicked girl and her gossipy tongue. Geertruid ran off laughing.

It's spawned in the black cherries that stick to your skin, squirming through bodies that die in agony, thirst and screams, in the houses, in the street, on the canals – wherever one can breathe the vermin. And while life and death go on, thousands of little worms dig their tunnels in the darkness of the wood.

The varnish splinters, the child swaddled in his mother's shawl and Mary and Joseph flee into Egypt. They're crossing a ford.

---

* Not long before the date planned for their wedding, Margaretha Tulp was 'abandoned' by Johan de Witt, an important Pensionary in the Dutch province (he was assassinated in 1672).

Joseph holds the donkey's reins, with the other hand, he tests the water's depth with a stick. The lines intersect in the copper, this evening, the weary travellers are resigned.

Carel Fabritius, Barent's brother, was your favourite pupil. That was during Saskia's illness and for a short time after her death. When you talk about him, it's like you're talking about a friend, not a pupil. He was there, right by you, sorrowful and attentive to you when Saskia went away. Now he paints in Delft and teaches more than five pupils in his studio. When he comes to Amsterdam, he knocks at our door. He's always loyal and his friendship is joyous.

From his box, he took out a little wooden panel and placed it in the light. Carel's eyes question you trustingly. Slowly you enter the painting, gently you smile: 'He's very real. He'll warble away forever.'

When I was a little girl, I used to go to the country with my brothers and, like them, I too had a sling. I know the birds, and I say quietly, as if my voice might scare him off: 'That's a goldfinch. At his bird table.'

'That's a goldfinch, and he sings beautifully. And this patch of yellow wall . . . You do my heart good, Fabritius. I need to see painting, and there's not much left in Amsterdam. It's not what the merchants want, not today's taste. Maybe in Delft . . . (He laughs sadly.) Come back soon with more paintings that are just as beautiful.'

You watched Carel Fabritius's figure disappearing down the Breestraat for a long time. I'm thinking of him this evening. I often think about him. Soon, he'd stop bringing you pleasure. But that evening your eyes were lit up by the light of his goldfinch, you didn't know.

Bathsheba's sacrifice will be more than just herself, it'll be in the child she will bear. The good Jewish servant-woman purifies her. You met her on the Houtgracht, right outside the synagogue. Crouched over my feet, she's not smiling any more: it's age, and her back. Like me: sitting still in this pose with my heavy belly is giving me pain below my left shoulder. You've seen the letter from King David in my hand, the lines written on white paper, and you believed in chance.

The letter arrived this morning, delivered to our door by a black-gloved hand just before we stop for a break. Closed with a glossy red seal. I broke it open, the letters swam before my eyes. The old Portuguese Jewish woman stretches her neck far back, her teeth set, lips parted around her pain. It's time she rested her back, time too that I share my fear with you.

'Rembrandt, this letter was brought three hours ago, but you were already mixing the colours on the palette. For three hours my heart has been beating so hard in my breast it's wearing me out. Are there more problems with the house? Read me what it says, I beg you.'

You're quick to pick it up, but gingerly, as if it carries the Plague. Glossy seals never bode well. Your eyes scan the lines.

'Tell me, read it to me.'

'The consistory. (You laugh – more like a sigh.) We're summoned, you and I. For a quiet Christian admonition.'

Your tongue gives special weight to the words. Your arms already twine about me. 'Nothing to fear, don't be anxious. Let them get on with it, the Church is not God. We're doing no harm, not even to the Church, let alone God. Not with your goodness.'

Your voice winds around me. I tell myself that I believe you, Jesus Christ is love, and I close my eyes. In this is charity; it's not that we have loved God, but that He has loved us and sent us His son.

Jan Six is getting married in three weeks' time. He knocked on the door of your studio, he doesn't wait, but comes straight in. Would Rembrandt paint his portrait? As a gift to his fiancée before the wedding. Will Rembrandt have time?

Yes, you've got time for a friend, yes, you can already see the picture, painted quickly, poppyseed oil in the palette and essence of aspic as a drying agent. Brisk strokes, your experience and your friendship. You know the man in this portrait, you know him well, and you'll depict his true nature. Jan Six hears the words he wants to hear. Tomorrow, he'll come and pose for you.

Titus is eating fat juicy, black cherries. Rembrandt wants me to keep my country fears to myself. I hold them in; deep inside, they take root. They're like lice, they turn into other things inside. Perhaps fear is the start of the Plague.

I knock at the studio door. I've brought marzipan and pancakes glistening with melted butter and molasses. Jan Six is wearing a red doublet, and the row of buttons on it look like brushstrokes. He thanks me without seeing me – it's a refusal, it's his upbringing. He won't eat, he won't drink anything, he's in a hurry to get back to Regent Tulp who's waiting for him. He looks down at Rembrandt, seated behind the easel, from his full height, already pulling on a glove, just one, today's look for people like him. It'll be a quick portrait of a man about to leave the room, an elegant man in a hurry to leave his friend.

Another messenger hands me another letter. The blood-red seal of another summons bursts open in your hands. Of course, you say, the men from the consistory have checked up and discovered that you're not on the list of the faithful who attend church. So I'm the only one summoned. So I can ask forgiveness for the sins that bring dishonour. Whoever invokes the name of the Eternal shall be saved. The words rise within me. Who shall condemn God's elect? My lips know and say it over and over again, quicker and quicker. I give My life for My sheep and I know them.

You bend down, plant a kiss on my full-moon belly: 'Too ignorant, rigid, stupid, they're all alike, they don't think.'

You tear up the summons. 'You shan't go.'

*　　*　　*

At the foot of the Cross, Joseph takes the body in his arms. He will wrap it in a clean shroud and place it in the tomb. Beneath your drypoint scratching and splintering the shiny surface, you can smell the tears, the end of the world, and the tortured body that's not yet stiff. In the middle of the lamentations, a white hand is raised. Clement de Jonghe took away the first prints; they were still damp.

I have to pay the dairyman. I ask you when Jan Six is going to pay for his portrait. You think the painting will partly repay him for what he lent you. But you've not talked to him about it, your price of 500 florins for a portrait hasn't changed since the easy years. Jan Six is a man with a good education. It isn't done to talk about florins with a friend who's getting married, a friend with a good education. Yes, I understand that.

   That evening after dinner I went into your studio on my own. Gripped by a fear I didn't recognise, deep down inside, beyond where the child was kicking. The candlelight flickered and, around it, the whole room and the painting on its easel flickered too. Jan Six putting his glove on. He's bigger than you sitting down, he looks down at the one who looks at him. He's so sure of himself; there's no light of friendship between his weary eyelids. There's a weakness at the corner of his mouth; it's a sign he can lie. Jan Six quivers on the other side of the candle flame. You know the man in the portrait well, you've depicted his true nature. You've seen the sadness behind his betrayal. It's the portrait of a farewell. I think, he's got one glove on, but he's not leaving the house, he's leaving your life. Maybe his own, too.

It's dusk and Barent Fabritius has come along the Breestraat. He's been walking up and down in front of the house for a long time. For a long time, he's been wandering about, with a heavy heart pitching at every step. Two days ago, the powderworks in Delft blew up. The sky was in flames, more than a third of the city fell in a welter of smoke and ash, bodies were torn apart, dismembered. In a few months Carel Fabritius would have been the same age as Christ when He died. His laugh and his talent went into the lively little goldfinch he painted; its warbling will never cease. Passers-by that night on the Breestraat saw candles burning behind the leaded window panes till morning.

Your first draft of the entombment was made on fine Chinese paper. The day had been long, the Virgin had fallen asleep, worn out with weeping. Then your drypoint cut into the copper. Bit by bit, criss-crossing strokes darkened the interior of the tomb hollowed in the rock. The last and only light radiates from Christ.

I've pushed away the cloth hiding my belly; my child is making waves under my skin with its tiny feet. In my right hand I'm holding the third summons from the consistory. You've read, you've hesitated, I've realised you've not told me everything, something was bound to be too unpleasant. Then you went over the phrase, putting in every word: '. . . Hendrickje Stoffels who lives as a whore in the house of the painter Rembrandt . . .' As a whore, my church. A whore.

A dark cloud hides the sun. My life with you is so sweet, my life for your sake and your work, for the sake of the gift God has entrusted to you. It's so pure, this life within me made of you and of me and that God has willed. He chose us before the world began so that we might be holy. God's law, I know God's law. And now I know the law of the church is the law of men. You wipe the tears from my cheeks, wipe my cheeks in a circular motion. In your arms, I hide in the shadow cast by your light.

You tear up the third summons. You say that the law of men is trying to attack you through me. I, the Lord's sheep, I who every day seek what is good and want to learn all that is good, I am called 'whore' by my church. I'd forgotten the word. If we were married, then life would be the same, yet so different. Sin entered the world through a single man, and death came through sin. And so death spread to all men, because all men sinned.

* * *

Jan Six didn't greet me, me and my belly. He was coming for his portrait now it was dry enough for the dust not to settle on it. He told Rembrandt he wasn't inviting any friends. Regent Tulp was playing host. Only Regents and grandees; the wedding was going to be very dull, he said.

I was drinking hot milk with Titus in the kitchen. It was too early in the morning, but someone knocked at the door; their knocks were too quick and too many. Titus puts his bowl down on the table, his eyes growing rounder with astonishment; if it weren't for his moustache of white foam, he'd look frightened. Nothing must disturb Rembrandt when he's working, so, quick, I must go and open the door. It's my shame, I know that already. I stare at the floor, I've become Rembrandt's whore. It's a lie that grows with each step, I'm a whore and there's nothing I can do.

On the other side of the door, standing in their black hats in a howling wind, three brothers from the district church purse their grey lips. Their eyes wander sternly to my full belly in spite of themselves, then slowly come back up to meet my eyes. Like black crows, the brothers watch me back off, a prisoner of their shadows. I give up, cast my arm about the space between us, and ask them in.

The one to speak has a pointed, hooked nose, like a bird's beak. 'Are you afraid that the neighbourhood will see the Church's brothers at your door? We will never enter the house of sin. Your fault is there (again their eyes weigh up the life in my belly), the Lord has publicly revealed your impiety. The pastor knows your shame and the Church has ordered an enquiry.'

Another brother mutters, rather than prays: 'Oh, God, do not allow sinners to be tempted beyond their powers of resistance. With temptation, He gives them the possibility to overcome it. And through the Holy Spirit, He revives them . . .'

The third opens his beak. 'Hendrickje Stoffels, the Church has decreed you a whore. You have not come before the consistory.

You refuse to hear your sentence, you have rebelled. Do you then fear your punishment so greatly?'

I shake my head, take a gulp of air. The waves break and roll, they wash over me. You'll be judged as you judge others.

The voice of the first brother was gentle, too gentle: 'One last time, Hendrickje Stoffels, you are summoned to the consistory. If you refuse to present yourself this time, your sentence will be pronounced in your absence and everyone will hear of it. Those are the wishes of the Church and the city.'

I think it was just then that the heavy tread of Rembrandt descended the stairs. (Titus had gone to look for him.) The brothers closed their mouths on my condemnation and withdrew. With no parting word (you don't say good day or goodbye to a whore) they turned their backs on me. Before closing the door, I watched their retreating figures grow smaller in the fog.

If the sentence is pronounced and I'm accused by the Church of being Rembrandt's whore, you too, my poor love, you too will be implicated. And if no more purchasers visit the painter who lives with his whore, you'll never be able to pay off your debts. I will go, I will hear the consistory's sentence. I believe in God's mercy, and I still believe in the indulgence of men and the goodness of the Church.

I walk forward under the frozen vaulting, each step resounding in the echo of the last. Mustn't step on the cracks in the paving. Right at the back, beyond the reach of the echoes, their faces framed by the high backs of their chairs, my twelve judges dressed in black watch me walk towards them, and watch the child swelling before me. They're growing bigger before me, too, as I approach; they look like the men in my nightmares, with dry, wooden fingers, sensibly placed on their leather writing desk, white-eyed, dry mouths, bursting pink flesh, judging me, but one day it will rot. The oldest speaks for the Church, he's lost all his teeth, he hardly seems to have any mouth left.

'Do you admit that you live with the painter Rembrandt van Rijn as a whore?'

I lower my head, but not from shame, no. And not so I can't see them any more. So I can't hear them. Who are you to judge your neighbour? Your riches are rotten, your clothes eaten by worms.

It was just a nightmare, the same two nights running. Voices whispered in my ear that I must confess. Gentle or harsh, in all tones. I must confess. My head and wrists are held prisoner in the stocks, my shift is whipped and striped with crosses of my own blood; I shake my head (as much as the stocks allow) without confessing. Sharp knives glint before the cauldron where the iron lies red-hot on the coals. Torture in peacetime is like torture in war. The first pain is a knife slash on my left cheek. Then the iron marks my left shoulder. Seated round the great table among the twelve members of the consistory, Regent Tulp and Jan Six grimaced at the sizzling and the smell of burning flesh.

Time slips by in my dream, no, I won't retract, my mouth screams out noiselessly at the torture. A peg clamps my lip, an iron burns my tongue. Then with an axe, one after the other, my torturer slices my wrists against the wood of the pillory; blood spurts from the stumps of my arms, but there's no pain, not yet. Jan Six wept. None of this stern gathering heard, like me, the displaced sound of his sniffing. Regent Tulp was accusing me, behind his flaming eyes, he was burning to hear my confessions.

Toothless, mouthless, his cheeks sucked in on the breath that would soon be his last, the elder pronounces the words (approaching death doesn't make men any better, then): 'You are living with him outside the laws of our Church. You may still be pardoned if you leave him and return to your mother where you will give birth to your child.'

'I can't, I need him and he needs me.'

'You are rebelling against the law of our Church. You are

seriously offending God. You are grieving the Holy Spirit, Hendrickje Stoffels. The Church and the city cannot allow it.'

Even in my dream I already knew how I'd be tortured by the United Provinces. After public exhibition, I'd be drowned in a barrel or buried alive. But first, they'd put out my eyes. They won't let me see my torturers. Regent Tulp wasn't talking to me, with his white eyes. Rembrandt was the one he saw; but he was using me to accuse him. He said he no longer wanted a member of his family mixing with Rembrandt van Rijn. He would warn all those who still did not know to keep away from an artist who prefers ugliness to beauty; to keep away from a painter who wouldn't paint in the style his dealers wanted, from a man who was different, too free. And he would use every means that power affords. All this fear and hatred woke me up. I don't know if dreams can divine the future. Dreams aren't the same as country beliefs, but I'll keep to myself these overheard words that single out Regent Tulp, that show he's the one willing all this, doing it. He's the one who condemned me.

The oldest man (the one death's nearness hasn't made any better) opens his toothless mouth: 'Henceforth, you are unworthy of supping at the Lord's table, you would profane the holy sacrament if you were permitted to take part.'

May God save me, I'm being sucked down into a bottomless mire, and there's nothing to hold me up. The air I breathe is growing thicker, what I see, less transparent. Who are you to judge your neighbour? The flesh of the twelve men in black is already foul with vermin.

My fingers search each other out and intertwine. When He had given thanks, he brake it, and gave it to his disciples, saying take, eat, this is my Body. The sentence is delivered in a few words. Like acrobats, jugglers and bankers, I'm thrown out of the Church I've belonged to since I was born. Unworthy to sup at the Lord's table. May all persons diligently try and examine themselves before they presume to eat of that Bread and drink of that Cup. Drink ye all this; for this is my blood. He forgave even prostitutes their sins. Even Judas the traitor, who hadn't yet kissed him, yes, even Judas took the Passover at His table with him. But I'm to be banished by Regent Tulp and shan't eat this bread any more. I'm unworthy, no more shall I drink His blood from the Church's cup in remembrance of Him.

'Behold the man,' says Pilate. The acid eats into the copper you've hollowed out, Christ is presented to the people. The people yell: 'Crucify him! Crucify him! . . .' His hands are tied, the light has gone out of His eyes, and Jesus gazes at the beyond. Sacrificed. The heavy cylinder of the press crushes the damp paper against the inked copper. I watch the first print, I see your compassion for ignorant folk. I see your disappointment and your sorrow.

My prayers will always be the same. It's the law of men that's condemning me, not the law of God. They're talking among one another now, the men in black. Church and city can't allow it. I'm drowning in their shadow. I can't breathe any more. Save me, God, the water's rising to my throat, I pass my hand across my face to crush the beads of sweat. I'm adrift in the water and the current is carrying me away. I bend, huddling over my child's heart so as not to think any more. Before the fever and nightmares begin.

I walked along by the canals; I know them but I don't recognise them. I heard what hadn't been said, I heard nothing. Little groups of people start to follow me, singing, dancing, raising their hands to heaven; there's laughter on all sides and a dance going on around me. The war is over, Holland and England have signed the Treaty of Westminster, the Westerkerk carillon rings in the new peace. The ten horns and the beast will hate the prostitute of the Apocalypse; they will eat her flesh and burn her on a pyre. Black insects start to hum in my ears, 'whore, whore': a chorus of dancers repeats the word over the bricks of the city.

While the fever ran its course, I didn't see the stork fly off.

She's not on our roof any more. Neither she nor her chicks. Maybe she'll come back another year.

He said the blessing. And it came to pass, as he sat at meat with them, he took bread, and blessed it, and brake, and gave to them. And their eyes were opened, and they knew him; and he vanished out of their sight. That's what your burin reveals: the invisible, and Christ's gaze and His glory.

Uylenburgh has moved house. He's not yet known to be bankrupt, but there is fear in his eyes. They fall on my belly in the hallway. He smiles, as if he's touched at the sight of it. Rembrandt's arm is round my shoulders, and I lean against his breast, lean my back against him, the weight's too heavy for me on my own. 'The war is over, but the local grandees are now used to keeping their money safely hidden away. Business hasn't recovered. It's very unfortunate you're out of favour, so many people are discouraged from coming here again . . .'

Rembrandt raises his head. 'It'll save us from being visited by fools, thanks to them I'll have more time.'

'Jan Six, has he visited?' asks Uylenburgh.

Rembrandt looks at me. It's not a pleasant thought: no, Jan Six hasn't come back to the Breestraat, not since I was banished from the Lord's table; not since the day he took away the barely dry painting, the present for a fiancée who perhaps didn't appreciate it, or anyway hasn't thanked him for it. It's no surprise: the loyalty of friends has its limits, especially for Regent Tulp's son-in-law. Hardly a disappointment.

Uylenburgh understands Jan Six's decision: Doctor Tulp, now Regent Tulp (who never mixed with low-class people anyway), wouldn't allow his relations (and certainly not his daughter's husband) to mix with people who have a bad reputation. Since Uylenburgh's trade started heading for bankruptcy, Regent Tulp has cut his links with him too. A bankrupt is a man who has been abandoned by God, a bankrupt is a sinner.

No one knows, not even you, my love, that it's probably

Regent Tulp who wished this evil reputation on me and, above all, on you. I've not got any proof, and I'll never say so out loud. And then, I'm so unworthy, who'd believe me? Nicolaes Tulp stole his name from the tulip. When I was ten, two *Semper Augustus* tulip bulbs were worth as much as the Breestraat house. Then the authorities called this market madness and took a decision. Prices fell, they fell by ten times. Mourning the tulip hastened bankruptcies, pinned nails to the wall for men to be hanged from. The tulip isn't an innocent flower, it contains a deadly poison.

'Anyway, did you know,' Uylenburgh goes on, 'Jan Six has just commissioned Govert Flinck to paint his wife's portrait?'

I can see you're stricken, you sag. Your back bends, your head falls forward. Almost imperceptibly, but I can see it. You'd rather have solitude than the company of men who've been selling their souls to business and glory for so long. But these little betrayals still make you sick, my love. I know. And the hurt they do makes your head heavy. It's me that replies; I say, Flinck will try to make Margaretha Tulp beautiful, but not even if he gives her a halo of flowers and foliage will he hide her rippling chin and her eyes that roll like marbles in her head.

With your brush, you give Bathsheba the last strokes. They tickle me lovingly but in my mind I keep repeating to myself that I'm a whore. You wanted to see the ache on my face. King David's letter in my hands . . . the sacrifice has been accomplished.

The collectors want engravings. Clement de Jonghe keeps saying so, it's his trade and his money. He also says that Jesus, and the love that radiates from him, is selling well. He was crucified at the third hour, his agony started at the sixth and at the ninth he gave up the ghost. Nine, the last figure, the end and the resurrection. He says that in these times of war and Plague, it's rare to find morality. And yet man needs it. And, when he doesn't forget that morality hides in him, he likes to have your engravings to reflect his goodness like a mirror.

*   *   *

That pain again, low in my back, on either side. I groan
against you; you're no longer asleep. The wave recedes, then
returns. Again and again. Nine times, the end and the beginning.
Suddenly, I realise that the baby has started to pass through my
body's tunnel, the way to us, its deliverance and mine.

Rembrandt has pushed back the sheets. He's shouting loudly,
walking quickly, he's woken the whole household. Geertruid has
gone running to the Zwanenburgstraat to fetch the midwife;
she's a handsome woman, for all she has gaps in her teeth. But
her smile is gentle on her closed lips.

I spread my legs on the birthing couch in the middle of
the room. The midwife tips up the little earthenware phial
hanging from a leather thong round her neck, and pours a
stream of oil into her hands. She rubs them over each other
till they're slippery. Her gentle hands can then slide, enter, and
reach the baby more easily. Her gentle hands know, they're
magic hands.

The sheets hide and protect me, over my drawn-up knees.
The midwife keeps changing them and wiping away the liquids
running out of my insides. Over my knees, I see the steaming
basins going from hand to hand. Judith and Geertruid go from
one side of the room to the other and back again, their faces red
and shiny from the steam. Freshly washed towels are hanging up
to dry over the fireplace in the room. I can't swallow air between
the pushes any more. Voices rumble, the whole room is full of
noise. In turn, curious neighbours and their servant-women come
and see if this birth entails pain, screams or misfortune. They
come to see, perhaps to help and remember as well. They give
advice I can't hear. Rembrandt offers them a glass of caudle*
and almond marzipan.

You've stayed near me, my love, as you did for Saskia's four
babies (three poor angels). You tell me it's a new idea put about
by the grandees to send men out of the room where a woman's

---

* Sweet white wine flavoured with cinnamon.

giving birth. You say it's the woman who's ripped apart by pain beyond her nine openings, but it's the man who can't deal with it. But you, you love this, you love these two lives and their blood. Your hand unsticks the hair from my forehead. I can't breathe. Fire is eating through the tunnel inside me, tearing me apart. Judith knows, like me, that bad spirits vanish when they see the colour blue. No one knows why, no one's ever tried to find out, we just know. Very quietly, so as not to disturb anyone, she whispers into my ear: 'The candles have a fine blue flame.' Lord, have mercy on Your sheep. And forgive me if I have sinned.

The midwife effortlessly slips her hand inside. 'Push,' she says. Don't punish me for the ill I never intended, that I didn't know I was doing. And I push. My whole red wrinkled face pushes round my tight-shut eyes. If the child is covered in scales or doesn't have an anus, don't let him live. I push and I shout so as to drown out the thunder of the pain. The steam from the basins overlaps and intertwines. So do the whispers and everyone's expectations. The resurrection of the flesh and eternal life. Amen. And if its entrails are hanging out of its body, may I die before seeing it.

The midwife has got her hand back. She's lying on me now, across me, pushing on my belly. With her full weight. With a great calm smile, she turns her head to my shouting mouth. With all her weight and all her strength, she presses on the great wave of my belly.

There, the head is out. From oblivion to life, from darkness to light. Red and loving, the faces watch the baby's head. Like it had never been, like it's already forgotten, the suffering; like it's all over as soon as the head comes out. The baby's body has effortlessly slipped out after it. You kiss me. 'A girl,' you say, 'it's a girl.' Yes, my love, a little Cornelia. After your mother and the two dead babies. We'll hang the red silk plaque edged with lace on the Breestraat door, with its centre of white paper which is all that's needed to say that the newborn is a girl.

I close my eyes, I don't want to hear all these voices chattering. 'A girl,' the midwife repeats aloud to everyone present, then cuts the cord by which I've nourished my baby, my child, for nine months. Little Cornelia, so little. A great wave of love lifts me up, quick, place her on my naked bosom and let me envelop her with my arms; but the midwife is already wrapping her in hot swaddling before putting her, as she cries her first cry, into the hesitant arms of her father. She speaks the words: 'Here is your child. May our Lord grant you much happiness in her, or may He recall her to Him quickly.' Rembrandt's ruddy smile says he hasn't heard what she said. And no more have I, not everything, at least. May our Lord grant us much happiness in her.

Neighbours, husbands of neighbours, families have come into the room, they're drinking and laughing. I close my thighs, press my legs together; slowly, I raise myself, till I'm half sitting. Rembrandt appears out of the steam from the hot water and the row going on, wearing the cap of the father of a newborn. Under the green and yellow feathers, his ruby-red face smiles a caudle smile. He holds his glass out to me, I just moisten my lips. He's proud, the father, ruddy and proud. He lifts the baby up high, so everyone can admire her. And then again, before the mother rests, before she nurses and rocks her as silence returns.

She's so small. I stretch out on our bed. She cries in her green straw cradle as I gently rock it with my foot. As soon as she's cried her first cries, she sees my arms held towards her, my hands like pincers that quickly carry her, little feather, towards the large, painful, balloon-like breast, bouncing free from its corset; with this red nipple, hard and tender at the same time, flaking a little and smelling of milk all day, with this nipple I'm now Mummy, putting to sleep the piercing pains of hunger. Until the next ones. I change her, I dress her, I leave her little arms and legs free to kick the air. Ephraim Bueno drinks a glass of caudle and raises it to Cornelia. He says he doesn't believe swaddling helps the bones to form properly. Aristotle was already saying newborn babies should be allowed to move freely and make all the movements they could. He said people who used splints to keep baby's bodies straight were barbarous. For nine months,

I've known I'll listen to his advice, I'm not going to make my child into a little packet, a little swaddled bean, like our mother did with us, like her mother did with her.

I don't sleep much, I'm a mother. Holding her in my arms or with my face bent over her, I protect Cornelia, our child. Your drypoint makes furrows in the copper's polished surface. My cheek gently touches hers. I listen close to her light breathing, the tiny breaths she takes. Sitting in a chair, I rock myself as I rock her. I won't go to sleep, just close my eyes in rest. You watch us through the window, you just watch, moved, you're like Joseph. The light falling into the room through the oval glass is other-worldly. It makes a halo above the two joined heads – mother and child. You engrave the Holy Family. The cat by our side sleeps too. Everything is at peace. God watches over us. The child is beautiful, the mother has committed no sin.

Then you drew the treacherous poisonous beast, the Devil's serpent. You gouged him out of the black varnish, and he appeared, from the shadowy grooves, in the shining, gilded copper lines. He slithers and disappears beneath my skirt.

I say to Rembrandt. 'Why this danger?'

'The danger is past. Your feet have already crushed him. Good has already triumphed over evil.'

You bend down, my lips first, then Cornelia.

The paint and smell of your painting have dried. Bathsheba is a victim. She is beautiful, she is pure, her fate has been traced. We can only love her and pity her. But I, I know that Bathsheba is a whore.

1655–1658

It was as if you'd done nothing else all those years, just sell. Fight, hope, then just let things take their course. The auctioneer's hammer goes down. Separating you from your objects and works, your own and those you bought for pleasure. Tearing you apart. The ebony-framed mirror in your studio shows the hollows in your face getting darker and darker round your nose that's getting redder and bigger. Glory to God alone. But it's not anger, and it's not fear yet, it's beer and gin that's doing it. I sit opposite you at the great table, too exhausted to go up and slip into our bed, I'm losing confidence. I've drunk my first glass; gin is the Devil's fire. Beer puts it out.

Again and again the auctioneer's hammer hits the table, the sound rings in my head with that little hollow sound like the empty glass I put down. You never leave your studio any more. With each painting, in the light of your brush, you breathe a new air, alone before your easel, miles from money.

A whole year I'll breast-feed Cornelia. Her little hands clenched tight on the nothing between her and me, her lips sucking empty space before clamping on my nipple. In the Oude Kerk, with its freezing echo repeating the prayers, she was baptised, our daughter, the child of Rembrandt van Rijn, painter, and Hendrickje Stoffels, whore. The Church was quite willing: so my exclusion from the Lord's table only interests the city.

By baptism, through His death, we have been buried with Him – the words fall from the preacher's mouth – just as Christ was resurrected from the dead through the Father's glory, so shall we lead a new life. Our child, born to parents who fear Him, is chosen by God. The water is cold on her forehead and on her little lips that crack when they scream. And, if He takes her from this life in childhood, baptism offers her salvation.

She seizes one of my fingers, traps it in her mouth, closes her lips on it, suckles it. A great wave of love behind my eyes. She sucks and breathes and my finger touches the darkness inside between her tongue and palate, the inside of my little girl's body, her damp, hot breath, the inside of her life. Later, with half-closed eyes and head lolling on one side, her half-open lips swollen and shining with the sweet milk from my body and with sleep, Cornelia will fall asleep. She'll draw long, calm breaths one after the other, I'll shut my eyes.

In the pupils' studio, Willem Drost and Bernhard Keil load their great brushes with animal-skin glue and carry it to the blank canvases. Then they mix the colours for the background, lengthily crushing the coloured powders in poppyseed oil. So that Rembrandt's time trickles slower through the sandglass. So that each of your brushstrokes is always the first, always the last. That's what Titus says with his big eyes. He watches Cornelia sleeping, he calls her sister and smiles at her without knowing.

Seated at his little desk with his new goose-quill pens, the sharpener, the ink bottle and box of sand to dry the ink – that's how Rembrandt painted Titus with swift sweeping brushstrokes. Your tenderness made this portrait, like so many prayers; love and fear were crushed under the brush on the canvas. With his big thoughtful eyes, Titus is still a child. He is beautiful, and I'm afraid of life for him, afraid of the cold and the Plague. Afraid for Rembrandt too; I know in myself that if the blood ceased to flow in his son's body, everything would stop for him. Life would stop.

When the lamp-lighters are lighting the lanterns at every twelfth house in the city streets, Abraham Francen taps a few times at the Breestraat door. There's the same kindness in his eyes as in Ephraim Bueno's, and I tell myself that doctors and apothecaries have the same eyes, maybe the same kindness. He goes up to the studio. He turns over the engravings without speaking, holding them in the best light, poring over them for a long time. His gaze stops. Rembrandt says he knows a good drawing, he knows when he's come across the miracle of a pencil stroke that's unique.

He often comes for supper. He uses simple words when he talks about art (the school for life), God and death. He takes several helpings of veal stew in melon juice. He also uses legal phrases, but stops when Rembrandt frowns at him not to worry me. He was the first person to mention, in front of me, the name of Thomasz Jacobsz Haaringh, keeper of the Chamber of Insolvents. Like his father before him.

At night as soon as I hear the first cries, quick, up I get and rub Cornelia's gums with juniper oil to ease the needles piercing her mouth.

I've opened the door, and let the cold spring sunshine come sweeping into the hallway. It's not a smile Thomasz Haaringh gives me, more like bottomless pity. My heart beats faster under my breasts and the blood runs quicker in my body. The stairs slope dizzyingly, less straight suddenly, the light goes white, freezing fear dries my mouth. By the time the stairs are back in place, Thomasz Haaringh is pressing my arm. 'Rembrandt is expecting you,' I tell him, and I felt soothed by his sorrowful kindness.

My two hands lift the great white shift woven by thick lashings of paint. In the limpid pool, my legs look cut off at the surface of the water, then lengthen beneath your brush. I've bent my head, I'm staring into the clear depths. Slowly, I walk forward, I'm going to bathe. Behind me, in the shadow of a rock, lies a heavy red-and-gold cloth, the one Bathsheba had when she was reading David's letter, yes, the same one, it always hangs on two nails on the wall of your studio, and it turns the water's glassy surface and the whole picture red and gold. The shadow hides between my thighs. I think I'm alone, but you're spying on me; in another moment, I'll be naked. King David watches Bathsheba just before she takes off her shift to bathe. Fate is sealed. The act has begun, the water is cold.

The dress is low-cut over a vast bosom, and the cloth below covers round white breasts, swollen with brown Rotterdam ale and the milk it's become in my body. The shapes under the shift are heavy, the thighs and calves thick-set. The years pass and I've got fatter. It's the child, the cold, milk and beer. Gin, too. A wan smile still broadens my face. You've painted me as you see me and as you love me. Life is always right for you, and you always love life better than lying beauty. For you, truth is beauty. That's what you see and what you paint, even when a garter's left marks on too plump a thigh.* You love all these warm lives; as long as they beat beneath breasts, they touch your kindness, but you know that the day will come when they'll cease. They'll fade from this moment when the blood still flowed within them, and the gluttonous worms will wake up and dig hundreds of tunnels where the stench will settle.

Time hasn't forgotten me. The skin on my cheeks is speckled with pink stars; I never used to have them before they suddenly appeared. My curls don't shine so bright, nor do my eyes. It's tiredness and the short nights caused by the child and by fear. It's time. Beer and gin have made my eyelids puffy. Two glasses and I forget, just like Judas the traitor, as he sat among the twelve disciples to the left of the Saviour, around the table I've been banished from. My cheeks are fatter, they look like they're melting; they've slumped below the line of my face between ear and chin. The drawing springs into life, the face is rounded out. The young woman in the shift is asking the painter if he still likes her best. But he doesn't hear her. Bathsheba thinks she's alone,

---

* Rembrandt was criticised for the realism of some of his drawings (including the woman referred to here), which his critics deemed in the worst possible taste.

King David has not yet seen her. Bathsheba isn't sad; unlike the painter, she can't foresee that she will soon be a whore.

I only know what Rembrandt doesn't hide from me. But I can see for myself that the debts are growing and that there's not enough money coming into the house.

The woman knocked at the door at midday. With that great wobbling tooth sticking out between her closed lips, and her holey black woollen stockings and muddy clogs, she must be the Devil's servant-woman. She won't speak to anyone but Rembrandt van Rijn. I ask her please not to move her clogs, and to stay in the hallway. Meaning on no account must she go into the other rooms in the house. A woman with a protruding tooth can't bring good news. Rembrandt put his brush down on the palette.

She's called Trijn Jacobs. Five years after the trial, she heard that her neighbour in Edam, Geertje Dircx, was no longer living in Amsterdam and was in the Gouda house of correction. Every word from her mouth makes her tooth wobble. It's the only thing I see in her face. I tell myself that one day it'll fall out without pain or blood, maybe without Trijn Jacobs even noticing, maybe in her sleep, maybe she'll even swallow it. She's on her way to Gouda to get Geertje Dircx out of there, because no woman (says the wobbling tooth), even one who is mad and in love, no woman deserves twelve years' punishment. Fear, like the past, can glide in front of the present in the blink of an eye. And even though her name doesn't mean danger these days, my throat tightens at the memory of Geertje Dircx's rage.

Rembrandt goes towards the tooth, goes right up to the witch. He tells her not to get involved, and that she's just as mad, that he'll alert the house of correction – they've already got Geertje Dircx in their care. She said a few words: Rembrandt was cowardly, and others, too. And I was a whore, Master Rembrandt van Rijn the coward's whore. And she left before Rembrandt could raise his arm; the door closed on our silence.

*   *   *

Abraham Francen brings news from the city to our house: Joost van den Vondel has gone bankrupt. His son has wrecked the family's silk-and-wool business like a ship in a storm on the IJ, and Vondel has paid off his debts. No one in the city knows what the young man and his spendthrift wife did wrong to make his father pay 40,000 florins – three times what the Breestraat house is worth – all his worldly goods. Holland's beloved poet has been abandoned by God. But not by men and the city Regents, no, not by the rich and powerful men whom Joost van den Vondel has been praising in verse for years (like Doctor Tulp or Jan Six). These men know how to return friendship. They've been good enough (what am I saying? says Abraham Francen, I mean, generous enough) to make him head accountant at the pawnbroker's in the Lombard Bank, the great warehouse on the Fluwelen Burgwal. Vondel will sit behind his desk and receive bankrupts. He thanked them, he was deeply grateful. Seated all day behind his little icy desk, he'll write endless columns of names and figures in a great account book.

Catching sight of yourself in a canal as you peer into the city's mirror-water cleaned by the rats, a pauper abandoned by God and everyone else at seventy years of age, it's not fair, that, not even for a bankrupt. We all agreed, all three of us, and no one laughed. Rembrandt said that Vondel would write; said he'd write more plays than he's written up to now in the echoing dust of the pawnbroker's.* Words between the figures, that's how he'd thank the city's generosity. And we did laugh a bit about that. Rembrandt poured another three glasses of gin. Under my breath, I said to myself that, in our present situation, Rembrandt might well end up going to see Vondel's dusty work, and that it might well be at the pawnbroker's that the two would meet for the first time. They'd talk about the

---

* There was a certain truth in Rembrandt's prediction, at least in terms of the quality of Vondel's work, if not of the quantity.

power of words and painting. I didn't voice my thoughts out loud, you can't always tell tears from laughter when they're mixed like that, not even under one's breath. Especially not Rembrandt's laugh.

The rich Portuguese Jew, Senhor Diego Andrada, has already paid for half the portrait of a young girl he's in love with. He kisses the rouged lips you've painted on canvas. At the end of every sentence, he sweeps the feathers of his hat through the air in a low bow. Must finish the painting so that Andrada can pay the other 250 florins as quickly as possible, and no, you won't set foot outside your studio, definitely not to go and visit the new Town Hall.

I put my *huik* round my shoulders, knot my scarf under my chin and walk towards the Dam, my head held high like all the Breestraat women – those who haven't been banished from the Lord's table. It was in the first days of June, when the stone polishers were finishing their work in the Great Gallery, that they settled on the 29th July as the date of its inauguration by the Regents. Earlier, no one would have dared suggest a date, a month or even a year – it brings bad luck. Everyone in Amsterdam, even those who can't read, knows that in Flanders, the city of Antwerp was destroyed the year of the inauguration of its new Town Hall.

I'm walking towards the Dam, head up. You're all saved by the Grace of God, by the way of faith; it's nothing you've done, it's a gift from God.

I want to see inside our Temple of Solomon the first day it's open; it took seven years to build and cost eight million florins and may already have bankrupted Amsterdam, although no one knows yet. And that includes the whale-blubber and cannon-powder merchants, and the Regents too. That's right, bankrupted without even knowing. They're the ones who haven't put Rembrandt on the list of Amsterdam painters to do the paintings for the

Council Hall. Not Rembrandt, no, but Jan Lievens, and your pupils, Ferdinand Bol and Govert Flinck.* And then, the men of the Guild of St Luke, who'll decorate the other rooms with their paintings. But not my Rembrandt, no, not my love. True, you don't work like them, you're always in your studio and you're not as knowing as them, you're not married to the daughter of a grandee, you don't dress in lace and stockings, glittering cloth and ribbons like in the French court. You're not always bowing and scraping.

Painting is always right, no matter who the model or who the purchaser. 'And, anyway,' you say, 'the great city decision-makers still haven't chosen the painters for the Great Gallery.' You're still hoping. You're hoping they'll remember Rembrandt van Rijn, who used to make rich people wait outside the door of his studio for months. Haven't they read the poem by the director of the city theatre, Jan Vos (another one who knows how to bow and scrape), where he salutes the city's painters? It's all thanks to Rembrandt, says the poem, that the fame of Amsterdam has spread overseas, right to the other side of the world. I walk forward, tiptoeing timidly in the black-and-white Great Gallery; it's much too big for me. No, my love, they've not forgotten you, they can't have. The Great Gallery's as big as they think they are, but it's not too big for you.

My eyes tell of fear and questions, and Thomasz Haaringh doesn't smile into them so much any more. Rembrandt is engraving his portrait and his sad smile. He's doing it as a way of thanking him for his counsel and payment. When he saw this man worn out by others' bankruptcies, the slow kindness of his old age, Rembrandt went to find a copper plate. None

---

* Jan Lievens lived in Leiden at the same time as Rembrandt, who was a year older than him. Constantijn Huygens met the two painters on his first visit. They were friends and very close in their art. Ferdinand Bol was a pupil in Rembrandt's studio between 1636 and 1642, Govert Flink, from c. 1633 to 1636.

of them was prepared with a ground. So he engraved it with the drypoint, then the burin, without using acid to eat into it first. He clasps me to him, whispering in my ear that Thomas Haaringh has the best advice and everything will work out fine. The drypoint gouges hollows in the yellow metal around sad eyes. There'll be no shame attached to bankruptcy and no one will stop you selling your works. I listen to the drypoint engraving the copper and I thank God for every day I'm alive on the Breestraat beside you.

I try not to think of the little worms digging their revenge in the wood. In the wood of thousands of piles underneath the Town Hall. But by the time I've thought of trying to forget them, it's always too late in the tunnels in my head.

Everyone who lives in Amsterdam can go through one of the three open doors in the grand frontage overlooking the Dam; then up the great stairway and across the black-and-white slabs. Even the quick steps of the grandees, so sure of themselves and where they're going, sound small on these giants' squares of Bentheim stone. In the burning rays of the sun, the Great Gallery is a white mirror for the clean shoes of the wealthy. But today, muddy shoes and clogs are also allowed to climb the great staircase and cross the new unblemished stone: rich and poor. Regents and beggars. Even the lepers have left the Leper House and come to the Dam; they're just as keen to see, before they get packed off by the guards, the wall of the House of God. The rich smile at one another; it's reassuring to see each other here, they're not so alone as when they look in their mirror.

No one really knows why, but it's true: the street fires that burn the miasmas in the air have driven off the Plague, and it's gone away. Ephraim Bueno says it's gone to kill elsewhere. Before it comes back, because the Plague always kills and always comes back. And he says the new war that's been declared against

England is stifling the city's trade, and that over 1,500 houses are empty, because the only people who are still trading and who can still afford to buy or rent them have already got one anyway.

On the top steps of the great staircase and on the first black slabs of the Great Gallery, everyone's meeting and watching one another. Everyone knows everyone else. I give My life for My flock and I know them. It's a blue summer's day, and the dresses of the grandees' daughters are made of pretty stuff in bright shining colours. They're not wearing high frothy collars like their mothers; no, they've got light Flanders lace round their long pretty necks and at the end of their sleeves. In one glance, they weigh up the dull fabric of my dress and my thick lace collar, my purse and my education. In one glance they know who I am, or they think they do. What they don't know are the treasures those Breestraat walls hide. Silk dresses from the East Indies, kings' shirts, doublets and cloth embroidered with gold thread and fur-lined jackets.

Framed by my white ermine, I look into your eyes. Your love for me enters me as I look, it enters the painting. You've seen and painted my desire to cry, but really it's happiness. My life's cleaner in these portraits, it'll outlast death, but I know that, when my life and the lives of the grandees' daughters are over, people who look at these paintings won't know me either. Dressed like a princess, for your eyes alone. They won't see the happiness in the eyes of Rembrandt's whore.

Abraham Francen says that Christiaan Huygens, Constantijn Huygens's son, has been looking at the sky through a long glass he calls a telescope. He's seen what no one else ever has: a shining ring in the black sky around a hard planet, like Earth, which he calls Saturn, and a spreading light reveals another one which he calls Orion. I know that the sky is big and we are little, all on this great Earth that maybe moves round the sun. I go down on my knees and thank God for creating life and giving some of it as a gift to all these little people, like you, Titus, Cornelia and me, those of our families who are still alive, those already dead and those who are not yet born. I hobble forward a short distance on my knees to ward off ever-dangerous death; sometimes I put my lips flat on a black tile of the bedroom, and lie on the freezing floor, repeating the names of those I love, and my mother.

Standing in the middle of the Great Gallery on its slippery floor, we women, alive at the same time and in the same place, we take one look at each other and look away. We don't know each other, pretend we've not even seen each other. I know that, in the short time between birth and death, the living are merciless to one another, but that's not what He wanted. He sitteth on the right hand of God the Father Almighty; from thence he shall come to judge the quick and the dead.

When Cornelia's little hands twist and turn on her belly, when I read pain in the faces she pulls, quick, I take her off to the kitchen. I melt pods and honey on the dying embers before placing them on her greedy tongue, and I rub her tummy button (the place on her belly nearest her insides) with a cloth sprinkled with essence of cumin and ragweed.

Senhor Andrada has refused the painting. Rembrandt had to defend his work. The Senhor won't pay the 250 florins he owes. No bows now, as he asks you to paint a new portrait of the young woman, a likeness this time. And if you won't, you're to give him back the money he's already paid. You roar like a wounded lion, the king of the animals is lying on his sore, in the depths of his cage away from the bars. A purchaser, a man who loves your art, is shamelessly calling on you to start a painting again. You, Rembrandt. They used to wait for months outside the door of your studio for their immortality to be painted by you, and you alone. Time erases glory, but not memories or insults.

    You burst out laughing, too loud, it's like a sob in your throat. 'He's never seen her, he's never really looked at this young woman who's helping him spend his money. He hopes she's white and pure, but she, she wants everything without giving anything. She's pure, but not white. And when she poses for a few hours, the gentleness and modesty disappear from her face. It's true there's a bit too much shadow in the two brushstrokes round the nose, but is it my fault if this dark-haired girl has a moustache where another woman would just have fine down on her upper lip?'

Rembrandt strikes his empty glass against the table rug. Abraham and I laugh, as long as he seems to be laughing.

He was crucified, He descended into Hell. He ascended into Heaven. I'd like to take your suffering on myself to deliver you, but I can only listen. I know you are always right. Love and the work of art are all that count. Because life goes on after us, and paintings do too.

I do my best to help you and take the burden off your shoulders. Make sure the house is clean every day. I massage your back every morning and evening. When Titus gets back from the Latin school, I play a game of *passe-dix* with him. I watch Cornelia who's learning to walk in her rolling chair. And when her screams tell me she wants to get out, I make sure I place the leather rolls of her bumper bonnet over her curly hair so that she doesn't hurt her head when she falls over.

Rembrandt, my love, sometimes complains he's too tired to be anxious. Too old, he says. My love, no, even if your teeth and gums hurt, you're not getting old; I know, I can see it every day, it's the light in your eyes, it's your humanity. Too old, you say, and also that life is dangerous for little children, and that loving one's children is suffering that never stops until the end. The day Cornelia fell against the corner of the big table without her bumper bonnet, making a bloody cut on her cheek, Rembrandt put down his brush. Ran downstairs, then sawed and planed off all the sharp corners of the house furniture. Tables, chairs, coffers, crockery cupboard and my linen cupboard all got rounded off.

*   *   *

Abraham came one evening with his brother Daniel, the surgeon. The same smile, the same gentle manner. I venture to ask questions, whispering the words very low so that the worms inside me won't wake up. The surgeon cuts into the body's meat, the skin and bones, then he sews it up and dries the blood with fire.

'Yes,' replies Daniel Francen, too loudly. 'The smell of life is outside, never inside.'

I hold the Breestraat door open. Rembrandt shakes Abraham's hand, then Daniel Francen's. He thanks them again. This evening you won't take the gin bottle out of the cupboard. Your sigh is calm. 'There are still good men on Earth because there are still good men in Amsterdam. Three thousand florins he's lending us, and yet he's not a man with wealthy customers. I was the one who wanted to add interest. He said, if I had the bad luck (which would be bad luck for art lovers, too) to find that I was still in difficulties, I could pay him back in paintings. So there are still men in Amsterdam for whom life isn't just about money. Kiss me, Hendrickje.'

The sound of children's drums and songs are coming this way. On the first day of September, the procession makes its way round the city; in every street, children run to join it, and it grows bigger and noisier. For ten years now, the city has opened the Exchange building in the first week of Kermess.* In the great square courtyard, Cornelia will stare in wonder at the pyramid of acrobats, Pekelharing the clown, the dolls in their bright and shining dresses made of pretty stuff (like the Regent's daughters) with lacy low-cut necklines, who lift an arm all on their own to the music of a spinet, and turn their head and part their lips in a smile of impossibly white teeth. Titus holds Cornelia's hand, he won't leave her, he promises, and they'll be back in two hours before the sun goes down. He knows, like me,

_____
* an annual fair or carnival

that all the child thieves and butchers are about in the Exchange court today, and they'd run the length and breadth of the city to get a little golden-haired Cornelia. I slip a pretzel over her bare arm as an amulet to protect her. She'll giggle when she eats it, craning her head and twisting her arm up to her face.

Daniel Francen's loan has paid for a few everyday debts and living expenses, but money leaves the house quicker than it comes in. You still haven't paid back Councillor Cornelis Witsen nor the merchant Hertsbeeck, and I can't see how you will; they're big sums of money and you can't keep hold of them, not with the everyday cost of living.

So, three months after his first visit, Thomasz Haaringh has helped you choose what to sell – the first sale, decided between you. Your pupils carried two marble statues by the Italian Raphael down the stairs, and twenty paintings, eight by you and twelve from your collection. They also brought your beautiful exotic table to the front door, turning it on its round foot; it's inlaid with coloured diamonds in Italian marble – red, green, white and blue – and you used to keep marble sculptures on it. You stayed in your studio. You didn't want to see your beloved artworks leaving the house, and you won't go to the sale, either. You already know that money isn't worth what it used to be, what with the war and business so slow, and you know you'll never get back the price of all this lost beauty.

Money's scarce, but life goes on. And while life goes on, your family mustn't go hungry, even if you've got debts. The day before the sale, Judith, Titus, you and I chose a carcass in the meat hall to give us meat for the year. And that day, while paintings and sculptures from your collection were being sold, you carried the great carcass on your shoulders on your own up the stairs and into the studio; sorrow gave you strength. All the way from the little courtyard, where it was waiting for Judith's knife, step by step you dragged it up behind you. Bernhard and the apprentices heard the powerful echo, heard it sliding over the wooden flooring, heard you panting with the effort. They couldn't make out what they were hearing, and Bernhard ran to your studio. And he supported the stiff, flayed beast on his back while you hung it from a beam; the back legs splayed out, like the arms of Jesus on the Cross, the rope as thick as your thumb knotted several times around its hoofs. You looked at the stiff, flayed beast for a long time, for a long time you screwed your eyes up at it as you looked.

Your brush spatters the canvas with paint and blood, vomits fat and scraps of dead meat onto it. The quartered beast collapses into the painting, where you've clawed bones and open innards with your paint. Death is red. I knock at the door, the way I always do. Then a bit louder; there's no answer, and I go in. Your shirt is red with the paint your hands have spread, striped with the colours your brush has splattered right over the place where your life throbs, like you've become the carcass yourself. Naked in your own blood, the two great shells of your open chest, spread wide either side of the place where life beats; suffering with each brushstroke. You've been flayed, too, and you'll give your throbbing innards to anyone who asks. Your suffering is silent. I didn't have any words. I stood watching you, admiring you.

The woman with the tooth sticking out of her face has come back. She won't come in, won't set foot in this house on any account, says the wobbly tooth. She's come to Amsterdam to tell the coward Rembrandt van Rijn that Geertje Dircx has been let out of the house of correction in Gouda and has gone home to Edam. Couldn't come herself and tell the news (good, isn't it?) because six years in the cold and the stench surrounded by raving mouths screaming from morning till night and from night till morning that they're still alive, these six years have made Geertje Dircx ill.

Thomasz Haaringh knocks at the door. He greets me affectionately and sadly. He climbs the stairs to the studio. He's not come to pose, his portrait has already been engraved, already printed. To my first question you reply that all these debts and problems are a nuisance; yes, the lenders want their money back now, and Thomasz Haaringh, who knows the laws and how to use them, is helping you gain time and money. You're not worried, but the time could be better spent painting and you're too tired to tell me all about it when he's gone. I realise you'll only tell me now what you can't hide.

It's not Titus who's got debts, no one can take anything away from him. And you, his father, you owe him 20,000 florins at the demand of the Chamber of Orphans. So that the Chamber of Insolvents doesn't take it from you in May, you're having your house placed in Titus's name.

In July, you ask for a *cessio bonorum* from the High Court of Holland at The Hague. The sun's glinting on the canals, but I'm cold, Latin words don't say anything to me, and their mystery even gives me the shivers. The children are in bed and slowly you explain. Under the protection of the High Court, you can no longer be threatened with prison by anyone you're in debt to, not Councillor Witsen, nor the merchant Hertsbeeck. Prison, my love, I never thought of that. You've won a reprise of six weeks to tell the Amsterdam Chamber of Distress how you're going to pay them back. Or that you want more time.

Thomasz Haaringh gives you his advice and some words to sign. Art today is not a good business. But you've got hopes of getting hold of money quickly another way: you're waiting to be paid back a large sum you lent a ship on business in the East Indies, which hasn't yet returned from the other side of the world. All Amsterdam knows that ships that travel halfway round the world can get held up, and that they and their possessions may even get lost forever in a storm. (Especially if neither they nor the loan of money ever existed.) It's worth lying like this, so you gain time to scan the horizon.

The woman with the tooth has returned. The words fall from her face. Geertje Dircx is dead. Titus hasn't come to the table.

Very quietly he said that, before she became what she ended up, Geertje Dircx wasn't evil, and that she loved him with a mother's love, for seven years. He doesn't hold it against anyone, he already knows that time erases memories.

A keeper at the Chamber of Distress always visits the house of the debtor and makes an inventory. The possessions described on the list no longer belong to him; he can keep them, see them on his walls every day, but they already belong to the Chamber of Insolvents. So he can get used to the idea, you say. After the sale (the 'liquidation', says Thomasz Haaringh), the creditors can't make any more claims, even if they haven't been paid back everything they're owed. I understand that it's the least of the evils. I can't get used to the idea; to make myself remember, I go through the rooms of the house with you, looking for the walls between the paintings, while I wait for the words to turn into a nightmare.

Early this morning, when it was still dark, a man knocked three times. Rembrandt was quicker than me: he got up and opened the door. In the shadow against the freezing wall, I saw the man in black, the crow that never stops looking for the whore. Almost the same black beak. He's not alone; the man behind him holds a book and a quill pen. They came here two days in a row, went round every room, looked at everything without seeing the beauty: walls, tables, cupboards, drawers and coffers. And every box of drawings. The man in black asks the question, always the same one: 'What's the name of this? . . .' or 'What do you call this? . . .' and you reply, sometimes enjoying the joke of giving so many details the two men can't think straight any more. They didn't ask what a giant's helmet was.

The list the second man makes is turning into a last work of art: a description of your years of collecting, of the years of love for these objects you'll never see again, sold and dispersed. This list brings them together forever, for an eternity that will outlast the sale and our lives.

For two days the quill pen scratched away at the paper. A

landscape by Rembrandt; another landscape by same; a trifling work touched up by Rembrandt; a painter's studio by Brouwer; a little landscape by Hercules Serghers; three little dogs painted from life by Titus van Rijn; a plaster head; four Spanish chairs covered in Russian leather; a little metal cannon; sixty Indian pistols, as well as arrows, javelins and bows; an Annunciation; the head of a horned satyr; a head by Raphael; a book of very rare engravings by same; five antique hats; the skins of a lion and lioness; the statue of the Emperor Agrippa; a statue of Tiberius; a Caligula; a Nero; a child by Michelangelo; a giant's helmet.

Transparent in the shadows, I seethe at the hands that point, the hands that lift, weigh, open and rummage, turn things over in the sunlight – they're filthy hands. They wipe out the beauty in your house, your works, your collections, your life. Maybe it's grief, maybe it's the cold, I don't know but I'm shaking. In answer to their questions, you even remembered your three shirts, six handkerchiefs, three table rugs and twelve serviettes, as well as a few collars and sleeves still at the dyeing mill, where Judith's husband works. As if my clothes have been torn off and I'm suddenly naked, I cross my arms and legs and huddle over my modesty, over what I want to hide from thieving hands.

Cornelia was crying gently, almost peacefully, and Titus was rocking her in her bed. Judith and Geertruid were cleaning the kitchen without a sound, they'd been cleaning it for hours; they didn't know where to go, that's why; the other rooms of the house had been visited and sullied by the men in black, and they knew these rooms were condemned. Life was forbidden in them for a few days, while they were aired of the burning memory. We sat alone at the table, facing each other in an inner silence that words can't share, and we ate *hutsepot* that had been cooking for two days but that our poor appetites hadn't been able to finish. You laid your arm across the table, placed your hand on mine.

'You deserve more than this life: I'm sorry.'

There were no words in my open mouth; I shook my head

to say no, and the drops started at the corners of my eyes. Tomorrow would be like today's nightmare, your work and all your beautiful objects struck off by a quill pen. Tomorrow, in the last rooms not yet profaned, tomorrow in the front room, in the antechamber to the art gallery and in the large pupils' studio, they'll go on writing, treasure after treasure, writing down the words that Rembrandt will dictate.

I swallowed my tears and said: 'Let's go out.' It was I who said it.

'We'll go to the tavern.'

'You're right. I always say no. Yes, take me there.' For the first time, I said yes, I'd go to the tavern with you. I washed the redness from my eyes in cold water.

Our steps rang on the bricks in the street. Voices in the night don't whisper; deeper than in the daytime, they breathe their words. Tonight, yours breathes what you'd never said before, not even to yourself.

'You've been so warm and so close to me for seven years, you too have grown attached to the house and its treasures . . . seven years. I never thought I'd be separated from them, I still can't believe it tonight.'

I look up at the sky to count the stars. The Lord takes away and He enriches. He abaseth and He exacteth. He watches over the steps of pious men, but the wicked ones perish in darkness. Gulls cry and echo one another, the street gets narrower, the lanterns further apart, we're coming to the port.

'I am insolvent, my love, cleaned out, that's what I am. Yes, tomorrow, I shall be the cleanest of men.' You laugh as best you can, but it doesn't even sound like a laugh any more. Two rats cross the road in front of us. Two fat black rats, full of the canals' vermin. A woman with a painted mouth comes slowly out of the shadows. The lantern light crushes her fat cheeks, flattens her naked breasts; all deflated and wrinkled, they dangle like two pears.

'When I gave the two men words that scarcely say anything,

and certainly don't convey any sense of beauty, I realised that if these works of art and objects, which are precious because I love them, belong to me (as our friend van Ludick says), I belong to them myself. Dispossessed, I shall be set free.'

In the light of the lantern, I can feel my eyes grow rounder. I can't find words. Dispossessed, he shall be set free. Further along the canal, three men are fighting, muffled sounds, curses, falling. Something metal shines in someone's hand. I cling shivering to Rembrandt. But we're already there, under the tavern lantern, music and laughter reach us through the blue-and-green leaded windows.

Rembrandt bangs his fist on the heavy door. In my first glance, I couldn't make anything out, just noise and smoke. Robbed, he shall be set free. The tavern is a great fireplace where the Devil's fire is cooking. In its flames men and women are roasting, their teeth weeping and singing over the music that's coming from a red-haired man, there at the very back, standing on a table by the wall; pursing his lips and puffing out his pale cheeks, the red-haired man breathes music into the black pipes sticking out of a fat cloth bag with a checkered pattern of red-and-green squares. The people at his table are looking up at him, clapping their hands.

I walk or float (I don't know which any more) through the cloud of smoke behind Rembrandt. Red faces, red lips. Dispossessed. Soldiers' boots strike the floor near a bare-headed woman whose breasts dance out of her dress. A sailor with a wizened face, his eyes permanently fixed on the horizon, is walking sideways like crabs do down at the harbour. He doesn't see the fishing nets hanging from the ceiling, and his head rubs against them; they hold drying hams and round cheeses with red skin, and little round, green sheep's milk cheeses. They've been hung from the beams to dry so they'll get their fine flavour and smell from the pipe smoke of Dutch tobacco with weed from the Indies hidden in it to make people forget, or remember differently – that's what you tell me.

Cleaned out, dispossessed, set free. Yes, from tomorrow, the cleanest of men. And misfortune: why can't we accept this, too, as a gift from God? No, Job suffered too much: he lost everything, all his children died, and he never complained.

Your hand on mine. I bang my empty glass on the table. Your words settle on the smoke and travel, like laughter. You ask for two more glasses of gin from the girl going from table to table, holding out a bottle.

'The important thing is to stay in the house that belongs to Titus, my beloved son, who loves you like a sister and a mother and who loves Cornelia like a sister. The walls of my house know me and speak to me. They talk of the rays of the sun, which I guess are there, season after season, before I see them. They speak of Saskia and you, of the children who crawl around bumping into them, of the babies that were taken away too early, and of friends who have entered your life and will never leave it.'

With his small shining nose and round eyes, a waiter puffs out his fat cheeks as he blows on the stone platter where the embers glow red and rekindle. He goes to each smoker and asks: 'Another pipe?' It's like a necklace round his throat – four little cloth bags hanging on a fine rope. He bends down to the smoker to hear his order, then chooses the tobacco from the bags, mixes it in the palm of his hand and stuffs it into the bowl of a long white pipe. He goes over to the embers and blows on them until the pipe spits out its first smoke.

Ephraim Bueno, who always smokes a pipe when he's in a Plague-victim's room, doesn't believe tobacco cures gout, gallstones or insomnia; but it eases toothache and cures worms, he's sure of that. I always make a face, and he always laughs. I'm sitting opposite Rembrandt at the end of a long wooden table, and watch as, one after the other, the men and women at our table swallow their pipe smoke. I know that, immediately, the worms in their insides will be suffocated.

You lean forward: 'The walls of the house tell of the years that have passed between them, of my sleepless nights when I walked up and down, casting my shadow over them as I passed. And they'll go on talking to me for a long time to come of the paintings I chose, almost for them, like jewels for a beloved wife.'

Another burst of music from the man with the pipes. There are as many women as men drinking and smoking, clapping their hands and singing, losing reality and gaining oblivion. The woman beside me at the table laughs alone, enlightened by alcohol; you can see bubbles forming and bursting around her teeth. Two flat-breasted women are chasing a little pink-and-grey pig between the tables, uttering long ear-piercing screams, longer than the pig's. They're so thin you can hear their bones knocking together. That's what Rembrandt says through a belch to his neighbour, a fat man who laughs with his belly.

Two black-skinned men are sitting in a cloud further away, and all I can see are their teeth and the whites of their eyes. I know they live on the other side of the horizon but, before this evening, I'd never seen any in the city. Every time they part their full lips, their white teeth shine, and you know they've got too many in their mouth. The music man has sat down between them. He calls to the serving-girl with the great pitcher. The froth falls from above like a fountain of white bubbles into the two black men's tankards. They nod a thank you, and the froth makes their lips look even bigger before bursting over their teeth, now even whiter.

'Welcome,' says the man playing the pipes. 'Welcome to our beautiful city of Amsterdam where a Negro who's been sold in the West Indies can become a free man. If he jumps from the boat that has brought him from Africa, if he can swim long enough to get to the harbour. A slave who sets foot on Amsterdam soil is a free man. Never again will these two Africans be slaves. Holland is a country of freedom!' The tankards clink, in a waft of alcohol the teeth repeat: 'Holland is a country of freedom.'

But again, Rembrandt is looking beyond the tavern walls and beyond the sale. 'You need a roof and a fire in the hearth for children to flourish and for old men to age less quickly. I can save the house, I must. The art and objects will be sold for more than the debts . . .'

'Are you sure?'

I don't know why I'm asking. He's so sure. But when I heard him, my tongue formed the words out of fear. Rembrandt laughs. Words are comforting and his train of thought continues.

'My possessions today are worth at least twice my debts. My treasures, all those works of art, all those precious objects that have made me happy for so many years. But one mustn't cling to things too much or they'll cling to you (as van Ludick says). You can attach yourself to the pleasure they give you, but not the things themselves. They've already given me everything, the pleasure is in me, it'll stay there forever.'

I realise that his sorrow isn't the same, and I think that I'd gladly drink a pipe of smoke. And at that moment, the woman laughing bubbles onto her teeth and into my ear suddenly stopped, the life in her stopped, her mouth opened and she stopped moving. I tell myself that drinking as we've all drunk this evening is a betrayal of God and that I'll talk to you about it tomorrow. After Noah had drunk the wine from his vines, his sons came across him naked in his tent. The youngest laughed and his father cursed him, both him and his son Canaan and his descendants. Which shows that Noah had drunk too much then and for the rest of his life. Slowly over the table, the woman coughs out her pipe and beer. Before my eyes, the smoky worms drown in the alcohol she's swallowed and regurgitated.

I thank God for guiding us that night, without the forgotten lantern and without us falling into a canal. I thank Him, I ask His pardon and I promise not to drink alcohol ever again, because it takes reason away from souls, as it took Noah's clothes away from him and took away the love of his children.

Christiaan Huygens, Constantijn Huygens's son, has stopped looking at the planets in the dark sky through a telescope. He's invented a clock with a pendulum. Time swings back and forth.

*   *   *

Doctor Tulp's successor at the Guild of Surgeons is Doctor Jan
Deyman. His visit was announced at the Breestraat door by an
assistant surgeon. Rembrandt sees a sort of superstition in his
choice of painter: it's twenty-four years since Doctor Tulp's
anatomy lesson, and Doctor Deyman is hoping for the same
luck, the same power, but also the same immortality as Regent
Tulp. The surgeon's lancets will probe the skin, flesh, bones and
innards of a hanged man. He's called Fleming Johan Fonteyn;
he's a thief who broke into a draper's shop one night and
threatened the draper with a knife, though he didn't kill him.
He's going to be hanged on the 28th of this month of January.
Does he know that before he's given to the earthworms, cold
and stiff, his body will be dissected, and that a painting will
tell how he was carved up? For three days the painter will look
at him, draw him, paste on the hollows and shadows. Maybe
immortality consoles a thief for his death.

The house is in Titus's name, but on the stairs, I heard Thomasz
Haaringh say that the creditors are angry and will have a share
(especially Councillor Witsen), and that this can't go on much
longer.

The armed band, led by Judas, approach in the distance. On
the Mount of Olives, St Peter, St James and St John are fast
asleep. The drypoint scores the black ground like it's drawing
with copper. The angel has appeared, supporting Jesus in his
arms, his mouth trying to wrest the anguish from His mortally
sickened soul. And in His agony, He prays still harder. Not what
I will, but what thou wilt. In the studio's smells of ink, the sweat
falls from Christ, like drops of blood falling to the ground. The
pupils turn the press. The great cylinder grinds against the tiny
copper plate.

Ornia has bought the acknowledgment of Rembrandt's debt
from Jan Six. Why, what favour is he repaying? Thomasz

Haaringh has no idea, he says you'll never know all the city's secrets. Ornia wants the debt to be settled today. He's one of the richest men in Amsterdam and the 1,000 florins plus the interest Rembrandt owes on it won't alter his fortune. Is he setting an example? Does he have some moral reason? Or is it the city, Regent Tulp? Yes, maybe Tulp begged Ornia to free his son-in-law from his last link with Rembrandt, and buy this bit of paper off Six, the whole of the acknowledgement of debt. But I've no proof of Regent Tulp's heartless banishment, nor of Jan Six's cowardly betrayal, and without proof I can't make my accusations out loud.

For three nights, I've woken up in the middle of the same nightmare; I'd completely forgotten about it. The great horses' hoofs pulling Regent Tulp's golden carriage gallop noisily over the bricks of the little street. I'm glued to the black slimy wall, pushing, disappearing into its shadows; I'll soon be imprisoned under the bricks, I'll fade away. But always the clouds disperse too quickly, always the round moon casts its shining white rays on my skin, my hands and my face. And on the canal's mirror-water, ships are slowly swallowed up by the city. Above the houses, their masts cast lengthening shadows that pick out the gables. The galloping hoofs ring deep in my ears, then inside my head.

Ornia has received his money, the 1,000 florins and 200 interest, from faithful Lodewijck van Ludick, Rembrandt's guarantor. In answer to your embarrassment and gratitude, he asks to be paid back in paintings of his choice, and within three years. A man of moral fibre, a rare friend, you say.

Again the agonising screams of the dying echo through the night. Again the Plague is killing in Amsterdam, with twenty-two dead last week in the port and in the Jordaan. The rats are dying too, from cleaning the canals of the disease. The militia guards keep shooting the cats and dogs fighting in the streets before they poison every house in the city with the miasmas of the Plague hidden in their fur.

Titus is sixteen; he says that during the Plague everyone alive makes a will. And it's true, with death so close life is more dangerous, and when there's Plague about, notaries write wills from morning to night and sometimes into the watches of the night. Titus wants to plan for the future and give Rembrandt back the house in his name, just in case. Lord, spare him, spare us. Rembrandt tosses these silent prayers about, then gives his consent; some members of the Uylenburgh family would have no compunction in seeing the beautiful Breestraat house come into their possession, and Rembrandt and his whore out on the street forever. Titus is no longer a child, I look at him, and seeing him so grown up, I tell myself that since I've known him, I must have grown old, too. Deprived, cleaned out, we've all grown old.

Tears wash away my nightmares. There's emptiness in the house, and in my head, and in my memories. They've come, they've taken everything. In their hands, the furniture, paintings, sculptures and curiosities crossed the emptiness in the rooms. For everyday living, they left the beds, the ladle and the great copper bowl in the kitchen, the cutlery and pewter tankards; and in the studio, two easels, canvases greased with animal-skin glue, pencils and brushes, the great pots of oil of thyme and turpentine, blue pigments, the artist's work.

They even took the cupboard, my cupboard, your gift. I said: 'You can't, you've no right, it's mine, we're not married, it's not his and you've no right.'

One of them looked at me, laughter in his eyes. His mouth was laughing too when he said: 'You can prove it to the auctioneer.' At night in the empty rooms your steps echo. You walk up and down the rooms, up and down in the emptiness.

Titus is posing for his father. His expression is resigned and gentle. He wears the red beret on his auburn curls, the doublet and the collarless sleeveless *pelisse*. Round his neck is a chain that seems to say: 'I am round the neck of a prince.' Resigned and gentle. I tell him so, I call him prince. A smile lights up his eyes: 'That's true, since my father is a king.'

When Cornelia is in bed, the three of us have supper. The empty house echoes with our memories, the remains of the past and our whispers. In his will, with Abraham Francen as witness, Titus leaves everything to his half-sister Cornelia and me; everything he doesn't have, and the house. Rembrandt gets life-rent, usufruct, like a fruit full of good sweet juice. The Uylenburghs are anxious about Titus. So they say. They're demanding that Titus's 20,000 florins be paid to the Chamber of Orphans, or else paid before the other debts. They're demanding to see the list of Rembrandt and Saskia's possessions before Saskia's death. The other creditors are also demanding proof of the figure in the will. But they're hoping the figure for the possessions will be smaller.

There was no marriage contract with Saskia, and the reasons for its absence don't look good. You've got to search, check everything, find witnesses, and the witnesses have to give evidence. Their portrait painted for 500 florins, was it really by you? ... the one hanging over their fireplace, on the wall to the left, their wife on the right. Even the ones in the background of *The Company of Captain Frans Banning Cocq*, mere ghosts at 100 florins a piece. You're forced to remember the jewels you gave Saskia too, her pretty fingers encircled by rings and the mother-of-pearl teardrops that dangled at her delicate ears. You already know it'll cost you time, all this, time and paintings.

St Francis of Assisi was thirty-eight when he died. One by one, your drypoint draws out the hairs on his head and curls an old man's beard round his lips. He kneels, hands joined as he worships Christ. Worshipping Him on the Cross in the foliage before him. And we see what he sees too. Time has stood still, frozen on the glazed metal. After the vision, for a few brief moments ecstasy will hollow out the stigmata in the saint's hands. You've aged him by more than thirty years. Does all the suffering lived through in time help one to see and pray better?

*   *   *

Cornelis Witsen has been elected one of the city's Regents. The same day he was elected, Regent Cornelis Witsen had your house struck off from the Chamber of Orphans. Titus's house, your house, my love. The Chamber of Insolvents can now put it up for sale. The house.

With his right to preferential treatment, he'll be the first to be repaid; Cornelis Witsen is sure now that you'll give him back his 4,000 florins (and the 180 for the right to preferential treatment). I hide my red tears from you. At a distance, I watch you cross the empty antechamber of the cabinet of curiosities. Empty. You walk up and down in the emptiness. I wake in the watches of the night, I listen to you breathe, your heavy sleep.

I'll never drink alcohol of the vine like Noah again, never again will I set foot in a tavern. But I'll spend these few months in a fog, where you can't tell fear from memories. Your possessions are not going to be dispersed in a single sale. It's not easy to separate them from you. There'll be three sales: the paintings and *objets d'art*; drawings and engravings; the house and furniture – everything they'd seized, taken, carried away. Even your studio, the house, your dear house. It's still at the end of the Breestraat, just before the Verwersgracht Bridge, because, of course, they couldn't move it, and it clings to its gabling still. And we can stay there till the sale, and till the buyer (if he doesn't pay for it in one go) has paid the entire sum.

For three days and three nights you didn't come home. For three nights I waited for you on the cold bare tiles, praying to the Lord that you'd come home quickly before I died of worry, that you hadn't fallen into worse company at the tavern, or into a canal in a gin-soaked stupor. And on those three afternoons, I pretended to Cornelia to go on living; let's go and throw bread to the swans – mind their snapping beaks. On the third night, in the cold empty house echoing even to Judith's whispers, I ran to you and, on your knees, you hid your weariness and your remorse, forgive me, forgive me, you kept saying. You buried your face in my breasts and between my legs. Forgive me. I stroked the locks of your hair. The lump in my throat wavered and, with it, useless words.

I didn't fall, no, I too sank to my knees. I drank your requests for forgiveness from your lips. Eyes shut, hair and tongues entangled. So sweet the calm after the storm. On my breast you roll your head down, further down where it rests on my belly. Your breath's warm in the darkness. I fall, no, I sit, lie down, my legs apart, knees up, your lips beneath my skirt between my thighs. Deprived. With each thrust of your hips, a groan sounds in my ears. Like St Paul, I know how to live in abundance, I know how to live in times of need. Noah got drunk, and in the Flood we're drowning together. Our lips and saliva mingle, deep inside, stuck together with the salt from our bodies.

Hendrick Uylenburgh has been received at the Town Hall by Regent Tulp. Abraham is quite certain; the 1,400 florins he owes the city of Amsterdam has been reduced. Now, he only owes 1,000, the rest can be paid back in services. I ask what sort of services. 'Art services,' replies Abraham, laughing, 'art services that Uylenburgh must do for the city.'

I go up to the studio, I stare at the emptiness and at the finished paintings, still reeking of garlic and glistening with paint. I put my hands on your shoulders, massage your neck and your back. You lean your head on one side, your cheek gently strokes my hand.

Stretched out on the easel, the dead man's hands are bigger than his feet. A lot bigger. They're thieving hands, assassin's hands. They're bigger than his feet, but much further back, on either side. Between the assassin's hands, in place of his belly, there's a gaping black hole. Only the top is visible, lower down it's hidden under a cloth.

The house has been bought by Lieven Sijmonsz, the shoemaker, and his partner Samuel Geringhs for 11,218 florins, 2,000 less than you didn't pay, but signed away twenty-one years ago.

I didn't mention the stork; it flew away a long time ago and it's never come back. I know your house was worth twice the price, but who'd believe any more that a stork on the roof of a bankrupt's house is a sign of good luck? Sijmonsz has only paid a first part. On this 22nd February, Cornelis Witsen went with Rembrandt to the cashier's at the Chamber of Insolvents. He was in a hurry, in a hurry to get it over with and forget his mistake (he said on the way). The cashier gave Rembrandt back 4,180 florins, which he immediately placed in Witsen's outstretched hands.

The Earth and its riches, the world and its inhabitants, belong to the Lord! It was He who founded the Earth on the waters and anchored it on the waves. In the darkest hour of the night of the 30th January, the great flood of the Alblasserwaard burst the southern Dutch dykes. In every church, on every square and especially in Rotterdam and Dordrecht, men and women sing psalms, God save me, the water's rising to my throat. I'm wading in a bottomless mire with nothing to hold onto. Again, images float in our minds of church steeples submerged in the great flood on the night of St Elisabeth in the year 1472. May God have mercy, may He keep the island of Rotterdam safe. There's no water so powerful at putting out the fire of God's anger as the water of repentant tears, which is God's wine and man's jubilation, like drops from the vine.

A hammer blow strikes the table: the hammer of Thomasz Haaringh, the insolvency auctioneer, comes down. 'Sold!' he repeats, and the word whistles to the back of the Kaiserkroon inn where the sale's taking place. The sun casts slanting rays through the inn's bright leaded windows, forming stripes in the dust and haloes on the collars and white lace of the wealthy purchasers. I've left Cornelia with Judith, and I take Titus's arm (he's grown, he's taller than me now) as we cross the city to Kalverstraat. I look for you, I know you're here in the inn, hidden in the shadow.

The sun slips behind the blue storm of Hercules Seghers's

landscape. The painting used to hang on the wall to the right in the hallway. But the collection's been blown apart like a powder store, the painting's been separated from it, and now it's in the Kaiserkroon, ripped off the wall. Thomasz Haaringh searches the rows of faces before him for bids and repeats the low figures. Behind the storm the sun is about to pass to the other side of the world. In the moment before rain and night, the sky still holds its heat and blue thunderclaps among the clouds.

I squeeze Titus's hand, we're walking up the central aisle. Heads turn, eyeing the comings and goings as much as the works.

'Thirty-four florins,' taps the hammer. There's no one left to defend the good of the profession. Had he lived to see this day, Hercules Seghers would have filled himself with gin, yes, and thrown himself from the top of his stairs.

One hundred thousand dead, 100,000 mouths open at their last submerged cry. Among the church spires, wading birds' nests float on the becalmed waters.

Since catching sight of me, Thomasz Haaringh's eyes have been asking my forgiveness. My sad smile says again that he's not to blame. That was one evening over a *hutsepot*, a week before your possessions were snatched from the Breestraat walls. Thomasz Haaringh said: 'There'll be enough for everyone. With all the art services to be done for the city, they could all agree not to bid against each other.' I didn't understand at first, not till Rembrandt laughed.

The pale yellow cloth is too big over his genitals, it hides his thighs and much of his legs as well. The soles of his feet in the foreground say for sure that Fleming Johan Fonteyn is dead. You can tell a dead man when he doesn't react to a needle stuck in the soles of his feet.

On his right, to the left of the painting, is the Master of the Guild, Gijsbert Matthijsz Calkoen, his shirt open at his stifling throat. In his left hand he holds a dish. He waits, holding the dish. Perhaps a brush will put a pink bit of the hanged man's body in it. Calkoen waits patiently, his right hand elegantly turned against his hip, so much more elegant, he thinks, than the dead man splayed out, forsaken.

On my right are Hendrick Uylenburgh, Jan Six and Regent Tulp; I hardly need to turn my head to see them. Behind me, the friendly voices of Ephraim, Abraham and Daniel Francen, struggling against the silence, against the plot; they're doing what they can to make the bids go up, they won't let Rembrandt's collections be stolen for so little without anger. In the next row, a mask of wrinkled wisdom turns round, I recognise Constantijn Huygens.

Regent Tulp casts his bid before looking about him with an expression that says: 'The first who dares after me.' Jan Six and his fat wife with red cheeks lift their fingers and shake their heads, them too; and Hendrick Uylenburgh as well, more often than his debts allow. Is he buying so much for others? Is he surprised by such low prices, or did he already know? My breath comes faster: is he one of those who have met and agreed, and is he doing the city a service, an 'art service', as Thomasz Haaringh said?

Out of the salty mud, along with the sprats, the fishermen will keep pulling up teeth, bones and skulls for a long time.

Weariness, or perhaps sorrow, has dulled the auctioneer's eyes. He searches the faces that look up at him for the buyer who will outbid the others. In the silence, his eyes continue to search. In the silence and the murmuring. The voices inch along the rows. I can hear, but have I really understood? 'An assassination.' Fifty-four florins for the Resurrection of Christ by Rembrandt. Thomasz Haaringh's dulled eyes. His right hand lets the hammer fall.

*   *   *

You saw, you were there. The dead thief with assassin's hands slept. Jan Deyman lifted the blade to the light, tested it with his thumb. Then he pierced the top of the forehead and sliced straight through the shaved skin on the head. He cut the skin, which split right down to the back of the neck. He pulled either side, and it came away with a little flesh (as fine as a *koek**) from the round pink bone. When the skin and flesh stick to the bone, he taps with the blade. Then he parts the two halves, leaves them, and slowly they fall either side of the sleeping face. Like long dressed hair, the skin on the head is torn back and covers the ears. Then the living man's hand closed over the saw handle.

The muttering grows steadily louder. The men and women look at one another; heads turn and then turn away. Eyes see me and glide off me. I don't like them. They've come to steal from you, my love, to steal your collection at meaningless prices. The eyes come to rest on me, on Titus, on me again. I don't look down, I don't turn my head, I look straight into their eyes and reply: Yes, it's me, yes, thieves, she's right beside you, Rembrandt's whore.

The sea is calm. From dry land on the top of the mountain, Noah watches the water subside. The water that has drowned men's sins, engulfed their wealth and washed away alcohol. And, in the distance, where a dyke on the Alblasserwaard has withstood the force of the waves, the sea has cast a cradle up on the land. A baby is crying, shaking the cradle which doesn't rock him. Cleansed of their sins, the Dutch are children.

On the platform, two young porters in grey cloth are carrying the cupboard. That's my gift that Thomasz Haaringh is now describing, the dark wood cupboard with a carved frieze of tulips. When the porter opens its doors to count the shelves, with the linen and two little silver chains inside, the left door

---

* A *koek* is a pancake, thicker than a French crêpe but thinner than a Russian blini.

creaks. It always creaked. Rembrandt's whore has a cupboard with a creaky door.

The back and forth of the saw has stopped and with it the music of the blade burning in the light. Jan Deyman has lifted the lid of the head and, not knowing where to put it, held it out to the person nearest. Standing before the painting, I don't understand at first. The dish in the young man's right hand is the lid of the head of the sleeping hanged man.

In my hatred I found courage. They have banished me from the Lord's table. They are stealing my cupboard. I stand up, taller than the sea of hair and pink skulls before me, and I hear my voice. The cupboard is mine. It's not one of Rembrandt van Rijn's possessions.

Under the lid, the inside of the dead man's head, with its skin of long hair, is soft and pink, his brains cut in two halves, like good and evil.

All of them, they've all turned round to see. Their lips part, not to smile, no, to air the little bones in their mouths, the only bones the body doesn't hide, yellowed by wickedness. The mutterings recognise the whore. Yes, the whore has stood up. With her profligate fingers she's touching her hair, touching the lid of her head, repeating they'll never sell her cupboard, that would be stealing. My head aches under its lid. All round me, behind their wicked teeth, their breath passes from their insides up through the stench of Hell. It's the whore's cupboard. Louder than in my head, I hear my voice. 'Yes, it's the cupboard. My cupboard.'

Between two waves, the shrieks swallow teeth. Little yellow bones.

Titus clasps my right hand. His solemn smile won't leave me. I hold my head higher, I look straight in front of me. On the platform, the lawyer Torquinius, the administrator of Rembrandt's estate, chosen by the High Court at The Hague, bows his head and whispers in Thomasz Haaringh's ear. My legs are quaking under me, too much for me to bend and sit down. The white collars float around me. Far off on the platform, the words of the auctioneer and administrator hold the key to the whore's cupboard, with its contents of a few linen and woollen shirts and two silver items of jewellery.

Does an assassin's brain look like an administrator's or a surgeon's? You'd never find the surgeon Jan Deyman groping about inside his own head. Will his fingers lift out all that pink crawling flesh, dig out a great hollow over the unseeing eyes, like they've already done in the black hole of the belly? Judas fell forward on the bloody Earth, he split down the middle, his intestines spilled out.

The man holding the lid of the head like a dish isn't looking at the surgeon's hands, and he's not looking at the dead man's open head either. No, his sad eyes lose themselves in the stinking empty belly. He holds the lid like a plate, he waits for the surgeon to put the brain in it upside-down.

The two porters carry the cupboard – the administrator's given it back to me. They carry it away, out through the door away from the hall. I sit down.

The light warms the surgeon's and assistant's hands and faces. The shadow round each of them and their black clothes make the light on the corpse shine even brighter. Like the engraving of Christ's entombment, the light that illuminates the picture comes from the dead man. The face of the hanged thief is sad. It's the sorrow of being dead. If he opened his eyes, he'd see the great black hole of his belly. His colour too, the transparency of death, it's not as brilliant as the cloth that covers too much of him, like the Holy Shroud. Like his bare legs were barer, more sickening than his empty innards.

For thirty years, the ebony-framed mirror, the mirror that hung on the wall of Rembrandt's studio, told the eyes that saw themselves in it that they were getting old. And the pink stars around them, and their ambitions, and their falling flesh.

The mirror of Rembrandt van Rijn's self-portraits. Thomasz Haaringh's gaze searches the crowd and loses hope. Fourteen florins for the mirror in the depths of which all Rembrandt's eyes meet, fourteen florins, a few murmurs.

The assassin's hands won't hold the knife again, they won't strangle delicate necks any more. Stiff cold fingers won't hunt their music in the air. In the white light that shines both ways through his flesh – from the inside out and from the outside in – the dead man has turned to stone. Hard as a tomb. His death is there, open; death is stone, like him forsaken, nothing but what comes after life. Open and gaping in the stench, he'll know no resurrection.

Surprised, Titus's voice starts to speak, launching itself over the tops of the heads that turn to look. 'Thirty florins.' Titus has changed, and this deeper voice, no longer the voice of a little boy and not yet that of a man, this unfamiliar voice says again, but lower this time for me alone: 'For the good of his profession.'

You are beautiful, Titus, beloved child of your father, love of his life, dear angel (you still pose for Rembrandt, always the angel). Your gaze is steady, it comes to rest sorrowfully on things, on people, on their eyes; he already knows that life leads men through many troubles. This old mirror, inlaid with rust and memories, this ebony-framed mirror in which no purchaser has seen Rembrandt's faces, you're buying it; with the thirty coins your father kept in a purse and gave you to buy whatever was most precious. My Titus, my child, my brother. You lean towards me. 'I want us to have this mirror now. I'm paying for it and taking it home.'

A thief has turned to stone.

Hammer blows. There, on the table, beneath the lid of my head. Titus walks down the central aisle towards the platform. Faces turn, then turn away. Titus van Rijn, his son, yes, it's Rembrandt's son.

A sculpture is being displayed to the purchasers, offered to the thieves. Two sleeping children, dug out, hewn from the white stone. Those stiff cold hands: are they dead or asleep? If that smile is death, then the death of stone children is peaceful. The thieves' voices are few, like they're shy, Thomasz Haaringh's voice is sadder.

Thirty years after the St Elisabeth flood, the fishermen were still selling dentists the teeth they'd caught.

Titus, my child, my brother, Titus with the transparent skin and eyes is carrying the mirror, where his father's self-portraits drew breath. He walks down the central aisle, he's coming towards me, holding the mirror straight against his chest. He goes towards the door at the back of the hall. Thomasz Haaringh's hammer goes down on the sleeping children. Titus stops in his tracks, the sound pierces his ears and body for a moment. Titus, his father's son, the faces turn to him and hold their yellow breath. Dirty faces, a black line above their bright white ruffs.

The screams of children mostly.

It's the smell. Always there. With each breath, the flesh of the faces is never still, slowly it loses its shape. Titus walks on, taller with every step. The crowd and that smell all the time. Lips open and shut, stars burst beneath their skin, the blue worms of their hands swell and tie themselves in knots. And in the middle of the dead man's hanged neck, the black mark of life.

Titus walks on. Slowly he looks to right and left. He turns to face the muttering. The mirror moves down the hall. Step by step. Row by row. For a moment it holds the image of their faces in reverse, then swallows them in its murky depths. The white light crushes the white ruffs. Their toothless smiles have been disclosed and drown in the thick mirror.

There was no impact. There was no sound. I was staring at the square of glass, seeing nothing but Rembrandt's painted faces that today had been dispersed. In your first portraits, you didn't like yourself, you used to hide the line of your young animated face in shadow and in your curly hair. As painter to Amsterdam's grandees, you greatly enhanced your face and fame, placing a piece of armour or a chain of gold round your neck. Then came life's first betrayals, early deaths, great griefs, eyes full of shadow, lines and chapped and puffy skin. And always that steady gaze in the mirror and out the other side, to the world where memories cast blame.

Until the still-unfinished portrait (you're working on it in a tiny frameless mirror), when bankrupt and robbed, seated very upright on a throne you can just make out because of its great arms, you're wearing a suit of gold cloth fit for a king, the collar studded with precious stones while, in a careless hand, you hold a silver-topped cane. Your lips are unsmiling, but you're not sad. Calm and solemn; wisdom in that man, that king. Tired from what you've seen and heard, your eyes still shine. You judge the one before you who is looking at and desiring this painting, and through him the others – all those attending this theft, this auction, but also those not yet born, grandees like their parents who, from generation to generation, and from century to century, will look like them. Lacking both beauty and goodness, their souls frozen.

There was no impact. There was no sound. Titus was coming down the central aisle. The muttering had stopped. The reflections of all those who met themselves in the mirror knew that the auburn-haired young man was the bankrupt's son. Their very words cleaved to the edge of their lips and waited for the silence to end. As if a split second earlier, we'd all known. As if, when we saw this mass of hair and pink heads, all these necks with the black mark of the hanged man, these faces perched on their ruffs (as stiff as white china plates) which entered and drowned in the mirror – as if we already knew.

No impact, no sound. Titus walks. In the cloying silence, the air he cuts in two is heavier, his steps slower. Without impact and without a sound. Slowly, for no reason. Like the sea splintering suddenly at dawn, the surface of the mirror took life. Its brilliance faded, in a sigh perhaps, less than a moan, a tear. The lines gathered and shattered the surface. Aiming its sharp corners at us, each little piece came away from the others. Without the back and forth of the saw, the wrinkled skin of their faces gently peels itself away from their skulls, stops for a moment in the air, then falls to the floor with a slight metallic ring. I believe in the Holy Spirit. Eyes without light, all uncomprehending, toothy smiles on the frozen surface. Then amazement half shut their mouths. Constantijn Huygens toppled, Jan Six's head melted in the thick liquid, Hendrick Uylenburgh looked deep into his eyes in a tiny square, before he tried to find himself, horrified at disappearing. And in the 1,000 splinters of exploded mirror, Regent Tulp just had time to pick up his lips before seeing his face shatter.

The stone hanged man cried out before he was drowned.

Christ's love embraces us, when we think that one man died for all and so that all are dead. All those who judged Rembrandt, his life and painting, all those who couldn't forgive him his freedom, that day they saw their souls vanish on the other side.

Titus can't move. At his feet he sees a carpet of silver leaves, skin and clotted blood. He looks into the hole of the frame, like the dead man, with his inner eye, the great hole of his empty belly. Titus, with burning eyes, gripping the ebony frame. Titus, who can no longer place one foot in front of the other. I get up, my lips already forming his name. But a great shadow has risen and enveloped him, a king in golden yellow clothes. Rembrandt has come out of his hiding place behind the pillar, where no one had seen him. He clasps Titus to him with love, stronger and surer now he'll never be alone again.

The father supports and guides his son to the door at the back, to the sun beyond. Father and son, lost in a world they're ill suited for, alone together. Thomasz Haaringh falls silent, the whole hall falls silent. I stand up without knowing. Run towards their departing backs. And me, don't leave me, I love you. Behind my back, the mutterings start up again. Thomasz Haaringh's hammer falls on the table and echoes in my head.

Death is stone, death is flesh-pink. Whether it comes after ten years, sooner or later, in the face of God's time, each death is nothing. Every nothing is dead. One after another, or all together when the powderworks blew up in Delft. Have mercy on us, love, dust and what will remain. Bones, teeth and your paintings.

15th December 1660

On this 15th December 1660, Titus van Rijn, attended by his father on the one part, and Hendrickje Stoffels, attended by an adviser chosen for the occasion on the other, appeared and declared that they were obliged to trade in paintings, graphic arts and engravings on copper and wood, as well as prints and curiosities and all other objects, and that they began in partnership over two years ago ... the lies always make me smile, it's only afterwards that I want to understand. Thomasz Haaringh said it – we can't claim the art business is new, something we're building up for the future. Barely two years after the bankruptcy, the daylight robbery of the sale, our debts not yet paid off – everyone'd know that was a lie. But trading, knowing what would please whom, looking the purchaser in the eye and daring to put a price on art, no, not after two years, even now I couldn't do it.

... and wish to continue as long as the aforementioned Rembrandt van Rijn is alive, and for six years after his death, on the following conditions. Snow has covered the city, it's cold enough to make a witch's nipples stand on end. 'The serious nature of the business will prove that it's genuine,' said Thomasz Haaringh, impossible not to mention Rembrandt's death. I'm cold, my love, forgive me, I want to die before you.

The notary, Nicolaes Listingh, rereads the contract. His bottom teeth are all I can see between his moustache and little beard. There's a transparent drop dangling at the end of his sharp nose, glistening against the dark background of his doublet. I can't take my eyes off it, it's going to fall onto the contract, splash onto a line of ink, and a word on the page will be drowned.

Yes, I want to die before you, alive I'm perjuring myself. I watch my child's laughter, I tell myself, so small, she needs her mother. But when you're out in the city buying blocks of colour and essence of aspic, when Titus has gone out and Cornelia is trotting along by his side or she's asleep, when I'm left alone in the house to wash, iron, tidy up or do the cooking, when there's no one but me to talk to and listen to, the numbers get confused. Noah sent seven pairs of animals and seven pairs of birds of the air into the ark. Seven and nine. And this isn't just a country superstition, Ephraim Bueno said he's afraid too. Nine is perfection, the last figure, and seven is God's favourite, the end and the resurrection. There were seven lions in Daniel's den, and on the seventh day Daniel was freed. Town and country folk alike know about life's great climacteric: seven times nine, sixty-three. I've been counting the passing years with every year that brings it closer. In nine years you'll be sixty-three. Anyone who gets past the great climacteric will live to a great age.

First the chattels that the aforementioned Titus van Rijn and Hendrickje Stoffels have acquired, alone in our little house, I'm counting numbers, telling myself stories about the sorrow of death. Making myself get used to the idea. In the bed in our chamber, the still-warm life in you has stopped; I'm already mourning your absence, from now on, forever. The house walls speak of life, the child, my age, but nothing can console me for the dull flatness every day without you. Sometimes, you come in too soon, and I bow my head to hide my red eyes, I want to die before you.

Every time the dangling drop at the end of the notary's left nostril is just about to fall, he gives a little dry sniff and breathes it up into the tunnel of his nose again.

. . . in which they have invested, together and severally since they began trading, furniture, real estate, paintings, objets d'art and curiosities, yes, Titus and I have invested – the lie makes me smile – yes, I've completely understood: if Rembrandt has nothing left in his possession, no one can take from him what he doesn't have and will never own again.

Every evening for ten days, Abraham Francen and Thomasz

Haaringh have come to the Rozengracht, to our new house. Three rooms where life is smaller, but every day it's the same as in a big house, and we have to eat (*koek* and turnips), sleep and above all, make sure your work's not disturbed. And then, every day it's not raining, I take Cornelia to play on the other side of the canal, at a children's park in the Labyrinth, and I tell myself that the Jordaan is a good place for children's laughter. Rembrandt and his two friends round the little table in the flickering candlelight, Thomasz Haaringh's quill ran on.

. . . as well as the rent and all expenses which they have paid, thus they shall proceed and continue in the same way henceforth. A lie: the money that bought the family life on the Breestraat and that today buys it on the Rozengracht has always come from the sale of your paintings or an object from your collections. The cupboard-beds we now sleep in, the pewter plates we eat off, Cornelia's wooden horse, the iron and copper candlesticks, even the warming-plate for heating the iron, it's all Rembrandt's and it's all ours (jointly), because none of us would take anything from the other for himself alone. But a contract has to be written up, even for what could never happen. Thomasz Haaringh's quill made crossings-out, and rewrote.

Louys Crayers, Titus's guardian, named by the Chamber of Orphans, believes there are truths hidden behind the lies, he sees different lies from those written and repeated today by the notary. Behind Titus's faithful love for his father, he hasn't seen Rembrandt's adoration and fear for his son.

Louys Crayers didn't write with Abraham Francen and Thomasz Haaringh, and he didn't come that day to the notary's. He hasn't seen the painting on the easel, the angel struggling with Jacob. A man rolls in the dust with him till break of day. In the paintings, the angel is always Titus; framed by his golden curls, his face and eyes tell of gentleness. God has no name, the angel sent by God won't tell Jacob his name. But Rembrandt's brush has attached two transparent wings to his shoulders, which Jacob would see, like us, if God wished it. The angel's right leg and his left hand on the man's waist meet Jacob's strength with equal force, but his right hand is gentle on the back of his neck, lovingly supporting it. Louys Crayers hasn't seen Titus's wings.

And when the light shines on a kindly face in a monk's hood and habit, it's still Titus the angel who is the saint beneath Rembrandt's brush.

In the winter of the office with its gloomy walls and lightless leaded windows, we're sitting opposite the notary Nicolaes Listingh, Rembrandt in the middle, Titus to his left, me to his right, and Nicolaes Listingh on the other side of his desk of pale wood. On my right is Jacob Leeuw, on Titus's left is Frederik Hedelbergh: the two witnesses. The transparent drop glistens under the notary's nose, *their contribution to their business in particular that which the aforementioned Titus van Rijn had retained of his christening presents, his savings, private earnings and all other capital.* The lies coil up in the room. Titus, my child, my brother, you've got nothing from your christening, nothing but a gold medal from your mamma, no private earnings, no savings and no other capital. Not yet. Louys Crayers is hoping, he wants to prove the truth of Saskia's will.

It's already a year since the witnesses came to the same office of the same notary to testify to what they remembered. Anna Huijsbrechts and her husband Jan van Loo (whose brother Gerrit has married Hiskia, one of Saskia's sisters) signed, in the presence of witnesses, that they were very close friends of Rembrandt van Rijn and his wife Saskia. That they knew for sure what Rembrandt owned before the death of his wife, and then on his own afterwards. Two strings of pearls, the long one for the neck, the smaller one for the arm. Two pearls shaped like pears, a ring with a fat diamond, two diamond pendants, six silver spoons, a prayer book inlaid with gold, a silver plate and jug, and other things that I've forgotten.

Jan Pietersz, the draper, and Nicolas van Cruybergen, the provost, signed that they had each paid 100 florins to be painted by Rembrandt van Rijn among the guards in *The Company of Frans Banning Cocq.* If the notary counts the heads (and the more expensive head of Frans Banning Cocq), he'll know how much

Rembrandt van Rijn was paid in 1642 for this great painting.*
And Abraham Wilmerdoux, director of the East India Company,
he too remembered having paid Rembrandt van Rijn 500 florins
in the same year to have his portrait painted (plus 60 florins for
the canvas and frame).

You leave the studio, you wander round the city. These are
wearisome weeks, like every time you're not painting. I can hear
your heavy tread on the stairs; in my arms at last you close your
eyes; I ask questions, you scarcely answer, the details are always
unpleasant.

At Louys Crayers's request again, Lodewijk van Ludick has
given evidence in his turn because he was familiar with the
Breestraat house and with Saskia and Rembrandt's possessions.
And it's true, van Ludick is familiar, in the sense that he's been
loyal to the family. (He was Rembrandt's guarantor, and gave
Ornia the money without a murmur.) He remembered and he
signed. Remembered that the graphic arts, curiosities, antiques,
medals and plants from the sea, which the aforementioned
Rembrandt van Rijn had in his possession between 1640 and
1650, were worth the sum of 11,000 florins. And that the paintings also in the possession of the aforementioned Rembrandt
van Rijn at that time were worth the sum of 6,400 florins. Each
of these figures being likely to be more rather than less. I can
remember all the words and figures they wrote down, and the
two together, 17,400 florins. He didn't add anything else, what
was the point? Anyone who sees this will remember the 3,094
florins from the auction of Rembrandt van Rijn's collections. A
theft, an assassination. Dispossessed, my love, of everything
except your goodness.

After signing, after leaving the notary's office, van Ludick
came to the Breestraat. In the bare-walled big empty house,
he said, as a lover of beauty, that he could see the ghosts of
the paintings in the marks left on the walls. And then I saw

* Seventeen figures at 100 florins each (and Frans Banning Cocq consider-
ably more).

myself, in the frame of dust where a mirror had been, the ghost of another life in the red hollows of my eyes.

Each of the parties will have the profit of half the proceeds, because everything was bought with the christening presents, savings and private earnings of Titus van Rijn, the bankrupt's son. The written words are the proof, and Rembrandt's paintings are further evidence of his love for his son, the bond of affection linking their lives.

The paint digs shadows in the light. On his curly hair, Titus wears the helmet of Alexander the warrior. The painting is red and gold. In the shining metal of the great round shield, the young conqueror sees his solemn face and the battles to come. Maybe, too, the lessons Aristotle taught him, lessons he'll forget so as to go and fight; and maybe, too, his early death.

For two years now in his book-lined library, the cultivated man of taste, Antonio Ruffo, has been admiring Aristotle before the bust of Homer. He couldn't decide between his desire for a portrait of Homer and a portrait of Alexander, which his tutor Aristotle wears round his neck. You had begun this portrait of Titus; you always love painting his searching expression. When Isaac Just translated the letter from Sicily, Titus in the painting immediately became Alexander. Round his face you sewed three other pieces of canvas, you painted the helmet and shield. It's a portrait of love; it's for the cultivated man of taste.

. . . *and will share half of the losses of this business and will act in good faith and trust*, we stayed on the Breestraat without paintings, *objets d'art* and curiosities or furniture, just the beds, cupboard and easel – all four of us and Judith, who wouldn't leave us, wouldn't abandon us, she whispered into the emptiness. The shoemaker couldn't live in the house until he had paid the whole sum to the Chamber of Insolvents.

But your work needs peace and a settled existence. And now that the storks have come back to the city roofs, we've left the empty house, the empty space between two homes. It was Abraham Francen, who lives in the Jordaan, who found us the house on the Rozengracht. With the help of Judith and her dyer husband, we moved our last remaining possessions. Alone in our pasts, without holding hands, we turned round at the corner of the Breestraat and the canal. Our four figures cast flat shadows that stretched down the road, as if they were going to break away from us and stay stuck to the shadow of the house after we'd gone. Again we turned our heads, several times as we crossed the bridge to the Verwersgracht. Each of us alone in his memories, even Cornelia; we didn't look at each other. Mustn't catch sight of anyone else's tears: other people's tears make you cry. Only Judith sniffed.

Each will oversee and encourage the interests of the business, but each will use them for this purpose. The words are ground out between the notary's teeth; my love you're smiling at me, all these lies will soon be over, that's what your smile means. Slowly your calm fills the room, slowly your confidence enters into me.

However, because both of them are in great need of aid and assistance in their enterprise and trade, and because no one is more suitable for this purpose than the aforementioned Rembrandt van Rijn, they agreed with him that he would live with them, and be freely nourished, and exempt from all domestic expense as well as rent, on condition that he would help his partners in all ways as far as possible and would encourage the enterprise. 'Freely nourished', my love, free board and lodgings and exempt from all the everyday expenses of daily life. It's all written down. You'll no longer own anything. Just your art, your work, your freedom from your creditors.

Yes, my love, we're all very much in need, Titus and I, in need of your help and assistance in art and even in trade. Because no one is more suitable: yes, you'll encourage the enterprise. A great urge to laugh or cry, I don't know which any more. There, they've stopped skirting around, they're pointing. Who'll believe it? *He has heard and accepted this clause in the contract.* Nicolaes Listingh's teeth move. The drop's about to fall. And yes, Rembrandt's heard and accepted, he even came up with the sentence with Thomasz Haaringh.

There, Rembrandt van Rijn, Amsterdam's great and famous painter no longer owns anything. Thanks to the charity of his son and the whore who shares his bed, he's got free board and lodging. In exchange, he'll advise their art business. The same words, the same phrases, over and over again every evening for weeks, till they were written down.

However, on condition that the aforementioned Rembrandt van Rijn will own no part of the enterprise and will have no claim to the furniture, chattels, objets d'art and curiosities, instruments and all related objects which might be found in the house at any moment, and to which the aforementioned partners would have legal right should anyone take legal action against the aforementioned Rembrandt van Rijn. So no one can hammer and holler angrily at the door any more, take from Rembrandt van Rijn what he no longer owns and never will again. So, the creditor can rage and kick the doors to the Chamber of Bankruptcies, Desolation and Insolvencies, to the notary's and Regent's office till they shake on their hinges. No creditor will get anything else from Rembrandt van Rijn who doesn't own anything any longer.

We hold our heads up, all three of us, sharing our confidence. Mustn't feel ashamed, the law exists to be known, maybe also to help those who know, like notaries and auctioneers, but also those who owe art services to the city, and those who make their life's trade out of money, power and laws, like Regent Tulp, Jan Six, the Uylenburghs and the Constantijn Huygens. Anyone who, without shame, has bought the bankrupt's collections at six times less than their worth.

The aforementioned Rembrandt van Rijn having been recently granted cessio bonorum, *for which reason he has abandoned all possessions and must be taken in charge,* that's why what was possible has happened; and who'd dare reproach a legal text for sticking to the law? *acknowledges having received from the aforementioned contracted parties, namely from Titus van Rijn, the sum of 900 florins and from Hendrickje Stoffels 800 florins, and each of these sums is to be used for necessities and food, which he agrees to pay back respectively as soon as he has earned anything for his painting.* Free board, you might be tempted between meals. You'll be able to eat, dress yourself, buy canvases, blocks of colour, powders and oils for work (your necessities), you won't have to explain the florins in your pockets when you go out into the city. Titus van Rijn and Hendrickje Stoffels (who have savings and private earnings) know that money must be earned and lent with interest, it's never given away, especially not the money of two people associated with a bankrupt. Now everything's been said, and we've just got to make it believable with a harsh phrase, that's what Thomasz Haaringh said. He chose the figures 800 and 900 florins on purpose. They're both nearly 1,000 even though they've got fewer noughts, they tell of the effort of those who give them, and make the words around them look serious. Who's not going to believe?

Before the mirror, you've put your black velvet beret on your curly hair. The cold makes your nose go red quicker, but these two years of bankruptcy and wasted time haven't hollowed or puffed out your face (not like mine). You know how the deaths of loved ones age us, you know real suffering, and this portrait makes it look like the change in your life has left you unscathed. Your collections didn't own you.

The drop at the end of his nose is coming unstuck. *To guarantee the two aforementioned sums, the aforementioned Rembrandt van Rijn has transferred and yielded to the aforementioned Titus van Rijn and Hendrickje Stoffels all paintings and the income deriving from them, which he shall paint in their house.* An extra security, you'll always be our debtor, Titus's and my debtor, first and foremost our debtor. All those who were at the sale, the thieves who stole your possessions, they'll be mad with anger.

I know it's your expression and your kindness but, if my last portrait was a mirror, I'd be afraid of myself. Perhaps you wanted proof: this is what you have done, this is what you've done to my woman. Like a confession too, I can hear you asking forgiveness with each brushstroke. It's not you, my love; it's the last year, the injustice, the too short, too cold nights in the empty Breestraat house, it's the milk, the herrings and the lukewarm beer which sometimes warms one up. It's unbearable sorrow that's made my head sink on my swollen neck. My skin has yellowed and my eyes no longer shine as they gaze into space hard by, closer and lower than the horizon. My swollen fingers belong to a hand that washes in icy water. My cheeks are less round; heavy and flat, they've collapsed into a second chin. My lips have closed on an unsmiling silence.

Behind our locked door, peace has gathered again round your easel, you're making up for lost time by turning out as many paintings as ever, and I'll do whatever is best for you, for Cornelia and for Titus. Together again, because this life's the best we know, we'll laugh.

I've stopped listening to this long recitation, it's useless and boring. Quick, a quill pen to sign. A contract is a prison; no one reading it would guess the trust and affection it hides. Nicolaes Listingh has breathed up the drop on his nose just before it slips off and splashes on the notary's words. *The three signatories promise to conform rigorously to the terms that apply to each of them and to act irrevocably and without infringement*, everything has been said and written, I'm not listening, *securing their persons and their possessions according to the law and the regulations*. I put on the red-and-white dress, I posed for hours near the well with my bucket, sitting really, my left arm bent, resting on a table. *Decreed in good faith in the aforementioned city*. When the man asks me for a drink, I confess my surprise that a Jew should ask for water from a Samaritan woman; Jews have no dealings with the traitors of Samaria. Christ answers that if she knew Him, it is she who would have asked, and He would have given her the living water, a well of water springing up into everlasting life. Then, so that she might recognise the One that knew all things, Jesus told her the names of the five men she had had and the one she now had who was not her husband either.

Decreed in the presence of Jacob Leeuw and Frederik Hedelbergh, witnesses, and the signatories, apart from me the notary, signing the minutes.

Silence at last. Rembrandt, my love, I shall take water from the depths of the well for you forever, I'll never let you know the suffering of thirst. For years, time has been ebbing away too fast, money, notaries and inventories have been stealing your paintings. We look at each other calmly. From now on, our door will be closed, I shall protect you, you and your art. But the good I can do for you is nothing beside the living water and eternal life that you have offered me each day for nearly twelve years. Jesus spoke to the Samaritan woman (who, with her five men and no husband, was not a whore) so that she might tell the people of the city that the Messiah had come.

Nicolaes Listingh places his hands on the three pages of the contract. Slowly, he looks at us, each one, one after the other. Slowly, his eyes look searchingly into ours and stop when they come to Rembrandt. Again, his lips part, does anyone want to change or add anything? Our heads shake our answer, and Rembrandt pronounces a very calm 'No'. While Rembrandt's reply goes into the notary's ear and pink brain, the nail of his middle finger scratches the tip of his nose. He shakes, then crushes, the dangling drop. Without knowing. He removes his damp hand, seizes the pen lying on the table between three fingers, sinks it into the black hole of the pewter inkwell, but his hand stops in mid-air, like it's weighing the air.

'You know, Rembrandt van Rijn, that your creditors will condemn you, but so too will the city, for the man who can't pay his debts is always judged ill. Some purchasers won't set foot in your house again.'

I heard your sigh. 'I've already paid, and several times, they know I have. I have no choice, I just want to save my time and my work.'

Abraham Francen and Thomasz Haaringh told you this too: the thieves won't think twice about judging the bankrupt who can't pay his debts. Titus counted, they've stolen from you six times, you've already paid twice. All you want to think about now are the paintings to be done. And sometimes about the paintings of the Great Gallery in the new Town Hall. Govert Flinck was chosen, elected by Joan Huydecoper, to do the twelve paintings for 1,000 florins each. He just had time to sketch out twelve drawings, twelve times he depicted the courage of the Batavians* and their rebellion against the Roman invader. Then he went to bed with a fever and was dead within two days. At forty-four. Your memories are sad. In your studio, Govert Flinck learnt to search the shadows; then he forgot everything in garlands of foliage and flowers. I believe in the judgment of God but I don't say so out loud.

The notary hands you the quill pen and the brown ink. He turns the last page of the contract round toward us. Everyone in the Guild of St Luke is hoping he'll be the one to get the commission for the paintings. You've counted twelve paintings, the painters able to do it, and those at the Town Hall who are still well disposed to your art. That was before our contract and your new freedom, before the thieves' anger, and I tell myself that you'll soon know if you're forgiven at the Town Hall, forgiven on Earth as (surely) you already are in Heaven.

You hand the pen to Titus. Our eyes meet, confidently. Titus holds the quill pen very near the top; it draws careful curves across the paper. Then he gives it back to you. You look at me. This is a solemn moment, your eyes say solemnly. And your whole face, your entire body smiles at me. The page slides towards me. At the bottom of the notary's dark lines, beneath the pretty curls of Titus van Rijn's signature, your finger comes to rest for a moment at the spot where I'm to sign for your freedom. I press the pen on the page. I scratch two crossing lines – a cross,

---

* Tacitus tells the story of the Batavians in his Histories. The narrative was developed in 1610 by two Dutch authors, Scriverius and Grotius, who emphasised the analogies between the patriotism of the first inhabitants of Holland (first century BC) and the patriotism of the Dutch in the 17th century.

my signature. The second line is too long; if our Saviour had been crucified on it, the wood beyond His nailed hands would have continued too far.

Then Rembrandt van Rijn traces the fine round letters of his name. He took on Himself our curse to deliver us; on my Cross, under my nose, I see Him. He was hanged from wood, for us He suffers, for us He dies. The two witnesses, Jacob Leeuw and the great curl that surrounds his name, then Frederik Hedelbergh who presses heavily with the pen when he brings it down towards him. The Saviour is no longer there. He is free, He has been raised again; and the cross marks the paper forever. The naked cross, drawn by Hendrickje Stoffels, the Lord's sheep, banished from His table. Eternal life gushes from the living water that He gives. Finally, the notary Nicolaes Listingh signs the minutes. Christ is no longer humiliated. He suffers no more. The Cross, made holy by His blood, resurrects the dead. The Cross is bare.

24th July 1663

Thus saith the Lord, choose thee: Either three years' famine; or three months to be destroyed before thy foes, while that the sword of thine enemies overtaketh thee; or else three days the sword of the Lord, even the pestilence, in the land . . .

David was quick to choose: 'Let me fall now into the hand of the Lord; for very great are his mercies: but let me not fall into the hand of man.

So the Lord sent pestilence upon Israel: and there fell of Israel seventy thousand men.

God's mercy is great, but the pestilence is the Devil's disease. It's the fault of the tailed comet that crossed the sky two moons ago. And of the rain and the flooded dykes, the fog and the locusts and toads that infest earth and water.

The first to get struck down by the Plague are always those who eat too much meat. Meat starts to smell rotten if it's left to get infected by the air, but it can also poison the body that digests it. If the body doesn't vomit it back up or doesn't cook it properly in its heat.

The first to fall sick are always those with too many worms inside them and those who fall prey to sorrow, fear or anger. Ephraim Bueno calls them the black humours. They rise when the moon's full. That's why the Plague always starts on a night there's a full moon. That's when it kills the most people.

And that's when it gets a hold, it takes over. The Plague takes over from life. Soon, everything gets forgotten, like life's never existed, like there's always been Plague in the city. Memories get wiped out by the smells and screams. That's why it's important to remember, so as not to die of the Plague without memory.

And when, day after day, the Plague goes on rotting life and people, you start to think it'll never go away. Except maybe when it's killed every living thing.

In the first days, with the first dead, I peeled four onions. Buried in the floor, in a corner where the tiling's cracked, they absorb the infections in the house. After ten days, they'll be all infected and I'll have to change them.

Between the contract and the Plague, for more than two years, all you did was paint. You were behind with your work, and you wanted more paintings; the contract and the new peace in your life helped. Before settling down to work all day in the tiny room you call your studio, you'd walk by the maze of canals in our district for an hour, where they go up and down from each of the Jordaan's bridges. You pass beautiful expressions, real faces you call them, monks, Christs, apostles. In a beggar's face, you met the old Greek poet. For a florin, some bread, a few herrings and three tankards of beer, he posed for you every day till nightfall.

Since we moved, Judith's stopped working for Rembrandt van Rijn's family, but she's not cleaning in any other house, either. She's offered her services in the kitchen of two merchants on the Keisersgracht. If it's not too late, she knocks at our door on her way home. She puts down her sponge soaked in vinegar, which she uses to protect her mouth and nose from the dangers in the air. She throws dice with Cornelia. She talks very low so as not to disturb anyone. Already more than 200 dead. The grandees are leaving town, they're the ones who leave the soonest, go the furthest and for the longest possible time; they go to the country which belongs to them. Where the foggy air is heavy with miasmas – that's what Ephraim Bueno says, Rembrandt believes him, and anyway, he doesn't want to leave his studio. What with disease and the melancholy of the country, I don't want to leave the city either. Wouldn't know where to go, how long for, where to find the money. We'll protect each other, the four of us will, I'm sure of it.

*   *   *

Every day the beggar climbed the stairs. Groaning at every step. He is Homer, Homer is alive. His eyes have lost their sparkle – he's seen too much. Words fall from his toothless mouth. His face is set in an expression of fear, maybe in a vision. His hands are poised in the air; they're telling a story. Seated by his side, staring wide-eyed at the lips and vision of the poet, the young scribe writes. War, love and the Trojan Horse – that's what men's lives are: a gift with poison in it, says Titus.

Sometimes Isaac Just came to see you. Mainly so he could see the portrait of Alexander the Great, and find out when you'd call it done, and when the stench of the hen's feather would be dry. Don Antonio Ruffo is a cultivated man of taste, and great patience too. It's six years since he paid half the 500 florins for the canvas, doesn't Rembrandt need money any more? Isaac Just completely understands that the bankruptcy and the move took time, he understands how much you love the Titus-Alexander portrait and your endless search for perfection as you make endless fresh starts; yes, he can see the beauty and pride of Alexander in the light of his shield and in the gold of the paste. But he'd like to come one day soon with its carrying case, when Rembrandt's signed the painting. He stands before Homer dictating to the young scribe, and says he's sure Antonio Ruffo will like it.

Judith says quicksilver in a filbert isn't enough to ward off this new Plague. She's waiting for a recipe. To make me laugh, she whispers, 'a witch's secret'. She also knows Alexander the Great's secret. The miasmas stick to a bewitched spider, and the air all round is made clean again. You draw a circle with unicorn powder and put the spider in the middle. Unicorn powder casts a spell and the spider stays in the circle. Alexander the Great spent a lot of gold on unicorn hunts, because they live in solitude in a desert at the tip of the East Indies.

Like these years when life was tough had taught you who your few real friends were. Kindness, that's what you sought each day, you saw kindness in the faces you passed in the Jordaan; in their eyes you saw tenderness, true generosity, their souls, you said.

People who really wanted to follow you with their kindness on the Rozengracht said they were happy to pose for Rembrandt van Rijn. I used to bring them cheese and beer.

'He looks like an apostle.' Your laugh is sad, no more and no less than before. You spread the colour thickly on the canvas. Their faces are sculpted by life and kindness as they sit before their writings, holding a quill or clasping their hands in prayer. You call them Simon, Bartholomew or Matthew. Titus murmurs angels' words to Matthew behind his back.

Lodewijck van Ludick used to visit; he often left with a painting, an apostle. It's because he's a merchant, but it's also because he's a friend. He stands back and looks at your paintings silently for a long time, then he goes close up, then stands back again. Then he says he's amazed, talks of his love for your art, his anger at fashionable taste. Business hasn't picked up; what with the new war against Portugal and the way the rich have grown too used to fear, he says, fear of losing their possessions. Fear like that drives out kindness, laughter, desire for beauty and morals. That was before the Plague.

Day and night at every house door, huge torches burn the Amsterdam air. They're burning the miasmas in the air. And in the shadowless streets their flames also denounce the Plague spreaders. They're the Devil's messengers. They make an unguent with the pus of buboes, then hide a knob of this poison in the palm of their hands, and grease the door knockers of houses they've marked out. They're thieves too and they pick out houses where they want the inhabitants' possessions and strike them down with Plague. Some steal from the rich, some from the poor; there are Plague spreaders on the Dam and in the Jordaan. They're the first to know when Plague strikes the marked house. Then they lurk close by, listening for the screams, especially at night. And, when the dying think nothing more can happen (they don't even think they're going to die when they're raving), as they lie on their beds in agony, the Plague spreaders go a-thieving. Mustn't get too far from the house or other thieves might get there first.

You're waiting with van Ludick and Isaac Just for the Town Hall's decision on the paintings for the Great Gallery. The Regents are taking their time. Each year, amid smiles and lies, the Regents cast their vote. It's like a trade in agreements that will hold until the following year, keeping some from power, and giving power to others. The paintings for the Great Gallery aren't the Regents' main business, but they can cause arguments and humiliate their enemies. I shake my head and you tell me again. Power's the most important thing, power and money. Only two commissions have been granted so far, only two painters chosen. Lodewijck says that Lievens and Jordaens don't upset people, that Lievens has found a way of pleasing everyone and also that he gives drawing lessons to Cornelis Witsen's son. It's not that I don't understand, but these tales about the Regents' power, they're all the same and very dull.

In front of the houses, torches are burning the Plague. Sometimes they burn the houses and the city as well. The buckets and ladders beside each door have been checked for everyone's sake, a few steps away from the water of the canal. Two or three times a week, with the first tongues of fire, the clappers set up their rattling to call everyone out, and you know there's trouble. Everyone comes running. Except those who can't any more.

Before Arent de Gelder arrived, Titus was your only pupil, in your studio he'd been your only assistant. He's known for a long time it's so that time doesn't steal a march on Rembrandt's painting. You were working so hard all the time, we weren't even aware of the smell any more. Before preparing the canvases and colours, Titus spent whole mornings cooking the rabbit's skin and bones in a *bain-marie* and the linseed and poppyseed oil over a naked flame with the garlic and hen's feather. We share our bedroom wall with our neighbour Andries, the potter, as well as the smells from our place and his, and one morning, he knocked at the door; he asked if he was going to have to lie down, sleep and wake up in the Devil's kitchen every day for the rest of his life. Even though he now has his goat in the back room and you can't tell our smells from the goat's, Rembrandt, Titus and I didn't dare say anything. Some people in the city believe that the stench of a goat gets rid of the Plague's miasmas, so there are a few goats in Amsterdam. If Andries is right, the miasmas that get into our house will be dispelled along with his own.

Ephraim Bueno and Abraham Francen come at supper time. Because they're friends. They've brought *koek* and molasses for dessert. They know on the Rozengracht they won't eat the *hutsepot* and stew with melon that used to bubble away for hours in the Breestraat kitchen.

It's because they're friends. Abraham lives in the Jordaan, but Ephraim has to come through the city and the Plague, holding against his face a big handkerchief soaked in red *oxycrate* mixed with rose water. After the fried turnips and Edam cheese, while the *koeks* are warming through on the hearth, he takes a pouch of golden tobacco out of his pocket and a few bleached brand-new pipes. He offers a pipe around, but Abraham and Titus don't smoke. Even during the Plague, no thanks. And Rembrandt has been painting so much, till nightfall, he already feels full of smoke. Unless that's the fumes of the neighbour's goat. He looks at his hands in front of him, stained with all different colours. He takes a quick sniff at them.

With a serious face, Rembrandt leans towards Ephraim. 'Never any lice, never any fleas. Maybe the Plague miasmas will also slide off the oils stuck to my skin.' But Ephraim's eyes follow the smoke he spits, it rises and hovers under the ceiling. He's not laughing. Not even a smile. He clenches his pipe in one corner of his mouth and speaks out of the other. Already over 500 dead from the Plague in Amsterdam.

Isaac Just has come with the porter. Rembrandt and Titus have rolled up the Alexander the Great canvas, long worked over, loved and dried. They've taken it outside, slowly rolled the painting, and put a piece of unused canvas round it to protect it. Rembrandt runs the ends of his fingers over it, same as every time a painting leaves the studio for the dealer's wall, stroking it with the fingers that painted it and brought it forth from nothing (nothing but a blank canvas, bladders of colours and the light in his head). Eyes closed. In prayer, wishing it a long life and the chance, perhaps, of seeing it again. But certain, too, he'll never go to Sicily.

And now they've rolled the unfinished painting of Homer. So that Ruffo can love Aristotle, Alexander and Homer and wish them a long meeting on his library walls. Five hundred florins each; plus the cost of the canvas and frame, the case and packing, the journey to Texel and on the ship, and the insurance of ten per cent of the price of the painting to Messina with insurance and change at Venice, all at the expense of the dealer. The porter has nailed down the case.

To get rid of the miasmas, you first have to disturb them in the still summer air. The air rings with the carillons and chimes of bells, shaking with the echo long after the ringing has stopped.

Maybe they heard the peal of bells, maybe they guessed they'd soon be free. Replete with sawdust in their tunnels (each in its own tunnel), the worms nibbled and regurgitated faster and faster. To get to the end. A little army in the darkness of the wood, but none of them knew, no worm ever hears orders.

The cart rolls over the city's bricks in the morning. The bell-ringer calls out, long and sad like the cry of an owl:

'Bring out your dead!' People hear him coming in the distance, especially those with a corpse, dead during the night, who have been watching for him from their window since dawn. They call back to him.

And so the bodies fall from upper-storey windows into the wagon of grey newly-dead bodies, bodies twisted like dead wood, bouncing off the other dead twisted wooden corpses of the night, heaped up, their arms and legs too long and awkward (the arms of the dead are always longer than those of the living). The Plague dead are nearly always naked. Because, before they die, they suffer terribly from fever, burning hot, their bodies parched with thirst; but it's also because they sweat so much they go raving mad, and don't know what they're doing any more. The slightest cloth or sheet makes their skin blaze with fire, and they can't bear it.

You recognised the apostle Paul in your own portrait, in the replacement mirror in the old ebony frame. His expression beneath his deeply lined and furrowed brow is clear, almost innocent. It says he lives equally well in abundance and in want but, under his white turban and threadbare cape that's seen too many winters, he's suffering. His hands are almost hidden, trying to keep warm, holding his Epistles. And his eyes are wide with astonishment that the suffering has to go on.

I'm afraid. The Plague is making life even more dangerous. Afraid for all of us, for you and your work, which will only end with you. The doctors know now. Abraham Francen is sure, the Plague dead have been dissected, yes, cut open and stinking, without the surgeon or his assistants catching the infection. Proof that you catch the Plague by standing next to someone breathing out who's sick with the Plague, but only the living breathe out. Yes, a dead person doesn't breathe, especially if they died of the Plague.

*   *   *

Arent de Gelder is sixteen with red eyes, and adolescent spots on his forehead, cheeks and chin. He takes a step forward. He's grown too quickly, he's too thin, he looks down at his clogs pitching forward and crackling through the light morning snow. The cold has swept a dusting of snow inside, but I can't shut the door, not before he's taken a second step.

He says 'Master' to Rembrandt, says it very quietly and his spots go red. The other pupils used to say the same word, but they smiled; maybe because Master Rembrandt was younger, less thick-set and heavy, maybe because he hadn't yet gone through all life's trials. In the evening, you say he's a great help but that he wants to please you too much and just copy.

So Titus asks if you've seen any other painting in his brush. He says, too, that Arent is welcome with his sweet disposition and that, now you've got an apprentice in the studio to save you time, he'll be able to travel for our art business (I always smile). Go on a barge to Delft, The Hague, Rotterdam. To buy and sell, especially to sell. And he'll suggest Rembrandt van Rijn's understanding of engraving to art lovers and print merchants.

I always wear the filbert of quicksilver round my neck; I'm hoping to get Judith's new recipe soon. God is just. And, because God is just, we all pray for eternal life. The first three Sundays of the Plague, we all got down on our knees on the freezing-cold stones in church, in our clothes of satin, silk or stuff, and we prayed fervently to God and his mercy, which is great. After three days of pestilence in Jerusalem and 70,000 deaths, the Lord beheld and he repented him of the evil. He said to the exterminating angel, 'Enough.'

Those who have been good will rise again for Life, those who have been wicked will rise for the Day of Judgment.

The Plague is killing the crowds. Once it's settled in the city, there's nothing but Plague, there are no more crowds. Behind our handkerchiefs or sponges reeking of vinegar and rose water, we all avoid meeting people. After the first weeks, preaching stops, church stops, and there's no more Exchange, market or city. In times of real Plague, nothing is sold, nothing is bought, everything carries miasmas, cloth, furs, fruit and vegetables, meat and fish, money and the air we share, everything is dangerous. The poor who don't die from the Plague die from their burning stomachs and famine. The rich who haven't left the city stay shut up the longest, surrounded by the stocks of provisions their money has bought.

Vegetables are forbidden on the Dam Square, the farmers sell their produce at the city gates. Everyone serves himself from wooden trestles, careful not to touch each other's hands. I won't buy cucumbers, radishes or black cherries – they carry disease. The merchant counts the coins in my hand with his eyes, I drop them one by one into a tumbler of vinegar. Under the eyes of the merchant, I count the change into the vinegar, coin by coin. The basket is always full and heavy, I walk in the other direction halfway across the city, with the sponge soaked in *oxycrate* before my nose.

Everyone hides from the miasmas behind his walls. There's no more city. No more school either, not even in Labyrinth Park where Cornelia was learning to read, write and count. Titus is teaching her now, he's better and quicker than the teacher.

Christian Huygens has invented the manometer. A manometer weighs air and gases. I ask if it can weigh miasmas, too. Abraham doesn't know.

The Plague doctor strides over the city's bricks, his face hidden in a sponge like a great red leprosy. You can see him coming by the white stick he holds out in front of him. Piteous voices call to him from infected houses. He goes through the same motions all Plague doctors do with their patients, the dying: he opens the buboes (it's quicker than nature) and brings out the poison from inside.

Between two houses, between two torches, he listens in the silence. I take another road, no one is sick in my house, and I get as far away as possible from the miasmas the Plague doctor carries from buboes to buboes.

You still love searching, always for life, for the same answers (you say) from the transparency of flesh. And the older the flesh and skin, the more you see through them. I even used to say to myself that painting old men would make you old quicker. You and your smile, getting sweeter and sadder all the time. Time that furrows, time that makes men fat and red and yellow: that's the weight your love of life carries. Van Ludick knows everything about Jacob Trip's fortune: it's in Swedish iron, and in the Polish saltpetre they turn into gunpowder, and it's in banks that lend to kings. There's no reckoning the Trips's fortune. And they never spend any of it.

One does not spend. That's what the tight-lips, the eyes like a knife, and Margaretha de Geer's* ruff say – stiff like a plate and bleached and out of fashion since the end of the 1630s.

The Trips sell gunpowder, but the woman wears the same ruffs as her youth, bought once for her whole life. She'll live her entire life half-strangled in that rigid double ruff of her youth. She's never wrong, that plate round her neck is the proof. Life's nothing but the moral of a story, learnt through life's laws since childhood. Her ruff is her morality: clean and white despite the passing years, hard as certainties.

And yet, life still beats beneath this yellow flesh that has lost the rosy hue of her inner blood. So close to the death which she's staring at straight in the face, to fight it off better. There's still life in Jacob Trip's face; behind your brush, he's paling with a new gentleness (the gentleness of doubt and fear); you won't finish his portrait until after he's dead. You can see death in Margaretha de Geer's sorrow, in her red hollow eyes that have sunk deeper from watching her husband's agony. But, most of

---

* When a woman was named independently of her husband, it was her maiden name that was used (thus Margaretha de Geer is the wife of Jacob Trip).

all, it's in the handkerchief in her right hand, proof that in her breast her heart beats still.

For nine days Cornelia, Rembrandt, Titus and I didn't see Judith, for nine days she didn't come to the Rozengracht. Her husband has died of the Plague. She didn't do what two neighbours on the Bloemgracht did, she didn't leave her house. She burned candles between herself and her husband, throwing into the flames rue, vine shoots and camphor. For three days she breathed the same air as him, but always through good vinegar. She didn't catch the Plague. Every hour, day and night, she helped him drink, supporting his head and parting his lips. Not the last hours. She stopped going into his room till silence fell. Couldn't bear the grinding teeth, the stench and the noise.

Judith stayed. If a woman abandons her husband who's caught the buboes, the neighbours nail down the door and shutters of his house till it's quiet. The man dies alone, abandoned and imprisoned. After four days of terror, thirst and madness. If a husband leaves his wife, or a mother or father deserts their sick child, the door and shutters are always nailed down on the miasmas inside. In other cities, the whole family of a sick person (even those who haven't yet caught the Plague) gets shut up in their coffin-house. The neighbours listen and, at the first real silence, they open the door and shutters. Then there's no time to waste; Plague-dead bodies have got more worms than other bodies and they change more quickly.

Ephraim has given us some good-quality vinegar. Rembrandt rinses his mouth out every morning with *oxycrate* mixed with rose water, half and half. It wards off the Plague, and it's good against toothache and sore gums.

From her window Judith called the bell-ringer. The dead body that had been her husband fell on top of the other husbands in the cart. She burned the straw of his bed and the skins. She most probably burned rats in the straw as well, live and dead ones. Rats are like men, more of them die in time of Plague.

Then the fumigator came. Though Judith hadn't called him. There are Plague trades: the fumigators follow at a distance behind the Plague doctors, who follow behind the notaries. The fumigator can tell from a long way off which house will soon need fumigating, and he comes along behind the white stick. He has too much work in time of Plague; and if he doesn't die from the danger of his trade, he doesn't have enough work when the Plague's over. He opens up the house of the Plague-dead, he airs, he shakes, he burns, he washes the walls with vinegar, and anoints the house with pungent herbs, camphor and secret potions.

In her nightmares, Judith waited a few more nights. Her fingers searched over her body, fluttering over the inside of her thighs, under her arms, on her neck and behind her ears, quivering at the places where God's arrows always strike. Then she rubbed her body, her face and the inside of her mouth with vinegar. I ask if she wanted to find the buboes and follow her husband onto the cart, so as not to be left alone. Her eyes grow red, she looks down.

Don Antonio Ruffo has received the case and canvases. He's written to Giovanni Vallembrot, the Italian consul in Amsterdam. The consul made a Dutch translation for Isaac Just, telling him to go and complain to Rembrandt van Rijn. The merchant defends the man of money and power against the artist. Rembrandt's voice, Isaac Just's answer, Rembrandt more and more convinced, Isaac Just repeats, louder and louder. Don Ruffo has discovered that the Alexander the Great portrait was painted on a canvas with three other pieces sewn on.

'He's not discovered anything,' answers Rembrandt. 'I wasn't trying to hide anything.'

Don Ruffo thinks and writes that the painting on the seams will splinter and come away from the canvas.

'You won't find better animal-skin glue or better oils any-where outside Rembrandt van Rijn's studio. My paintings will never crack, they'll live for centuries.'

Ruffo already likes the half-painted portrait of Homer, the flesh and skin that have already lived half a life. He understands that, with the Homer painting, Rembrandt is making up for the faults in the Alexander portrait; and that he doesn't want to offend or lose his collector, a cultivated man of taste.

Don Ruffo will return the two paintings to Rembrandt. For the Alexander painting, the painter is to repair as necessary and repaint it. Or else send his money back, the 250 florins already paid. And the Homer dictating to a scribe – he wants this one, but not for 500 florins, no, for half that.

The Plague makes the sick mad, it makes the mad dangerous. I don't trust the person coming towards me in the distance, beside the same canal. People with buboes but no fever yet go about the city and hate God and the living. They throw their arms around passers-by, men and women alike, pressing their lips to them, rubbing a fresh bubo against the skin of those God wanted to spare. The bodies fight and writhe amid shrieks like slaughtered pigs (especially when the first bubo has appeared in an armpit or on the neck). The sick and insane breathe their rotten breath, push their infected tongue into all the openings where it can make the Devil's grimace. They pick on people at random, who are then cast into the pit a few days after themselves.

It wasn't the Plague yet, but the miasmas had already set in. They drive men mad before they attack and burn the body. He didn't have any buboes, but Antonio Ruffo had the plague of power; it had travelled in his letter all the way from Messina in Sicily to Amsterdam.

The house walls shook, the potter's hands shook at his wheel, everyone on the Rozengracht heard the lion roaring; his blood was up. You reply speedily without discussion, Isaac Just is hard put to erase the anger from your words. Oh, yes, really very

surprised, and if the painting is held in a good light, no one will
see the additions stitched in, and I can paint another Alexander,
at your own risk and at your expense, and 500 florins, and the
same for Homer, Your Honour, I await your reply. Don Ruffo
read, he, too, heard your anger. He understands that the artist
has the right, everything is permitted him. Some things are vital
to his art, like additional pieces of canvas. Yes, Don Ruffo likes
the Alexander, he'll put it in his library in a good light. And
the half-finished Homer portrait will travel again, from south
to north. With time and the 500 florins you asked for, you'll
finish the painting.

You have to kill the cats and dogs as soon as you see them. All
cats and dogs in the city off the leash and without a master.

Antonio Ruffo has brought on a black humour in your head.
I tell myself that time is precious, and that God shouldn't let
wealthy men steal time from artists. An artist doesn't only
work for those who live at the same time as him; what he
gives people is worth more than the time of his little life on our
vast Earth, more than all the money a man of wealth amasses
in his time.

Ruffo's letter had made the black humours rise in me too.
But I'm only thirty-four and I can bear it. It's for you, my
love, that I'm suffering. In six years you'll be sixty-three. Seven
times nine, sixty-three the climacteric age. It's a perilous year,
everyone knows that, and everyone's afraid of it. Anyone who
gets past the climacteric age will live for a long time.

I screamed. For the first time in fourteen years, Titus heard
me scream. It was fear. It's not their teeth or their wild eyes,
it's their fur where things can hide. No, Titus is not to bring
in every cat and dog off the leash from the city streets. It's
them or me. No, I won't see those I love die; no, I won't die
myself to save furry animals. Or else we'll leave, Cornelia and
I, shrink into the sunset to the end of the canal, we'll run away

from the cats and dogs with their fur full of the miasmas of the Plague.

Rembrandt laid his hand on his son's shoulder, they took a few steps outside. When I left the bedroom, the furry animals had gone from the back room. Titus too. Your arms enfolded me and held me to you. Your sigh smells of vinegar, all of us, we all smell of Plague vinegar. Titus came home before nightfall.

Ephraim never drinks the city's water and advises against it. The miasmas sink into it, but they don't die. They go on killing the rats in the depths of the canals. Between two pipes of smoke, he only drinks beer. Between two tankards of good warm red beer, Abraham says that the Plague kills alcohol drinkers (and everyone alive drinks alcohol) and alcohol will kill them if the Plague doesn't. But Ephraim's not laughing. He stares into the distance at the torchlight dancing against Amsterdam's starless sky. Already more than 1,000 dead.

Men are stealing your time, the Plague steals the air and light. And I'm powerless to help. Thinking up meals to cook each day, cleaning the house, listening to Titus, who's watching the pretty girls, making Cornelia laugh and making sure you hear and, each day, kissing you. In my arms, on my breasts, I've got to hide you from a world that's lost its kindness and its values. I want each kiss to tell you of my happiness next to you, fully formed words, my mouth ever wider to engulf you.

No surprise, just a sigh of delight. The familiar flesh, the same heat, that's where the surprise is. In our mounting desire. Like you were still searching in spite of so many years, burning in me, my love, like a long cry. For so long my only man, yes, I come to meet you. Not so quick. And our eyes are always waiting for each other, always the same surprise, there, now in the same light.

Rats don't scream, that's why they die in clusters, tightly packed together. In the country, city men think they've escaped the Plague, but they always take it with them, it always catches up with them. No one left to help them drink, no one to hold their hand, close their eyes, tie a cloth round their face and smother before God their shrieking teeth. No one left to make their coffins and bury them.

Judith's brought a present for the family; there's a smile in the depths of her red eyes. Four little cloth bags to carry over the place where life throbs in our breasts. Surer than the filbert of quicksilver, not as rare as the diamond, they ward off the Plague. And, if you're too late, they'll cure it. Not the cloth of the bags, but the balls Judith has put in the bottom.

It's a witch's secret. Catch a fat toad, in its prime, the fatter the better. Tie it by its hind legs with a string and hang it in front of a low fire. Place a waxed dish beneath its mouth; before it dies, the toad vomits little worms, green flies and earth. Dry the dead toad's body over the low fire, until it turns to powder. Press hard with both hands and mix the powder and vomit with the melted wax. Then rub the mixture between two fingers to make little balls. Not difficult to ward off the Plague. Judith cried. Seeing her tears, I cried, too.

Before the Plague, for our art business, Titus used to visit the studios of city painters. Not the ones who paint for the Regents, no, but those who work beside their wife and children, in interior courtyards or in their shadowy houses. They look about them with love, these painters, and they know what it is to have difficulties. Titus can only tell us what he saw in the paintings, he can't buy them. In times like these with trade so bad, who'd want to buy these paintings of everyday life? Like Gabriel Metsu's little boy, whom he saw just the other side of Lauriergracht, with burning eyes, laid low with fever on his mother's knee, or the little girl he saw at Pieter de Hoogh's, almost ugly, just about to leave the shadowy house to go and play *kolf** in the sun. No, life at the moment isn't good for

---

* Dutch *kolf* was a precursor of golf.

loving artists, for artists who aren't painting for money and glory as short-lived as their own lives. That's what Titus says, weary with sorrow and vinegar.

I'm de-lousing Cornelia's head on my lap in front of the peat fire. One by one, lice and nits get drowned in molasses. A man eaten alive by his lice, life is perilous. Long deathly screams pierce the night over the lapping waters of the black canals. At each scream, the neighbour's goat butts with its horns, and the walls and flames tremble. The flames cast pink haloes round Cornelia's hair, caressing her forehead, the down on her young cheeks and her long calm lashes. I'm so afraid. So afraid when I look at the life from my belly; I've given her death too. I don't know why any more. What's the point? I ask myself, what's the point of so much suffering, what's the good of it?

I believe in God, the Father Almighty, I believe in Jesus Christ, His only son our Lord, I believe in the Holy Ghost, the Forgiveness of sin, I'm afraid for my child, my little one, in this world of Plague. Have mercy, Lord (face down on the broken tiles), Thy will be done, the resurrection of the flesh, the eternal life, amen. May I not be one of those mothers who see their child's little coffin lowered into the earth and whose bellies bleed to the end of their days. Ten times as many as die in war, that's how many the Plague has killed; and it'll go on killing as long as there are men. As long as our little lives encounter it.

A messenger from the Town Hall knocked at the door. You were expected the next day at ten o'clock in the Regents' hall. The new Great Regent, Vlooswijck, finally wanted to give you one of the twelve commissions for the Great Gallery. Your painting's to be the first in the history of the first inhabitants of Holland, the Batavians – twelve paintings showing their revolt against the invader. Each Regent defends his chosen painter; getting a commission accepted is a way of proving his power to the others. You never sought to please Joan Huydecoper, you never bowed to him, you didn't turn up at the St Joris Doelen evening in honour of St Luke. He was pushed out of power by the very last vote. And he's ill in bed. But the new Great Regent wants you. I understand what you tell me. All these stories of power, petty triumphs and great treachery, they're very dull.

I couldn't help it, I just screamed. Our house! I saw him, the man in black, he planted the Plague on our door. I put down my basket loaded with cabbages and scream after him again as he runs away. Andries caught him, Andries's goat butted him against the wall between his two horns. Rembrandt and Titus come up to us. Cornelia's behind them, frightened, and she's not got her sponge to breathe through outdoors; go home! I shout at her straight away to go back into the house. The man says again that he stopped outside our door because he had a headache. Everybody knows Plague-spreaders lie. But if some of what he says is true, he's a Plague-spreader who's got the Plague. I step back. The man's eyes are rolling in terror. He must see terror in my eyes too. The municipal guards will question him and he'll confess, they always confess by the end of the night. He'll have both hands cut off, then he'll be hanged. And if he doesn't confess, he'll be hanged with his hands. He won't go Plague-spreading any more.

In the Regents' great hall, respectfully bowing your head, you said 'thank you'. It'll be your biggest painting, bigger even than *The Company of Frans Banning Cocq*. Yes, you can paint it in a Town Hall room, yes, a great empty hall with a key, and no one will come in. And yes, there will be good light. (They answer you hurriedly.) But make sure you've got the door shut so those dreadful oily odours from your painting don't poison the entire Great Gallery with their stink. You didn't hear their offensive words, best not to answer. The men of power pretend they've agreed, it's a game they play. A few words, a mere detail can remind them that this game is their war. My love, in their war of power and petty triumphs, you're a mere detail.

      *   *   *

Along the canals at sunset, we don't say 'good night' to each other any more; just a nod and a hoarse whisper, 'good resurrection'.

You were forgiven at last by the other living beings. Forgiven on Earth as you surely already were in Heaven. Bankruptcy, the contract, debts that will never be repaid. Forgiven and offended on the same day, I think quietly. Men never change, Batavians and Regents alike. But long after their delicate noses have ceased to smell things, not even their own smells (an eternity after their bones and dust have disappeared), long after the stink of oils has dried, the light of your painting will still be enlightening new eyes. I don't always say what I think out loud.

You've asked for 1,000 florins, not less than your pupil Govert Flinck, who painted twelve commissions for that price. You said it very quickly, so no one could argue and so everyone would forgive you the right price in advance. You didn't say aloud that with Titus and Arent's help your work would progress so well and so quickly (spending months painting nothing but Claudius Civilis), that the Regents of the Town Hall will love it and ask you, beg you, please, to paint other paintings. One thousand florins, they've heard your demand; their honour doesn't need a contract, their word's enough. And even their silence. On the 25th of this month of October, in a quickly sketched little drawing, you saw the great painting. On the 26th, Regent Huydecoper died in his bed.

The Plague-ridden air is stifling, and the windows are open onto the night – those that haven't got their shutters nailed down. Under the summer stars, among the gin-sodden songs, shrieks fill the night, the shrieks of the dying and the living. Sometimes you can't tell them apart. Good resurrection. While there's life until morning, let's take its pleasures. Gin and love. One day the Plague will go away; but no one believes it any more and no one knows why. Some months later, the Plague babies are born into a world of clean air. Rings of dancing children to replace the ones that have fallen down. Even women who have always been sterile give birth. Twins or triplets.

Two little glasses of gin clink together, yes, the men on Earth have forgiven you. To thank them, you're going to paint a great and beautiful painting, the first one to be seen at the top of the stairs to the Great Gallery. Everyone will come and marvel at it, the whole city, the men of power, the rich and the poor. Another glass of gin with your friend van Ludick; you promise him a quarter of the payment for Claudius Civilis (no less than Govert Flinck, no, no less than him) to pay him back what you owe on the guarantee. The money will be welcome, the shadow of bankruptcy hangs over honest van Ludick. He says that, one day soon, he may be obliged to sell his house.

The Batavians love God. In their long hair, the men find the strength and courage of Samson with which to fight for their freedom; the women are always chaste before marriage; men and women never change, the Batavians are Dutch.

Headaches and nausea.

Notaries, both false and true, cross the city behind their handkerchiefs. They follow at a distance behind the Plague doctor. When they hear a great scream as the doctor cuts open the bubo, when the doctor has gone, they knock at the doors. Anyone who hasn't made their will against the day they're taken by the Plague, anyone whose heirs died a few days before or who, in the despair of their diseased soul sees their immediate circle as other than it really is (and it's true, friends and family are often no longer there), these people pay part of their inheritance to the notary of their last will and testament.

Perspiration, a little wave of fever.

All day till nightfall, you painted the portrait of Jacob Trip, who had just died in the Triphuis, the great Trip family mansion on the Kloveniersburgwal. You'd glazed his wife's portrait, and now you were finishing the painting of the dead man from memory. Neighbour Andries has seen my white sweat, but I didn't listen, too afraid of the fever, no, I won't go to bed. The sun on my fever as I cross the city will be the last effort. The neighbour held my arm till I got to the office of the notary Nicolaes Listingh on the Herengracht. Why change to another notary when you already know one?

I vomit in pain. Go to bed.

Nicolaes Listingh has seen me infirm of body, but able to walk and in possession of my mind, my memory and my words. My one possession, my share in the art business that provides Rembrandt van Rijn with board and lodging, not to be yielded to the laws of the Chamber of Orphans. My child, Cornelia van Rijn, to inherit what can be transported but also what cannot. That was two years before the Plague, but a notary can see further than God's mercy. And, if my child should die without an heir, have mercy, Lord, may Thy will be done, my little one, her possessions to become those of Titus van Rijn, her half-brother. The aforementioned child's guardian will be her father, who will have every power, even to sell. And now you're protected by other laws against laws, my love. Nicolaes Listingh's words continue to roll around . . . if the child should die before the testatrix and without issue. The fever's rising. I sign. I like signing, I draw two straight lines. A bare cross, Christ is risen.

The bed never shook like this before. I can hear the fire-clapper, it echoes in my head. It's my teeth chattering.

The Romans lost battles. Then, thanks to a traitor, they invaded our beautiful country. Led by Claudius Civilis, the Batavians rebelled and put the invaders to rout. Abraham said that Civilis had won the battle. But Ephraim thinks that Civilis had made a treaty with the Romans; mustn't forget (his name proves it, he said) that he had spent twenty-five years fighting for the Roman army. Abraham says, no weakness casts its shadow over Claudius Civilis; the Batavians are a people brave and free, the Batavians are Dutch. Your painting will be the first of the twelve, it'll show the moment the conspirators took their oath.

Sleep a bit more. I can see your kindness hovering over me, and your furrowed brow, your concern. And your hand approaching, cool on my forehead. I love you, I smile at you. My eyelids are heavy, my body is heavy, my arm's too heavy to lift the frozen shift sticking to my skin.

Put the invader to rout, yes, the swords swore they would. The wine kindles courage, the Batavians know that. They have drunk the wine of courage from a great goblet, the blood of Christ. Other men sit by the walls and watch. But there are twelve of them round the table, twelve turning towards Claudius Civilis. Civilis comes of royal lineage, the crown on his head makes him taller still. He's taller, stronger than all of them. His shut eyelid hides battles and fire and the blood from his gouged-out eye inside his head. He has seen death close up, in his eye. Stiff as a stone statue, he faces the twelve by turn; with one eye he sees their oaths, face to face. But why does the eye look out of the painting? Why is it already looking at deaths and mourning beyond this moment and the promised victory? Why is it looking at me?

Cornelia comes through the light. Her white teeth laugh, then disappear in shadow. A tiny figure against the wall. She stops laughing and shakes her head, and Titus pulls at her hand, now she cries out; Titus-Samson-Civilis, with splendid fiery hair, puts his arms about his half-sister. He bends his head over her. They cling together, rock one another, share the same grief. I turn my head to the left, and with one eye I see you upside down, my love.

Sleep a bit more, till tomorrow morning. Your lips whisper the words, they tell me it's already tomorrow. It's morning.

The Plague-spreader.
It was the Plague-spreader. I believe in God the Father Almighty, maker of Heaven and Earth; And in Jesus Christ his only Son our Lord who was conceived by the Holy Ghost, born of the Virgin Mary, suffered under Pontius Pilate, was crucified, dead, and buried; He descended into Hell; The third day he rose again from the dead, He ascended into Heaven; From thence he shall come to judge the quick and the dead. I'm thirsty.

In the dark. I open and close my eyes. I think I'm opening and closing my eyes. I think. It was the Plague-spreader. And it's me.
I couldn't sleep any more if I wanted to, the ringing in my ears is getting louder and louder. The flames sweep up like a great wave, and the fire in me slowly rises. The Lake of Fire, it's the second death. Why, Lord? My teeth are chattering, the bed shakes, the walls, the whole house, the neighbour's goat. And, you, my love, your shoulders are shaking, you're shaking against Titus's shoulders. Inside, the fire burns what it wants, outside thousands of needles are piercing my skin.
Then the train of burnt foam meets the sea, slowly the sea draws back. A little breeze gets up among the leaves fluttering on their stems, a vast weariness blows over me. I've stopped shivering, I've stopped moving, I sink into my bed. Great peace. Waiting.
Candles are burning the miasmas in the air between me and those I love. I see your grief, that's what's pulling your eyes down, hollowing out your face and making bumps on it, forgive me. The burning air of my body has dried my tongue, but

words are still chattering on. Vinegar. Yes, the red handkerchief between you and me. Vinegar is the smell of life.

I spread my arms and legs, in the pit of my sweat, I've felt the first shiver. Between each fire, during the gentle breeze, I know now that the wave of flames will return.

I did the best I could. Always, all these years beside you. I did what I knew with unguents, powders, quicksilver and onions to protect us all. I washed the door in hot vinegar after it had been soiled by the Plague-spreader. The sins of men have raised God's anger, in anger God is quick to choose. But to leave you, not to see you before Judgment Day, I'm missing you already. It's not death or pain, it's love.

I saw my scream in your eyes before I heard it. It's not the fever, not the pins, it's the burning embers in my flesh. It's a bubo. I can't turn my head now, I can hear terror beating in the blood in my neck. The tips of my fingers tell me it's a cherry, already a plum, it's growing. Inside my thigh, as well. Swollen with black blood, it's hot, rotten.

Abraham the apothecary and Doctor Ephraim, thank you, friends, for being here. But don't look like sad friends, make dying easier for me. The bitter taste in my mouth is making me vomit, my body's poison keeps rising to my mouth.

The Lord will make them rot when they're all still standing on their feet. Their eyes will rot in their sockets, and their tongue rot in their mouth.

The cupping glasses, yes, I say, I want them to make the buboes bigger, make them ripe. I'm naked before you all, but I'm not ashamed. Perhaps because I'm not that other firm body of Bathsheba; yellow and flabby today. Infected by fat black leeches, and covered in red and black carbuncles like fleas. Across the room, through the thick fog, Judith's face appears for an instant and smiles at me. Don't let me rave, or only when I'm in pain, so as to forget. The cupping glasses burn, pull, tickle too. But at the same time, in the pit of my stomach, the pain gathers, ready to burst; my belly's being gouged out, arms and legs huddle round it.

* * *

My eyes are growing blind in the light. The white cloth is like a mirror that swallows up the light. The watching faces round Civilis are engulfed in flames, the bright blades of their swords cross on their oath. They hadn't yet gone into battle, but they were already drunk or solemn, already they'd drunk their victory.

Thirst.

My nine-year-old child is a tiny thing beside her father. Her mother's death will have taught her about the Plague, but the Plague isn't life. Nine years old. Thank you for these bubbles of beer that scratch my throat and tongue. Nine times seven, sixty-three. The climacteric year, but also the numbers of this year. So it's me that God's numbers were threatening. My ears are ringing, but Ephraim's voice is clear: 'Too early to cut them, the buboes aren't big enough.'

My voice is hoarse and drowning. Don't let me die full of poison, worms and smells.
   Fever grips my throat: 'Rembrandt, yes, listen to me, nearer, yes, but not too near. I, too, think that all the oils that have got into your skin will save you from the Plague, but life in this room is dangerous. Burn some thyme in the candle flames, too, and rue, vine shoots and camphor, anything that will hide your nose from my stinking body.'
   I hope your memories smell better than this perspiring death. Our sweat stuck to the damp sheets, the end was near; you didn't have to tell me, not even in a whisper, I already knew. Each night since the first night of summer, clasped in your arms between your thighs, I perspired under you, on top of you, I perspired whichever way we were. So as to forget the Plague. If the preachers are right and mating from the rear like beasts is a sin, then this last month we've sinned each night like it was the last, the last sin before the Plague in the morning.

Good resurrection. As I waited for your surprise, as I heard your lion's cry that would've woken the goat next door, each time I said to myself that it was the last, and that one night life would stop, you in me, me crushed beneath you.

Vomited again.

Sometimes you used to work till you fell asleep. The yellow, red and white paint marks on your great gold shirt clashed like the conspirators' swords. The next morning, I'd cross the city and the Dam with Cornelia to bring you, Titus and Arent your daily beer, herring, cheese and bread.

Mustn't die without remembering. That was a year before the Plague, outside the Town Hall, when the grandees' daughters in their pretty colourful satin hadn't yet left the city. They hadn't yet seen death behind life, they cast secret glances at one another, laughing between the mother-of-pearl drops at their ears.

Cornelia was hopping over the black-and-white tiles of the Great Gallery on one foot. She looked Claudius Civilis straight in his one eye. Then she slowly turned her head to the left. But the eye didn't leave her.

I'm hungry in my belly, but my throat contracts at the thought. And you're holding the *susenol*,* certain I'm hungry, certain it'll do me good. The plate comes closer to my nose, I've got to turn my head away quickly so as not to vomit.

It took the worms fourteen years to do their work. They're taking longer and longer to digest the sawdust.

I don't know what's me any more, inside and out. The water in my swollen belly, sweat everywhere, my body throwing up the poison in it from every opening. We were what you are, you

---

* *Susenol* was a breakfast food, eaten particularly in the country. It was thought of more as an energising remedy than as a dish, consisting of beer with eggs beaten into it.

will be what we are. Have mercy. Don't let the little worms in my head kill me from madness.

Judith has come into the room carrying three chickens. Chickens from the Indies. Rembrandt, my love, you shake your head; Judith speaks less quietly than usual, not because she wants to disturb anyone, but because she's sure. I whisper that, yes, I can bear it, that the doctors' cupping glasses haven't done it, that Judith has friends who are witches, that it's well known that chickens from the Indies can raise buboes.

Even if the poison kills them. That's why you need several of them. It was the last day of the last glaze before the varnish; I know that peace on your face, when the painting resembles your vision, when, after a long search, your brush has taken you further. Three or four grains of salt in the chicken's back end. Immediately, it opens wide and closes again. When it's shut tight, it scratches. Judith holds its body in one hand, the head in the other. With the same hand, she hides its eyes and closes its beak. A Regent would knock at the door, no reply, he'd go in. Judith places the chicken's backside on my armpit, over the bubo. He'd see the empty room, the rows of pots and bladders of paint, he'd see the great painting on the wall. He'd smell the stench. Against the black pain, the heat of the chicken's backside, burning with the salt, is soothing for a moment. Better than the glass of the cupping glasses, the hot breath from its belly draws the poison. Plague and death completely sucked into its backside. It shakes its head, wanting to cry out like me. The Regent will call others, they'll gaze admiringly together. In a day or two, they'll send a messenger to the Rozengracht to summon you; or else, without waiting any longer, they'll come themselves to thank and congratulate Rembrandt van Rijn.

When I was a little girl, I used to make my teeth chatter; it sounded like a grinning skull. My mother thought I had a fever, sat me on her knee, told me stories about Spanish tortures, the old man who drank his own blood as it flowed from his neck.

She told her stories, I chattered my teeth, but my bed never shook like now. Thirst.

Rembrandt van Rijn, my husband for life, two years ago you sold the little tomb, where Saskia's been vanishing into dust for twenty-one years, to Pieter van Gerven, the Oude Kerk gravedigger. With the money, you bought a new plot in the Westerkerk, nearer to the Rozengracht. Had you foreseen this Plague?

Through the vinegar, Judith smiles, red-eyed. She wants to say everything, she thinks I'm afraid. She doesn't know that pain and madness kill fear. Now the chickens have raised the bubo, bring it to maturation with the poultice. Take out the centre of an onion and fill it with theriac. Bake it in the ashes. Crush it with pork fat, mustard seed, a pinch of pigeon droppings and lodestone. Place on the bubo and keep it carefully covered; tomorrow, they'll make the incision.

Thirst. All night my body dry-retched. When the wind dies down, I gaze into the candlelight and wait. In the distance, I can hear the shivers of the first foam.

Ten days later, the Regents' silence became unbearable. Perhaps they didn't like it. Impossible, the wounded lion kept saying, pacing his cage. How could they, the Regents? The Regents are all-powerful, even over their own cowardice.

Van Ludick has come hastily to the Rozengracht from the Dam to the Jordaan. He sits down. Sadly, he smiles to say 'no thank you, no gin tonight'. His questions have met with no reply. Nothing has been said, nothing true, nothing transparent, just uncertainty. Cornelis Witsen is Regent again. Does he bear Rembrandt a grudge? He was the one who had Rembrandt's house withdrawn from the Chamber of Orphans, and Cornelis Witsen had the Breestraat house sold. He's not a man to waste his money, and he alone has been repaid his 4,000 florins (and his right to preferential treatment). The Regent upholds the values of money and power. The man who uses the law to avoid repaying his debts will never be forgiven. Even if those who judge him today have stolen from him, they were so sure they'd killed him, him and his stinking painting, him and his shadows.

The blade of Ephraim Bueno's lancet glitters in the light.

And then, one Regent doesn't abuse another Regent who's been pushed out of power at the Town Hall on account of a vote. He insults the painter chosen by his enemy in power. Petty stories of petty lives. That night, a bitter taste rose to my mouth, like I'd already caught the Plague. I call lives 'petty' when they've lost their souls, the ones that will burn in the Lake of Fire.

I shan't be damned, no I shan't know the eternal inferno. Only the lancet in this abscess.

The great banquet of Claudius Civilis has been taken down from the Town Hall wall, rolled up inside out (the painting hidden inside, splintering down the middle) and returned to the painter, Rembrandt van Rijn of the Rozengracht. No payment, no letter. Just a few words one of the three porters passed on to him. I remember what they were: 'the painter to repaint real people in real colours, not that man who looks at life out of only one eye'.

I still see, I still hear; if I'm still alive after my flesh has been pierced, it'll be because Ephraim has made a good cut in the shape of a crescent moon. Through the haze of vinegar, you're taking heart. Yes, the black infection is leaving the sick body. Another tankard of warm beer against my mouth, set rigid by chattering teeth. Another few bubbles on my thirsty black tongue. Before the cauterising flame.

If I can still remember after that, perhaps I shan't die, not tonight. One gin-soaked evening, you wanted to unroll the great painting. For the first time, you wanted to see the conspirators' supper again, the messiah Civilis and his apostles, and you wanted to find the traitor and denounce him. That's what you said. You kept saying that you'd aided the plots of the Town Hall's cowards, who didn't even have a single eye to look at your painting. The house was small, the front room too small for the great painting. So, on the great roll, on the back of the rolled-up painting, you slashed the traitors and conspirators with your knife, slashed the cowards and the blind men. With words, with time and kisses, Titus and I guided you to bed. Then, in the pink light of dawn, Titus unrolled the painting on the bricks outside. You'd taken your revenge with those knife slashes. They'd cut through the background, they'd sunk in, ripped the area round the table. They were all round the conspirators, but they'd not made a single hole in the conspirators themselves. Not one.

There's no air left to breathe, the cauterising flame sucks it all up. Only my cries to swallow. The living know that they shall die, but the dead know not any thing. I'm falling into a bottomless pit, I claw at the sheet with my long nails. The jaws of the dragon of the Apocalypse, the fiery jaws of the dragon's seven heads are devouring me. Will You work a miracle for the dead? Will the departed rise up to worship You?

We'll be together again, forever. I know we will. But before, I'll miss you, I miss you already. I'm still not afraid. I know God's mercy is great. Rembrandt, Cornelia, Titus, it's not one of you on this bed before me. Thank you, Lord, it's not I who am suffering as I watch one of them leaving my life and my sorrow.

Only men attend burials. This will be my first funeral.

The insult will be even greater. The Regents are going to get Jurriaen Ovens to paint the first painting of the Revolt of the Batavians after Govert Flinck's drawing. In four days. For 48 florins. I wait for the first shiver. I can hear it shuddering already.

Between the Batavians and the resurrection, our lives are so weightless. I've learned to stand back during these years beside you, and to feel pleasure or pain as further away instead of right inside me. Yes, already I've broken away, from my life and my death. But not from the pain beating in the colour of your face leaning over me upside down. Nor from my child, whom I won't see grow up, my flesh and blood, and her laugh.

'Abraham, dear Abraham Francen, yes, come closer, but not too close, keep the flame between us. Asking you to help Rembrandt. You and your kindness, will you be Cornelia's guardian? You'll always know what's best, and never against her father, but thanks to you, without the laws of the Chamber of Orphans.' Dear Abraham, thank you. You lower your eyes several times to reply, to hide your tears too.

Pain gathers in the pit of my stomach, bursts out, courses through my splayed-out body, my arms, my legs are too long. The Communion of Saints; the Forgiveness of sins; the Resurrection of the body, and the life everlasting: it's a flood that's torturing and shaking me.

Rembrandt, Cornelia, Titus, your beloved faces are slipping away. So it's easier to leave you, so my sorrow's blunted and lets go of me. My hands close over the sheet, then slip off. My breath still comes in a hoarse whisper. But in the shaking bed I feel lighter. I know the soul leaves the body and rises after death. On His right the sheep and on His left the goats. Those on His left will go to eternal punishment, but the just will go to eternal life. It's a bottomless pit, I'm afraid, Rembrandt's whore is afraid.

They'll always be there, the grandees and Regents with their quick profits and their lies. And, when they've gone, their children, still the same petty lives stewing in the same money and the same power. But Rembrandt will always be there. God will always choose one.

Rembrandt, thank you, I haven't said it often enough. I've never dreamt of another life since I've been with you. Life began in your arms. I was born to another life, in your eyes, fourteen years ago on the Breestraat. You taught me beauty and goodness, and even death.

I shall have lived for you, for our child, my love, and for all that's left behind. Thanks to your brushes and colours, my life shall continue through the eyes of the living for a long time to come. Night is in the room, but it's pierced by a silver ray. The moon is full, I can hear it. The Plague kills most when it's a full moon.

After this, Jesus knowing that all things were now accomplished, that the scripture might be fulfilled, saith, I thirst. When Jesus had received the vinegar from the sponge on a stick, he said, It is finished: and he bowed his head, and gave up the ghost.

Come, ye blessed children of my Father, receive the kingdom prepared for you from the beginning of the world. The bed is drying around me. Or perhaps I'm already rising above my sweat.

I don't know if it's the poison rising in my head. My mother used to say that at the gates of eternity life still throbs, memories grow. She didn't say you could also see the afterlife. Two fingers close my eyelids over my eyes, two fingers smelling of good poppyseed oil. Judith is already veiling the mirrors and turning the paintings against the wall.* No, don't cry, you don't know, but I can still see you. My child, my pretty one, yes, Titus, take her out of the room, away from death and ugliness.

Rembrandt slips a cloth under my chin and ties it over my hair; my upper and lower teeth meet for the last time. Thank you, my love, for closing my last cry, so God may see peace on my face. Quickly, under the stones of the Westerkerk, so that you may look into the light of your palette again. The thick paste that smells so good, the great blinding knife strokes. I see paintings and I hear sorrow.

I can hear children laughing, their stilts clattering over the city bricks.

---

* A tradition after a death.

I can see the ends of tunnels dug by the army of worms in the wood. Fourteen years they've been working, leaving behind more emptiness than wood. Blinded by the light of the sun on the water, they stop for a moment where the sawdust ends, then go on again. They don't know that water drowns little worms.

With a sign of the cross, St Nicholas stuck together the pieces of children in the butcher's salting-tub and brought them back to life. Children are on Earth so we may hear them laugh, and to sing and celebrate St Nicholas's Day. But the Regents and all men in black have forbidden it, forbidden the feast of the children's friend, forbidden too the selling of gingerbread dolls, or there's a three-florin fine.

The cloths soaked in rose water and myrrh soothe away the last needles in my skin. Titus, my child, my brother, I hear your tears. And I hear the sorrows of the Plague. The broken laughter of a woman and the cries of a child alone on the Earth. Since my birth fourteen years ago on the Breestraat, I know that if you die before him, your father's life will stop. Seven times nine, at sixty-three, life is dangerous.

They're beating drums, beating on the doors of the city, burning the Regents and preachers with their laughter.

He rose again from the dead, He ascended into Heaven. Under the stones of the Westerkerk, my face turned to the east, I shall see the sun rise on your life each morning. I shall count each day that brings us closer. Seven times nine.

Lighter than a wave, less salty than the foam. Your fingers on my face are caressing.

The wood will crack. The wood of the dykes.

Faced with the children's anger, the Regents will give up.

Thousands of gingerbread St Nicholases. Faced with the angry children's sweet tooth, this time the Regents will step back.

The thunderclap will be so loud that no one will know if it's the breaking waves or the shattering wood.

Your fingers on my face are cool.

Only afterwards, when God has flooded the sins of Holland, will His anger abate. The waters will subside, and those who have survived the Plague and the Flood will see thousands of little tunnels dug by thousands of worms in the burst wood of the dykes.

It's not a sigh. It's not a cloud I'm passing through. It's your tears on my face. Your fingers have gathered them at the corner of your eyes. You're sharing them with me, who has left you.

Postscript

As Hendrickje lay dying, the grieving she heard was for the deaths to come.

On the 10th February 1668, Titus married Magdalena van Loo, a cousin by marriage. On the 4th September in the same year, Titus died, probably of the Plague. Six months later, on the 19th March 1669, Magdalena gave birth to a daughter, whom she called Titia.

Thirteen months after his son's death, Rembrandt van Rijn died, on the 4th October 1669. He was sixty-three, the age of the great climacteric. He had suffered too much. He was buried in the Westerkerk.

On the 17th October, two weeks after Rembrandt, Magdalena died. Her daughter, Titia, was not yet a year old.

With her guardian, Abraham Francen, as witness, Cornelia married a young painter, Cornelis, and went to live in 'Batavia' (now Bali) with him. There she gave birth to a son and a daughter, whom she called after her parents: Rembrandt (born in 1673) and Hendrickje (born in 1678). All trace of them was quickly lost on their island on the other side of the world.

Titia died without issue in 1728.

Author's Note

I think I may say that in this novel everything is true. Nothing has been invented, neither the trials, recipes, smells, the cupboard, nor the mirror, nor indeed the works of art and Rembrandt's kindness. The proof exists in legal documents, letters and paintings, but it would be pedantic to provide the complete list.

Apart from biographies, I have read documents; studied contemporary accounts and contracts; pored over paintings and engravings; compared the misfortunes of Rembrandt's life with the expression in portraits and with the years when he didn't paint, and I have revisited the families' hopes and fears. I also came across the Plague.

I was touched by Hendrickje Stoffels's fate because of the unfair judgment that was cast upon her and because of the way she had to suffer for it. Rembrandt's portraits of her reveal the nature of her soul and her generosity. To get to know her better I went to meet her, and with her tried to remember.

S.M.

Works by Rembrandt Cited in the Text

The Company of Frans Banning Cocq (The Night Watch) (painting) 1632. Rijksmuseum, Amsterdam.

The Hundred Florin Coin (engraving) 1649.

Medea (engraving) 1648.

Bathsheba Holding King David's Letter (painting) 1654. Musée du Louvre, Paris.

Man in a Gold Helmet (painting) 1650. Gemäldegalerie, Berlin.

Jan Six (drawings and engravings) 1647.

Self-portrait (painting) 1652. Vienna.

Town Hall the Day after the Fire (drawing) 1653.

Clement de Jonghe (engraving) 1651.

Aristotle Contemplating a Bust of Homer (painting) 1653. Metropolitan Museum of Art, New York.

Mary and Joseph in the Stable (engraving) 1654.

The Flight into Egypt (engraving) 1654.

Jan Six (painting) 1654. Jan Six Collection, Amsterdam.

Descent from the Cross (engraving) 1654.

Ecce Homo (engraving) 1654.

Supper at Emmaus (engraving) 1654.

The Holy Family (engraving) 1654.

Titus at his Desk (painting) 1655. Boymans van Beuningen Museum, Rotterdam.

Abraham Francen (engraving) 1657.

Hendrickje Bathing (painting) 1655. National Gallery, London.

Thomasz Haaringh (engraving) 1655.

Hendrickje (painting) 1660. National Gallery, London.

The Slaughtered Ox (painting) 1655. Musée du Louvre, Paris.

Christ on the Mount of Olives (engraving) 1657.

Titus (painting) 1658. Wallace Colection, London.

St Francis of Assisi (engraving) 1657.

The Anatomy Lesson of Dr Jan Deyman (painting) 1656. Rijksmuseum, Amsterdam.

Self-portrait (painting) 1658. Frick Collection, New York.

Jacob Wrestling with the Angel (painting) 1659. Gemäldegalerie, Berlin.

Titus as St Francis (painting) 1660. Rijksmuseum, Amsterdam.

Alexander (painting) 1655. Gulbenkian Foundation, Calouste, Portugal.

Self-portrait (painting) 1659. National Gallery of Art, Washington.

Hendrickje (painting) 1660. Metropolitan Museum of Art, New York.

The Good Samaritan (painting) 1660. Gemäldegalerie, Berlin.

Homer Instructing his Pupils (painting) 1663. Mauritshuis, The Hague.

St Matthew Inspired by the Angel (painting) 1661. Musée du Louvre, Paris.

Paul the Apostle (painting) 1661. Rijksmuseum, Amsterdam.

Jacob Trip and Margaretha de Geer (paintings) 1661. National Gallery, London.

The Oath-Swearing of Claudius Civilis (painting) 1661–62. Nationalmuseum, Stockholm.

WORKS BY OTHER ARTISTS

Landscape, by Hercules Seghers (painting).

Goldfinch, by Carel Fabritius (painting).

Margaretha Tulp, by Govert Flinck (painting).

Acknowledgments

I am grateful to Hendrickje Stoffels for being the attractive character she was and will remain forever in Rembrandt's portraits of her. I hope I have been faithful to her. Thank you, also, to Rembrandt and Titus van Rijn; I had plenty of time to become fond of them too.

My thanks to Charles, Léonard and Jules, and to friends and colleagues, for having supported and put up with me during this enterprise.

I should like to thank Muriel Beyer for her unfailing and affectionate support.

I should also like to thank Elisabeth de Laubrière, Anne de la Baume, Sylvaine Parmeland, Marina Kamena and Jacques Baratier for their devoted and careful reading. I am particularly grateful to Elisabeth, who, from the outset of my research on Rembrandt, led me to libraries and worked on all the documents with me.

Thank you to Charles Matton and Serge Clément for everything that may be seen and smelled in a painter's and engraver's studio.

My thanks, too, to Sebastian Dudok van Heel, a researcher in Science and History at the Amsterdam Archives, and to Anneke Kerkhof, archivist at the library of the Dutch Institute in Paris, for their kindness and support, and for offering me leads and clues.

My special thanks go to Jacqueline Brossollet for so generously sharing with me her outstanding knowledge of the Plague and its human and social consequences.

Thank you to Armelle de Crépy, Zime Koleci and Suzanne Andriessens.

Also to Toby and Yves Gilbert for the pretty tears.

And to those who have taught me kindness and compassion: F.F. and C.M.

Select Bibliography

Jacqueline Brossollet and Henri Mollaret, *Pourquoi la peste? Le rat, la puce et le bubon*, Gallimard Découvertes.

Jean Calvin, *Catechism of the Church of Geneva*.

Jean Chevalier, Alain Gheerbrant, *Le Dictionnaire des symboles*, Bouquins/R. Laffont.

J. Cottin, *Traité de la peste* (republished in 1721).

Daniel Defoe, *Journal of the Plague Year*.

Pierre Descargues, *Rembrandt*, Lattès.

La Bible et les Saints (Tout l'Art), Encyclopédie Flammarion.

The Bible. Old and New Testament.

Pierre-Jean Fabre, *Remèdes curatifs et préservatifs de la peste* (reprinted in 1720).

L. Gagnebin, A. Gourmelle, *Le Protestantisme, La Cause. Les Canons de Dordrecht*.

Jean Genet, *Le Secret de Rembrandt*, Gallimard.

Jean Genet, *Ce qui est resté d'un Rembrandt déchiré en petits carrés*, Gallimard.

Guides Gallimard, Amsterdam.

Bob Haak, *La Peinture hollandaise au siècle d'or*, Dumont.

Cornelis Hofstede de Groot, *Die Urkunden über Rembrandt*.

J.J. van Loghem, *Le Rat domestique et la lutte contre la peste au XVIIe siècle*, Masson et Cie, 1925.

Les Maîtres de Delft, Waanders Publishers.

Jan Mens, *La Vie passionnée de Rembrandt*, Intercontinentale du Livre.

Emile Michael, *Rembrandt, sa vie, son oeuvre et son temps*, Hachette, 1893.

Johannes Nohl, *La Mort noire*, Payot.

Rembrandt eaux-fortes, Musée du Petit Palais.

Rembrandt, le maître et son atelier, Flammarion.

Simon Schama, *The Embarrassment of Riches. An Interpretation of Dutch Culture in the Golden Age*, HarperCollins.

Gary Schwartz, *Rembrandt, his Life, his Paintings*, Penguin.

Seymour Slive, *Dutch Painting 1600–1800*, Yale University Press.

Seymour Slive, *Rembrandt and his Critics*.

Tout l'oeuvre peint de Rembrandt, Flammarion.

Christian Tümpel, *Rembrandt*, Albin Michel.

C. Vosmaer, *Rembrandt, sa vie et ses oeuvres*, 1877.

F.P. Wilson, *The Plague in London in the Time of Shakespeare*.

Paul Zumthor, *La Vie quotidienne au temps de Rembrandt*, Hachette.

FILMOGRAPHY

Ingmar Bergman, *The Seventh Seal*.

Carl Dreyer, *Ordet*.

Pier Paolo Pasolini, *The Gospel According to St Matthew*.

Lars von Trier, *Breaking the Waves*.